Elizabeth Marchioness of Westminster

# Diary of a Tour in Sweden, Norway, and Russia, in 1827 with

## letters

Elizabeth Marchioness of Westminster

**Diary of a Tour in Sweden, Norway, and Russia, in 1827 with letters**

ISBN/EAN: 9783743337633

Manufactured in Europe, USA, Canada, Australia, Japa

Cover: Foto ©Andreas Hilbeck / pixelio.de

Manufactured and distributed by brebook publishing software
(www.brebook.com)

Elizabeth Marchioness of Westminster

# Diary of a Tour in Sweden, Norway, and Russia, in 1827 with letters

# IARY· OF A TOUR

JERS.

OF WESTM

OLUME.

N:

HUE...TT, PUBLI
OUGH STREET.

# PREFACE.

THE following short Diary consists of literal extracts from one kept by me at the time of our Tour, and of letters of the same period addressed to relations at home. I have thought it better to give both, though necessarily involving some repetition, as the letters are often more ample than the Journal, while the latter preserves the sequence of events. They touch on no scientific or political subjects, merely giving an account of such incidents as happened day by day. The way of travelling at that time, fifty-two years ago, may be amusing when contrasted with the present easy and rapid means of transport in distant countries; and some interest may be found in the brief notices of sundry great personages who afterwards filled distinguished places in the history of the countries through which we passed.

E.M.W.

Motcombe House, Shaftesbury.
August, 1879.

# DIARY OF A TOUR

IN

# SWEDEN, NORWAY, AND RUSSIA.

ON Saturday, May 19th, 1827, we started from Grosvenor Square for our expedition to Sweden and Russia. We had sent the carriage ready packed to the Tower Stairs, close to the Custom-House, on Friday afternoon, and this morning Belgrave* and I, his servant Gartner, a native of Riga, who had been our servant in the Spring, and my maid, left Grosvenor Square at half-past nine, and reached our place of embarkation at ten; when we immediately got on board the 'Hylton Jolliffe,'

* My husband, Richard, afterwards second Marquis of Westminster, but who was then Viscount Belgrave, in the lifetime of his father, Earl Grosvenor.

B

Captain Downie, and weighed anchor at eleven o'clock. We passed the greatest part of the day in sailing down the Thames, between its ugly banks. We remained most of the time upon deck, dined in Belgrave's cabin, and drank tea there in the evening.

There were a good many passengers, principally foreigners, returning home, and some English. We undressed at night, by which time we had got out to sea, and went regularly to bed, and slept quite comfortably till morning. Belgrave called me at half-past ten, I was soon up and dressed, and went to his cabin where we breakfasted; but the sea being a little rough, and as I was *rather* uncomfortable, I lay down in my cabin while Belgrave dined in his own. I came up afterwards, but it was cold and disagreeable. In the course of the day two little birds alighted on the deck, apparently quite exhausted from fatigue; one of them flew away again, the other was caught and put into a cage; but it also died in half an hour afterwards.

*Monday,* 21*st.*—A very fine day; the sea was quite smooth, and the weather hot. We were off Heligoland about four p.m.; the most miserable looking place that can be seen. We stopped off Cuxhaven for an hour, about six, while some of our companions went on shore in a boat to get some eggs and milk. The sail up the Elbe this evening was beautiful; the river full of ships of all nations. We met a Danish ship, the passengers in which, recognising some of their friends on board our vessel, gave them first a round of cheers, and then fired a salute; at the same moment an American ship was passing on the other side, which afterwards crossed the Danish ship's bows; and the effect, together with the smoke, and a splendid setting sun, was beautiful. We anchored about ten o'clock in the river, after taking in an intoxicated Ostade pilot, whom we afterwards exchanged for one of greater respectability; but, the river being full of sand banks, it is not safe to proceed up it by night.

*Tuesday*, 22nd.—Everybody was up early, impatient to arrive at Hamburg; the shores of the river became very pretty, and we saw a fox running about on the sand. The banks are covered with villas and gardens, and small villages; there is a good deal of low wood, but the soil is all sand. We passed Altona, a singular and handsome looking town, enlivened with plenty of shipping; the houses as usual, very tall, with ornamented gables, and a large admixture of trees. Arrived at Hamburg before twelve. The ship was very soon cleared of its passengers; but we remained till the carriage was placed in a boat, and we proceeded with it to a landing place belonging to a timber-yard; but seeing that the horses, which one of the passengers had promised to send, were not there to meet us, we desired the man to row us to the usual landing place. We, therefore, went on up a very curious part of the town, with enormously tall ornamented houses, like those in the pictures of Venice; the canal was positively crammed full of boats, so that we had some difficulty in getting on. The Custom-House, where all passports are examined, is at the entrance of this narrower part. We were kept waiting an immense time before we could get up to the place where is the machine for disembarking carriages and heavy weights; but there was a boat in the way which had to be unladen first, with two enormous green trunks bearing the Russian Imperial Arms upon them. This royal obstacle being, at length, removed, our carriage was soon disembarked, and we sent for the horses; a pair of long tailed chestnuts soon conveyed us to the Hôtel de Russie, where we found a comfortable apartment.

We ordered dinner for half-past five, and Belgrave went out to find a Monsieur Stächer, who had been recommended, poor man, as being *useful*, by Mr. W. Wynn;* he also paid a visit to the Bank to arrange for some supplies of money. Towards the conclusion of dinner arrived M. Stächer, full of good intentions, which somewhat failed in the execution, seeing that he did *not* order horses, as he had promised to do, and gave us a vast deal of intelligence as to roads, payments, &c., the whole of which turned out, in the sequel, to be utterly wrong.

In the evening, we took a drive in a *calèche* with a pair of long-tailed black horses, round the environs of the town, which are extremely pretty, full of villas with gardens of lilacs, laburnums, tulips, &c. Almost every one of these houses had its large centre door wide open, with a table covered with a white table-cloth and with refreshments, as if their owners were expecting visitors. We met many open carriages, full of people, going out on pleasure expeditions. Our drive took us by the Alster, a fine wide river, flowing through very green rich-looking meadows; the verdure and

---

* Mr. (afterwards Sir) Henry W. Williams-Wynn, a younger brother of the late Sir Watkin Williams-Wynn, Bart., M.P., and of the Right Hon. C. W. Williams-Wynn, M.P. He was British Minister at Copenhagen from 1824 to 1852. He died in 1856.

thickness and height of the grass was remarkable; the trees also were in full foliage. When we returned home, we had lemonade, and the additional solace of receiving a very heavy bag of dollars from the Bank.

Hotel de Russie,
Hamburg.
Tuesday, May 22nd, 1827.

My dear M——

How glad you will be to hear that we have had the most prosperous of voyages, the most comfortable of cabins. Belgrave had one, and his servant another upon deck; and I and my maid one in the State cabin. We had the very smoothest of seas. Saturday was delightfully fine, the sea being like glass the whole way. On Sunday came a little swell, and I was a very little sick in the evening. Yesterday, Monday, quite delightful, and sailing up the Elbe charming. We were obliged to anchor in the river last night, as it is dangerous to thread one's way up it at night, from the sand banks; but that did not signify, for we slept like tops every night. We got here before four p.m., being retarded by the disembarkation of our carriage; thus we unluckily could not get up to the pier, where are thousands of boats, on account of the unloading of an enormous panorama of St. Petersburg, conducted by a bear of the true Cossack sort.

This old town is very curious, full of ships, carriages, and pompous horses. Our hotel is very good, and there is a most excellent *cuisine ;* we have had just now for dinner, among other things, " the thing I eats with mutton-chops," and the mutton-chops themselves, besides Rudesheim wine and Vanille ice. Belgrave is just gone to the Bank with a most civil old Mr. Stächer, a sort of burgomaster, recommended to us by Mr. W. Wynn, he does nothing but kiss one's hand and make the most civil speeches ; and we are going to take an evening drive in a *calèche* round the ramparts. How you would like to see these curious old houses ! We go to-morrow to Ploen, forty miles off, next day a very short distance further, to Kiel, where we are to embark, at four in the afternoon, for Copenhagen. We are to make this part of our journey by steam ; it will take us about twenty-four hours, and Mr. Wynn expects us at Copenhagen.

*Wednesday, May 23rd.*—We got up at six; but as we had another visit from Mr. Stächer, and as

Belgrave had a good deal to learn from the master
of the hotel about money, which is very difficult to
understand, we did not get off till half-past eight,
by which time all was ready. We found our carriage drawn by four long-tailed, grand-looking
horses, without blinkers, and driven by one postillion, who rode the near wheeler and drove the other
two before him ; both driver and horses displayed
great prudence and sagacity. We drove through
some of the streets, which have all the same curious
picturesque and clean appearance, and, at length,
arrived on the high road, which certainly would not
be admitted for one yard as a part of the King's
highway in any cross lane in the most unfrequented
part of England.

It is impossible to describe the unvarying bed of
sand, diversified with enormous stones ! Our best
pace was four miles an hour; our first stage was
one of twenty-four miles, which we performed at a
foot pace, our horses occasionally stopping to eat a
little brown bread by the way. One of the leaders
chose to kick prodigiously, till the driver changed it
and rode it himself, when it became quite quiet.
Our good-natured horses arrived at the end of their
first stage, Aldersloe, without being apparently tired,
and we waited about an hour for the next relay,

which conveyed us by the same admirable roads to Segeberg, our next post, about eight English miles, here we had to wait the usual time for our *unordered* horses. We had intended to sleep at Ploen, and in fact, we had been recommended to do so; but being so retarded, we found that we could not possibly reach it till one in the morning; we therefore decided upon taking our chance of accommodation at a little unknown village, Bornhufte, about ten English miles from it.

We went over a road as good (or bad) as before, and through the most extraordinary wastes and deserts of sand I ever saw. It was getting very dark, and as we came suddenly to a full stop, we asked what was the matter. We were told " the bridge is broken," we were, therefore, obliged to make our way through the water; our servant got down to turn the leaders, who did not seem much to understand the ceremony, but were quite willing to do anything in their way to facilitate our progress; we got through very successfully, threaded our way through a pine-wood, and then came out on the wildest of commons, where there seemed to be no road, but only a number of different tracks. Here we stopped again, and ·were told that the driver was not sure of his way, but was gone to look. This must have done him much good, or, at all events, it must have been a difficult matter, as it was quite dark; however, he soon came back, saying all was right, and we speedily arrived at Bornhufte.

Here we had some little difficulty in making out the inn, where we were received by loud barkings from two irritated mastiffs, who were, however, soon appeased. The people of the house, who were all gone to bed, were roused up, and showed us into a tidy room with two very clean beds, which was a joyful surprise. The servants were also comfortably lodged, and even the carriage, for we were surprised on opening our bedroom-door to find it close to us; the fact is, that it had been placed in a sort of archway which ran through the centre of the house. We found our beds very soft and comfortable, and after supping on our own provisions, we slept till six next morning soundly.

*Thursday, May* 24*th.*—We had the young mastiff, a most amiable animal, to breakfast with us; and saw a great many people going to church, it being Ascension Day. The women were tolerably well dressed, in close caps, gilt at the top, and, generally in black petticoats; the men wore loose coarse coats, and ill-made, dirty boots. The postmaster had a long but friendly dispute with Belgrave to prove that he had paid him too much for the horses, which is not a common complaint.

We set off soon after eight on our next stage, twenty English miles in length, for Kiel, where we arrived at two, after passing along rows of hedges nearly devoured by those horrid reptiles, enormous locusts, who were in such numbers as to cover the trees.

The whole of Holstein is flat, dull, and un-interesting, very green, rich-looking fields, with hedges like the uglier parts of England. The vil-lages are very few, but many large farm-houses, with enormous roofs and one great gateway ; in most of these the house seems to consist of one parlour, and all the rest is one large room ; in the centre is the fire-place and kitchen, and the rest is partitioned off for cows, poultry, &c. The family sleep in small cabins ranged round like those on board a ship. The roofs are of thatch, very steep and picturesque. The houses themselves are constructed of a mixture of brick and wood, like an old Cheshire house, and very pretty to look at. There seems to be an all but universal taste for flowers ; every win-dow is filled with nosegays of lilacs, daffodils, tulips, ranunculuses, lilies of the valley, &c.

On arriving at Kiel, Belgrave's first care was to get the carriage on board the steam-packet, which was to sail at four; but it proved a very difficult matter, for the captain at first refused to take it, saying it was too large; at last, however, he was persuaded to consent, but the men were very awkward about it, taking it off the wheels, and nearly letting it go into the water. At length, however, the work was performed, and Belgrave came up to the inn (Hôtel de Hambourg, Fischer,) to dine. The inn was remarkably nice, and the dinner excellent. We should have much liked to have seen more of Kiel, which is a very pretty and clean town, but we were obliged to go down immediately to embark.

Our vessel was the ' Caledonia,' built at Glasgow, the captain Danish, but speaking English, and a Scotch engineer. At first there were several passengers, but they soon left us to go to some place on shore, a few miles from Kiel, and we luckily remained a small party, only a few gentlemen and two ladies, and both very good-natured Danes, one of whom spoke French ; they were returning to Copenhagen on the death of their sister.

The Baltic looked wild and gloomy, but it was not rough, and Belgrave passed the night very comfortably in the carriage, as being more fresh than going down below. At ten I went down into our cabin, which was a most comfortable one, with four large beds, of which the two Danish ladies, my maid, and myself, were the occupants.

*Friday,* 2*5th.*—As I wanted to be up very early this morning I did not undress, but slept without waking till six, and then went upon deck. I found we were getting among the islands; we coasted Zealand the whole of the way to-day, the islands are pretty and well wooded; but it was rather a gloomy morning, and no sun, so they did not look to advantage. People came upon deck by degrees; I sat in the carriage and on deck alternately, as there was rain, and about half-past one we all went to lie down, as there was a bit of rough sea. We speedily sighted the Swedish coast, and at half-past three we had a very good dinner in the cabin; and when it was over were soon in sight of Copenhagen.

In approaching it we saw many vessels, (though nothing like the numbers in the Elbe,) among others a large English ship laden with timber from Prussia, which had run aground near the shore, and could only hope for a high wind and a high sea ever to move again. Before arriving at Copenhagen there is a tremendous battery of great strength.

The passengers, of course, all disembarked as soon as we got near the pier; we stayed for our carriage, which they managed to land better than at Kiel, and it was soon put on shore. A Mr. Baines, a fellow-passenger in the steam vessel, had sent down horses to meet us, and we had no difficulty in settling ourselves in the Hôtel d'Angleterre by nine; the drive thither through the streets is very pretty, and the town looked handsome and gay. We had a good supper, and arranged our apartments, which seemed very comfortable, and went to bed about twelve.

*Saturday, 26th.*—We had a good long sleep, which was very refreshing, and immediately after breakfast set to writing our letters, as the post for England was going that evening. I afterwards wrote all this journal, for which I had plenty of time, as in the afternoon it began to rain, and continued in torrents through the day, which we, therefore, passed at home.

Copenhagen,
Hotel d'Angleterre.
Saturday, May 26th, 1827.

Dearest M——

Never were such lucky people as we are with our sea-voyages! We have had a most excellent passage from Kiel of twenty-six hours, the sea not at all rough enough to make one sick, a very nice extremely clean little steam vessel of twenty-eight horse-power, and very few passengers. The name of the vessel was the 'Caledonia'; she had been built at Glasgow, the captain Danish, though he talked English very well, and the engineer Scotch. But I must begin where I left off, at Hamburg, which we left about quarter-past eight on Wednesday morning; such perfections are the roads of Holstein that we were fourteen hours in going between forty or fifty English miles. The roads are the deepest sand that can be conceived, interspersed here and there with enormous stones; but they baffle all description, so I won't try to picture them. They drive very carefully and well, one postillion managing all the four horses, who are grand creatures, with long tails, like those in Wouverman's pictures; they seem uncommonly gentle and good-natured, and go

trotting on (or rather *walking* in these roads) long
stages of twenty-four miles, more or less, without
seeming the least tired, and only eating a little
brown bread now and then. One of our drivers,
however, as nearly as possible overturned us by the
strangest invention of suddenly turning out of the
road down a steep muddy foot-path, and running
us against a tree ; after we were extricated from the
danger, he gravely drove us down into a small river,
and up the middle of it for some way, then suddenly, by a sharp turn up again, into the road ; on
our inquiring the cause of this wonderful proceeding, and why he did not go by the natural road
over a very good looking bridge, he said he thought
it was a pity to go over the bridge as it was quite
new ; on which our servant cried out in a transport
of indignant contempt, "*c'est excellent, il veut
ménager le pont !*" We got on as best we could, and
our carriage stood it all perfectly ; it is a very pretty
dark green nice carriage, and a very strong one too.
We could not have got to Ploen before one or two
in the morning, so we stopped at a very small village, which we reached at half-past ten, having
passed through the most desolate district of sand
which can be imagined. In the middle of it we
stopped in the dark, the postillion fearing he had

lost his way; but he was right, which was lucky for us; so there we arrived, and found every soul gone to bed, except some angry dogs, who were making a great noise; they were, however, soon appeased, and the people got up and gave us a clean room, with very clean beds, which was pleasant, inasmuch as we did not expect to find any such luxuries. The next morning we had some fine tubs of clean water, and a very good breakfast; a good-natured young mastiff came to breakfast with us, and then we set out for Kiel, where we arrived, by the same sort of roads as before, about two o'clock; got the carriage on board the steamboat; had an excellent dinner at the nicest and prettiest inn possible, and embarked at four.

Kiel, I should tell you, is a beautiful little town, full of picturesque old German houses. The hedges during the last part of the journey were devoured by locusts—nasty beasts. The country very flat and dull, but excessively rich, and green to a wonderful degree. The gardens were all full of lilacs, and the windows quite gay with nosegays of ranunculuses and lilies of the valley. Our only lady companions, on board the ship, were two very good-natured, innocent Danish women, who were returning to Copenhagen; they grew very fond of me, and we

c

all got on very well together in an excellent cabin
with four large beds. I slept all night, and got up
very early to come on deck to see all the islands
that we were swimming among. We saw Zealand
all the way. This place is approached through a
tremendous battery, which is said to be " untake-
able." We got safely lodged, our carriage disembarked, and everything arranged by nine o'clock ;
had a very good supper, and found our hotel very
comfortable ; we have a very handsome apartment,
like a French one, lined with crimson silk. I am
writing just after breakfast, so have not seen Mr.
Wynn, or anybody else, as yet; he is at his country-
house, about nine miles from here, but is expected
in town this morning, as the King has a review in
the evening; I dare say we shall go to it, but till
we have seen Mr. Wynn we cannot settle how long
we stay here, or anything. This town looks very
gay, and has many large and handsome squares, in
one of which we now are, and magnificent curious-
looking houses, quite different from what I expected.
I am as well as possible, and have got a large nosegay
of lilies of the valley.

*Sunday,* 27*th.*—After breakfast we read the morning service, and then took a walk down the Oster-

strasse, the region of the shops ; we were scandalized
to find them all open, but found that they were all
kept by Jews, and would therefore naturally, I
suppose, have been shut on Saturday. We came
home about two o'clock, dressed, and went in a
hired chariot and pair (of slow horses) through nine
miles of horrid road, the first seven through a
hideous country, to dine with our Minister, Mr.
Williams Wynn, at his country-house at Fredericsthal,
a house which he has hired of Count Schulin. It is
situated in the middle of very fine woods, close to
two beautiful lakes ; the house itself, however, is
most miserable, it has bare unfurnished rooms, with
no communication except through each other, these
are hung with English prints and a few wretched
pictures. The garden would be pretty if well taken
care of ; but it is now very like a neglected Scotch
" policy," with nettles and long grass growing all
over the strawberry and flower-beds. Nothing, in
short, could be more forlorn, or give one the idea of
greater desolation, than the house and grounds,
though beautifully situated in the midst of wood and
water. We dined as soon as we arrived, and then
went out walking about the grounds, then took an
open carriage and drove to a villa of Madame
Brune, where we got out and walked about, and

then drove back to Mr. Wynn's, had tea, and came home in a regular rain; we arrived about half-past ten.

*Monday, 28th.*—Got up rather early and breakfasted. Mr. and Mrs. Wynn came at eleven and gave us information about our future journey. Mr. Wynn and Belgrave went to the bankers, Mrs. Wynn and I to several shops in the Osterstrasse to buy gloves, ribbon, crape, &c., &c. We met Mr. Wynn and Belgrave in the street. I came home with Belgrave, and we went again at two to Mr. Wynn's, and walked with him again down the Osterstrasse to see a curious old round tower built by Christian IV., round the inside of which is a road so broad that a carriage and four might drive to the top; however, we stopped half-way to see the University Library, and a collection of curious old things which had been found in the Tumuli, flint-knives and spear-heads, (before the use of iron, and the consequent improvements in metal,) old swords, spears, &c., &c. We then took leave of Mr. Wynn, and came home for a short time; set out again and went to Mr. Been's, a very good shop, to lay in a provision of tea, which is remarkably good here, sugar, and arrow-root for our journey; went on by the palace and to the pier, then had a beautiful walk round the ramparts, whence we had the most magnificent view of the harbour, the sea, (which was quite blue,) and the Swedish coast at a distance. On the other side, the town, with its trees, picturesque houses, and old towers, looked particularly well in a bright sunshine, and the walk was delightful, though I was thoroughly tired. We saw the Queen returning from witnessing the review ; she was in a small *calèche,* drawn by six very pretty, long-tailed, little black horses. We came home exhausted and hungry at a little before seven, dined at half-past seven, passed the evening in paying our bills, writing this journal, &c., received a visit from Mr. Fenwick, the Consul at Copenhagen, and then went to bed.

*Tuesday,* 29*th.*—We had had our carriage raised and repaired in some trifling details by an English coachmaker, and again set forth in it this morning. On our departure from Copenhagen at half-past eight, we went by the same road along which we had gone to Mr. Wynn's at Fredericsthal, consequently the first part was dull as well as ugly ; but at about eight miles from Copenhagen the road began to be wooded, and we very soon improved in point of scenery. At the village of Limbye we picked up some letters from Mr. Wynn, and also

some sheets, with which Mrs. Wynn very kindly
provided us, and continued our journey to Friedericsberg through beautiful forests, principally of beech,
forming part of the King's *chasse*, and containing
*chevreuil*. On arriving at Friedericsberg we walked
to the old palace, which is a very handsome building, surrounded by three moats, and approached by
drawbridges and gateways. It is built of dark red
brick, the cupolas, minarets, and very steep roof
are all of copper ; the palace itself is something
between Burghley and the French castles of the
time of Francis I. The towers are very handsome,
the house is built round three sides of a large square
court ; the doors are very much carved, and the
most remarkable of the many curious things within
is the chapel, which is long and narrow ; the ceiling
of the King's pew is a mediocre performance of
King Christian's own hands, made of ebony and
ivory. The pew is lined with curious panels, painted
on copper, with subjects from the Bible; at the
further end is a sort of modern throne in very bad
taste, on which the King was crowned. All the
Danish Kings have been crowned here. But the
most remarkable part of the whole is the ceiling,
which is of white and gold, but so rich, so delicate,
and so much in relief, as to resemble a piece of

jewellery; it is the most beautiful thing possible of the kind. The doors of the pews are all in marqueterie. The shields of the Knights of the Order of the Elephant* are hung up in this chapel; among them was that of the Duke of Wellington. Over this chapel is "The Knights' Hall," one hundred and sixty-five feet long, but not high enough in proportion. The ceiling is perfectly flat, but so strange and so extraordinary, that it is difficult to describe it in any way. *En relief*, over the whole of this enormous space, and there is not an inch but is covered with birds, beasts, fruit, flowers, men, angels, stories from the Bible, representations of trades, &c., all richly carved, coloured, or gilt, in strangely formed compartments. The effect is singular and rich beyond description, and is like one large field of enamel, or of Florentine wood. The walls of this, and of many other rooms, are covered with pictures, principally portraits, some very bad, but many very singular and entertaining; and I should think among them must be some very

---

* This chief royal Danish Order dates from Christian I., A.D. 1458, though some writers claim for it a still higher antiquity. Originally religious, it is now secular, like our own Order of the Garter. It is under a presidency of a Chapter of the Royal Order, established at Copenhagen in 1808. The annual festival of the Order of the Elephant is January 1st.

curious ones, but we had not time to look at a hundredth part of the collection; of those which we did see, the portraits of Christina and Charles XII. were the most remarkable. We saw the room inhabited by poor Queen Caroline Matilda,* and written by her on a pane in the window,

    "O keep me innocent, make others great."

There are fine gardens belonging to this palace, which, with some care, and a good deal of additional furniture, might be made a delightful habitation, surrounded as it is by its beautiful forests; but the Royal Family never go there.

We returned to our inn, and soon went on by Friedensbourg, another country-seat of the King— a common, modern looking house, with fine woods and a lake. Thence on to Elsineur, a sandy road all the way. It was near six o'clock when we arrived; Belgrave went to find Mr. Chapman, a merchant, to whom he had a letter from his brother, who was a passenger on the Hamburg steamboat with us. Belgrave soon found him, and he took us to see the Castle of Cronberg, which is a beautiful building, and finely situated; it stands quite by itself on the sea-shore. It is of brick and stone, with fine

---

* Sister of George III., and wife of Christian VII. of Denmark.

towers, and built entirely round a court; it is now used for barracks. We mounted up to the top of one of the corner towers, which commands the most beautiful of views over the town, the sea, and shipping, and the Swedish and Danish coasts beyond. We also went into the chapel, which is now entirely dismantled and used as a gymnase for the soldiers. We then went to Mr. Chapman's house, where I waited some time while Belgrave and he went to see about embarking the carriage. This was at last effected; we embarked ourselves in another smaller boat, and, as there was no wind, we rowed over four miles to Helsingburg ; we went to Mr. Mohlberg's inn, where, though the town looked poor, we found a very clean and comfortable apartment. Belgrave went down again to see the carriage landed, and was kept a long time by the tiresome slowness of the Custom-House people; at length he returned to supper, about eleven o'clock, in a large, clean ball-room, and then went to our beds, which we found very comfortable.

*Wednesday, 30th.*—We breakfasted on some of our own tea ; the bread here was very tolerable, and the eggs excellent. After breakfast Belgrave set out to find the Commandant, Major Katterholm, who came here with him, with a very fine pointer,

exactly like Dash, at Eaton.* The Commandant
talked bad French, but was very useful in providing us with a hussar to drive us through
Sweden, for it is very necessary to have a trusty and
good one. Lord Bloomfield† had written, asking
for one to meet us, but as it was only the day before
we came away, our hussar could not possibly arrive
in time. Fortunately we also dispatched a *forebüd*
to order our horses on the road, who set out at
two to-day, and Belgrave bought a carriage, to take
part of our luggage and the peasants, who must be
conveyed, in order that they may bring back their
horses. Belgrave was very busy writing and settling
matters all the morning, and I wrote letters, and am
now writing this with the help of a great thunder-
storm, which is growling and rattling incessantly,
the rain also pouring in torrents like a water-spout.
In the afternoon we had a visit from Mr. Turing,‡
who was very civil, and very kindly lent Belgrave
some money, of which he found he had not enough
to get on to Gottenburg. While I was writing my

---

* The Duke of Westminster's seat near Chester.

† Benjamin, first Lord Bloomfield, G.C.B., &c., then Minister-
Plenipotentiary at the Court of Sweden. He died in 1846.

‡ The late Sir J. H. Turing, Bart., many years Her Britannic Majesty's Consul at Rotterdam. He died in 1860.

letters I had a pain, which came on suddenly in the muscle below my knee, which increased so rapidly, and swelled so much within an hour, that I was hardly able to move for the rest of the day.

Helsingburg.
Wednesday, May 30th, 1827.

Dearest M——

I am obliged to write on nasty inn paper, as I have let Belgrave go out after the Commandant with the key of my writing-case in his pocket, and as he has gone to settle about a hussar to drive us, (for Lord Bloomfield's coachman cannot, we think, get here in timé,) and an *estafette* to precede us, heaven knows when he will come back, so I won't wait.

We went to dine on Sunday at Mr. Wynn's, nine miles from Copenhagen; he has got a place situated in the most beautiful and luxuriant woods, close to fine lakes; in fact, nothing can be prettier than the exterior; but the interior! Imagine all you can that is most comfortless and forlorn in a combination of an unfurnished Scotch and French house, and you will have it; for living-rooms, an *enfilade* of three or four apartments, which have no access but through each other, and about seven bedrooms, also *en suite*,

to which there is no access but "through each
other," but in which they, six children, maids,. &c.,
contrive to rest, all packed together. A few English prints and some bad pictures serve for all
decoration, and a garden, which would be pretty if
it were not full of long grass and nettles. They
can get the house at present for only a year; so it
is not worth while to do much to it, and they make
the best of it as it stands.

On Monday, we walked, I believe, all day. Mr.
and Mrs. Wynn came to Copenhagen, where they
have an excellent town-house; so I first made, in
her company, a round of the shops, which are very
bad; then we went to an old round tower built by
Christian IV., with a broad drive up, so that a
carriage and four might go to the top. In it I saw
a curious collection of old Scandinavian arms; then
I went to other shops, and Belgrave and I took a
long and most beautiful walk on the ramparts,
whence the views are splendid. We saw Her
Majesty the Queen* coming home in a very small
green *calèche* drawn by six very pretty little black
horses, very slow, with very high action, a very fat

---

* The Queen of Denmark. Her Majesty was Princess Sophia of
Hesse-Cassel; she was the wife of Frederick VI., whose reign lasted
from 1808 to 1839.

coachman, and one *avant-courier.* The Hereditary Prince,* and a pretty Princess, whom we saw in England some two or three years ago, were just gone off to Lubeck. We found that we had seen all that there really was worth seeing at Copenhagen; and as we wanted to get on, we left it yesterday morning. Mr. and Mrs. Wynn were most kind; and she has been of the most essential use in providing us, besides information, with a further supply of sheets, towels, &c., for our northern journey. There are very nice gloves to be had at Copenhagen, but with such an odd smell that it takes off from their merits; however I am to have some by the winter, and if the smell goes off and you like them, you shall have some too; but they are not so nice as the Dresden gloves. The tea is beyond anything good at Copenhagen; we have a whole store of Pekoe with us, besides arrow-root, &c.; and as we find *nothing* at the inns, in future we shall lay in provisions of meat and bread when we find them; and besides my bed we have sheets, mattresses ready to stuff with clean straw, &c., so I daresay we shall do very well.

On leaving Copenhagen yesterday we found the country at first ugly, till we came to the most beau-

* Afterwards Frederick VII., King from 1839 to 1863.

tiful forest, almost all of beech; magnificent trees, in short the prettiest thing that could be imagined; and at about twelve miles from Copenhagen we stopped to see Friedericsberg, a beautiful old palace of the Kings, built by Christian V. I wish I could describe it, but I cannot. It is six times larger than Chenonceaux, with rthee moats round it; the palace is of dark red brick, and it has a copper roof terminated with beautiful cupolas and minarets. It has also a great deal of stone work, statues, and arcades, something in the way of Hatfield;* but much more picturesque and decorated, with towers of all shapes and sizes surrounding a large courtyard. The chapel is very handsome; without any exception it has the most magnificent, refined, and finely-worked ceiling of white and gold, in high relief, that I ever saw. That of the gallery at Northumberland House,† is as nothing in comparison of it. Above this chapel is " The Knights' Hall " above one hundred and sixty feet long; with the most extraordinary ceiling I ever saw, a sort of Florentine work *en relief* with coloured fruit, flowers, angels, and long stories from the Bible and history all over

---

* Lord Salisbury's seat in Hertfordshire.

† The Duke of Northumberland's town-house at Charing Cross; demolished in 1874.

it; not an inch but what is highly worked, coloured, or gilded; the effect is wonderful, like one of the enamelled bracelets; the ceilings at Eaton are meagre in comparison, though this, from being flat, has not the same effect which they have on the eye; but no description can give any idea of it. We saw Queen Caroline Matilda's room, and some of her hand-writing on the window; and rooms without end full of the strangest and most extraordinary, and I should think, very curious, old portraits of everybody connected with the Royal Family of Denmark, and many others. We had not time to look at one hundredth part in detail; there are curious portraits of Christina, Charles XII., &c., and delicious old family pictures; there are also fine gardens, and a park adjoining the forest I have mentioned, and a stud, with, I believe, some good horses. It is a delightful place, and might be made both gay and comfortable for living in; though they never go here to stay, but prefer Friedensbourg, a little way from it, with fine woods and lakes, but a common modern looking house.

We came on to Elsineur, where we found a very obliging Mr. Chapman, to whom his brother, whom we met on the Hamburg packet, had given us a letter. He took us to the exquisite old castle of

Cronberg, which is most curious.  We saw Caroline
Matilda's three rooms where she was imprisoned;
and more *triste* ones cannot be imagined.  We went
up a very high tower, and from the roof, just as at
Dunrobin,* we had a pleasant view of the sea, the
shipping, and the Swedish coast.  We then embarked,
and soon made our passage of three miles over to
our present quarters, a poor town with an extremely
good and clean inn; we stay here to-day as we have
many arrangements to make.  Belgrave has bought
another carriage, which is quite necessary, as the
peasants whose horses take us, must be conveyed in
it in order to bring back their horses, as well as
part of the luggage.  We go with six horses, the
carriage with two, and our *avant-courier* departs to-
day.  We are to get to Gottenburg the day after
to-morrow, and then we go on to Christiana.

The Commandant has just been to visit us with a
charming great brown pointer, and he has provided
us with a very trusty hussar who does *not* drink,
and is a very good driver.  There are country
people selling fish, grain, &c., in long narrow carts
drawn by tractable ponies something larger than
Scotch ones.  I have just bought some beautiful

---

* The property of the Duke of Sutherland, in Sutherland-
shire.

flowers, tulips, daffodils, and lilies of the valley. The head waiter here is a Scotch woman; but she has lived so long abroad, that she is become quite a foreigner, and talks a very Swedish patois of Scottish English, if you can imagine such a thing.

*Thursday,* 31*st.*—When I got up, I found my leg equally swelled and painful; but nothing could be done, so we departed soon after eight o'clock, and came through a prettyish country with fine woods for eighty-five miles to Falkenberg. The stage before reaching that town is beautiful, made up of woods, and a great deal of wild ground interspersed with birch copses. The woods were full of gentian, lilies of the valley, wood-anemones, &c.

Our equipage was arranged as follows—we had hired a coachman (Hüberg), recommended by the Commandant Katterholm at Helsingborg; he sat upon a wooden seat, constructed at Helsingborg, and placed upon the fore-trunk with room for another by his side, where sat one of the peasants to whom our post horses belonged. These horses were like a better sort of highland pony, but in bad condition, having been half starved by the heat of the preceding summer. We had bought our own harness at Helsingborg; it was very simple, mostly made of leather, though the reins were of rope; the horses had sometimes four shoes; sometimes two only, on the fore feet, and sometimes none at all. We had six horses to our carriage, and two to the little one; they were harnessed four-abreast next to the carriage, and driven by the coachman, the two leaders being managed by a postillion; the latter was usually a great heavy peasant, who rode without a saddle or stirrups. In spite of the primitiveness of our *attelage*, these little animals went very well, and securely, at the rate of between seven and eight miles an hour; the roads were very good, and our coachman was a very good driver. At one place, however, we found the bridge across a river completely broken down, and we had to cross upon a temporary bridge made of planks, which lay level with the river; all the horses were taken off except two, which brought us very successfully over the bridge. We had to wait for our horses at each stage, as we performed them in a shorter time than we expected, and we found at the end of the day that the *forebüd* was not far enough before us. The stages were short, generally of about nine or ten English miles. At ten o'clock we got to Falkenberg, famous for a large salmon fishery near the mouth of the river. A baddish inn, the people could talk only Swedish; we had an indifferent supper, and I slept for the first time in my own bed, which we carried with us, and which I found very comfortable.

*Friday, June 1st.*—We left Falkenberg at eight, a.m., came through a bare country, extremely like parts of Scotland, only in some places more wooded; towards the end of the day had to wait for the horses as before, but reached Gottenburg about eight p.m. Here we were kept a little time at the Custom-House, but referred the searchers to the imperial. This, as I should have mentioned before, travelled in the little open carriage of the country, which Belgrave had bought at Helsingborg, and which contained my bed ; and was drawn by two horses, which Gartner drove occasionally at a furious pace, accompanied by one of the peasants, the owner of some of the horses. The peasants are very anxious to go on these tours along with their horses, in order to bring them back ; and besides the three, who regularly went with us, another would sometimes run by our side the whole of the stage. When we arrived at Gottenburg, where Gartner soon followed us without anything having been opened at the Custom-House, Belgrave immediately set out to find Mr. Dickson, to whom we had a letter, in order to get some advice

for my leg, which was still very painful and
much swelled. It was pouring with rain; but
he soon discovered an English physician, Mr.
Lambert, who came to us without delay, and
prescribed rest, and promised that he would see
me again the next morning. Our apartments were
tolerable.

*Saturday, June 2nd.*—We had an early visit from
Mr. Dickson, and soon after another from Mr.
Lambert, who said that I might put on leeches,
and must keep my leg up; accordingly he sent
eight leeches, and more voracious animals never
were seen. I could hardly prevent them from
biting my fingers in taking them out of their glass;
and they fixed the moment they were applied,
biting like pen-knives; we put on seven, and never
saw anything like their size, and the quantity of
blood they took away, as well as what rushed out
for some time afterwards. I remained all day
on the sofa, and Belgrave went to dine at Mr.
Dickson; he there met Count Rosen, and his
two sons, and Mr. Hainson, the English Vice-
Consul.

Mrs. Dickson was a Swede, but speaks both
English and French. Mr. Dickson is Scotch. Mrs.
Dickson sent me some Vanille Cream and dessert

in the evening. When Belgrave came home, we drank tea and went to bed.

*Sunday, 3rd.*—I was better, but Mr. Lambert would not let me leave Gottenburg before Tuesday. Belgrave went, after breakfast, to Mr. Dickson, and returned before one to dress, in order to go to dine in the country, about seven miles from Gottenburg, with Mr. Wyk. Count Rosen's son came to fetch him. Bokedal, Mr. Wyk's place, is a villa prettily situated about eight English miles from Gottenburg on the Stockholm road. Belgrave was conveyed there in Mr. Dickson's barouche. He met there a party of about thirty, who entertained him very hospitably. They dined at three o'clock, and drank toasts after dinner, the first being the health of the stranger who visited their country; they then sang several songs and national airs; the morning had been wet, but they walked out for a short time after dinner, and Belgrave then returned home, accompanied by Count Rosen, in Mr. Dickson's carriage, reaching Gottenburg between eight and nine o'clock. I remained all day on the sofa. Belgrave came in with Count Rosen, who made us a long visit after that we had tea and went to bed. We found the bread, butter, and cream at this hotel

(Segerlinds) very good.  *La cuisine*, otherwise, only
tolerable.

*Monday, 4th.*—This morning arrived Setterberg,
the coachman recommended by Lord Bloomfield,
having travelled six days and nights to catch us
up; he had been down to Helsingborg, and then
had followed us up to Gottenburg; we were, at
first, rather puzzled, being already provided with
Hüberg, but finding that our new friend spoke
English, and was highly recommended as a useful
servant as well as a very good driver, we determined on taking him.  Hüberg then requested to
be allowed to go on as *forebüd*, which answered
very well; and we found it, in the sequel, very
useful to have a regular *forebüd* of our own.

When I got up I found my leg so much better,
that I was able to walk without the least inconve-
nience, and therefore accepted Count Rosen's
invitation to dine at his house.  In the morning,
we had visits from him and his daughter, and Mr.
and Mrs. Dickson.  At half-past three, he sent
his carriage to take us to dinner; we found a party
of about twenty-four, consisting of himself and
Countess Rosen, their three sons, Mademoiselle
de Rosen, Mr. and Mrs. Dickson, Count Platen,
a Baron d'Argleswelt (from L'Ostro-Gotha),

Captain Schultz and several more gentlemen and ladies.

The *avant-repas* of salt fish, tongue, brandy, &c., was served in the outer room; but we very soon sat down to dinner, and as Swedish dinners are, I suppose, all alike, I will give the description of this, once for all. The dessert is placed upon the table before the meal commences, and the dinner is carried round, dish by dish, all ready carved, and offered to each person, beginning with dried salmon; then followed macaroni, stewed or roast beef, eggs and ham, or veal, soup, some other meat, fish, chicken and blackcock; then cream, which generally concludes the feast.

There are a great many sorts of wine here, and the gentlemen drink a great deal during dinner, which from the dishes being carried round singly, with an interval between each, is rather a long proceeding. But, *en revanche*, they are a very short time at dessert, and both gentlemen and ladies go together back to the drawing-room, where coffee is served. Before they move, however, the gentlemen frequently sing one or two songs; and at Count Rosen's, Captain Schultz sang a beautiful little Swedish song, without music, before we left the dinner table. After dinner, a Monsieur de Berg

came in, and sang a great deal, quite beautifully,
having a very fine voice, and great taste; Captain
Schultz, whose voice was almost equally good, also
sung frequently; and the national Swedish air—
answering to our " God save the King"—sung by
him and Monsieur de Berg together was beautiful.
After some time we had tea, and the evening passed
most pleasantly between singing and talking, till
half-past ten, when we returned home. 1 forgot
to say that after dinner, Count Rosen proposed
our health with a " short" and appropriate speech,
and Belgrave then proposed that of Madame de
Rosen, before we got up from dessert.

Nothing could exceed their kindness, and the
perfect ease, and pleasantness of the whole evening.
Count Rosen's house is a good one and very prettily
situated, looking out on the sea; the rooms, like
all foreign ones, were perfectly bare, with only a
sofa and a few chairs ranged against the wall, and
those such as would hardly be admitted in an English inn; but such is the custom, and one never
thinks about it. Count Platen,* whom I mentioned as one of the company, is a very distinguished person; a fine good-natured old man of
about seventy.

* The father of the late Swedish Minister in London.

*Tuesday,* 5*th.*—We got up at six, as I was quite well enough to continue the journey, and received from Mrs. Dickson two bags of excellent rusks; we had also laid in a provision of tongues, some salt beef, chocolate prepared with Iceland Moss, some wine, and plenty of white bread, besides what I formerly mentioned. As we were going away, we met at the door, one of the gentlemen who had been our fellow-passenger from London to Hamburg. We fared very well at this hotel; all its passages, staircases, &c., were, as usual, horribly dirty. We found the horses much thinner, and in worse condition to-day than heretofore; but our new coachman managed them extremely well, and we went on at a great pace. We passed through Lilta Edit, where a new canal was being cut, and got to Trothälta by about six. We found a very nice apartment in a house close to the inn, and belonging to it—it was a mere country inn; but our rooms were decently clean, and so there was nothing to complain of. We ordered dinner, and then proceeded with Mr. Allen, the superintendant of the saw-mills, to whom Mr. Dickson had given us a letter, in order to see the falls of the river. They are more beautiful from their number and variety than from any one great volume of water, and are, therefore, not to be compared to those of Schaffhäusen. Still they are very fine, and from the saw-mills being built over the middle of the river, one can stand exactly *over* some of the falls, which has a very fine effect.

The rocks in them and around them are magnificent, and the banks are very high, and covered with masses of fir wood. There is a short bit of what was intended by Christina for the line of the canal, excavated between rocks of an amazing steepness. The work, however, being suddenly stopped in the middle, there comes a straight fall, perfectly perpendicular, of a very great height. Some adventurous women insisted on wading to nearly the edge of the fall to poke down for our amusement some large trees which had become wedged in the rocks ; it seemed to me the most frightful and dangerous work ; and it was not till after repeated signs, nor finally till we had beaten a retreat, that they could be persuaded to give up their object.

We went down the canal in a boat, getting out occasionally to see the most remarkable places; we then rowed about two miles further down, and again landed to inspect the locks which are very curious, being constructed between perpendicular rocks of great height, with a path and railing carried

along the edge of the precipice on one side.
They are eight in number, three adjoining the river,
and five up the side of the mountain; and were so
made in order to raise the water to the level of one
hundred and twenty feet above the river.

We rowed back again and took leave of Mr.
Allen who is a very sensible intelligent man; and
returned to our inn, where we supped soon after
eight on salmon.

*Wednesday, 6th.*—We set out at eight a.m.;
passed through Wennersborg at the head of the
Lake Wenner, and through Odesvalla. The country
about this place is extremely pretty, with woods,
rocks and lakes, all of which seem never to come
to an end. As we advanced, the country became
less pretty and more barren; we got to Hide about
seven. Before arriving at Hide, our off leader fell
down, on which all our assistants—the coachman
excepted—went into a most dreadful fright, and the
*purring* noise which they immediately set up is not
to be described; all in various tones of horror and
lamentation. Pr·r-r-r-r-r-uh! being the kind of
sound with which they stop their horses. The
horse, poor beast, was up again in a moment, and
no mischief done.

We found our *forebüd* who told us that the

inn was full with a Justice meeting, but that at a smaller house, about two hundred yards from it, we should be provided with a couple of rooms. We accordingly went there, and found two very decent apartments ; one for ourselves, and the other for my maid. Gartner and the coachman were accommodated at the other inn. We had a supper of black-cock, potatoes, and six lobsters, all of which were excellent.

*Thursday 7th.*—We got up at four a.m., and were off by a quarter past six ; it soon began to rain, and poured in torrents, which did not cease till after we had crossed the ferry of Swinnesund. This separates Sweden and Norway, and is a very beautiful pass. The bridges are constructed out of the bodies of trees placed across and covered with a little earth, and each one has generally in it two or three or more holes passing completely through it, so that the water below is perfectly visible, and it is a miracle how the horses gallop over without falling, in which case they must be killed, or at least break their legs, as it would be impossible at the pace they go to stop the others. It is often necessary to put a drag on one wheel, and very frequently on two.

The rain began to clear away as we approached

West Goard, and by the time we reached the inn, the day was quite fine. We found this inn much better and cleaner in appearance than most, and after eating some cold meat, Belgrave and I got into our little open wicker carriage to see Fredericshall, about four English miles off. Setterberg went with us in another little carriage with one horse. We had a pair of very good steeds which Belgrave drove; the view from above Fredericshall is very pretty, embracing the town, the sea full of islands, and the fortress which stands in single masses of two or three distinct bodies of buildings perched on high rocks immediately overhanging the town. Fredericshall looks as if it was a new settlement, from the quantities of new houses which are being built, the greatest part of it having been burned last year. The houses are almost all of wood; as indeed is generally the case in Norway.

We drove through the town, up a steep paved road, half way up to the fortress. Here we left the carriages and walked up through the Castle, taking a soldier as a guide to the spot where Charles XII. was shot. This spot is marked by a very small shabby white obelisk with a concise inscription and the date.

The situation of the fortress is delicious, with

green banks, woods, and beautiful walks; behind
it the view from it also is splendid, looking up into
the interior of the rocks and mountains of Norway;
and on the other side over the town, the sea and the
islands beyond.

The place where the King was killed commands
this view, and looks straight at the fortress, from
whence, however, it is too distant to be reached by a
pistol bullet. The ground was covered with wild
flowers, and particularly heartsease, with which the
fields along the whole of the road were often quite
purple.

The pavement of the town is horrible; we got
back to West Goard soon after three, and proceeded
again in our own carriage as before; we went
through Fredericstadt, a small pretty fortified town;
crossed a ferry there with very little trouble, as the
men understood taking in and out the carriage.
We continued our journey on a very fine evening;
but the roads were not so good as usual, owing to
the quantity of rain which had fallen; and in one of
the jolts occasioned by the numerous holes, the iron
bars which support the hind seat became bent.
We were, therefore, obliged to proceed slowly and
with caution, till we got to Moss at a little before
twelve. We were disappointed in the inn which

we had been told was very good, but *indifferent* was all we could say for it. We went to bed at half past one, somewhat sleepy. It is but fair to say, that though we had been warned that we should get *nothing* to eat at these inns, yet with the assistance of our *forebüd* we mostly found a good dinner, and that the eggs, and cream, and milk were very good ; we, of course, ate our own bread, as that of the country is disagreeable ; but with this, and our own tea, our fare was as good as travellers could desire.

*Friday, 8th.*—As we were to have but a short journey to-day, we did not get up till eight, and had the advantage of tubs of very fresh water, which we usually found everywhere; at Hidè, instead of one of the usual kind, I had a *slop-basin* besides. We set out about ten o'clock, and came through a very pretty country of very fine rocks, covered with woods—all full of wood anemones— green fields, and beautiful lakes, the whole looking like a magnificent park, and the hills most abrupt, indeed, almost violent ; the horses, too, became much improved, being fatter and in better condition. We have had some very nice horses since we came into Norway, most of them are dun, with eel backs, and however wild their manners may be, the moment they are in harness they are perfectly quiet, and go without any tricks, pulling very evenly, and with all their might. Our road, in the latter part, lay through woods, and was very wet. On descending Mount Egebert, the view is one of the most superb that can be conceived; the whole district lies around you and at your feet likē a panorama.

The town of Christiana is immediately below, at the head of a large bay, with many ships and many islands; the country around stretching out in a large fertile plain till it reaches a boundary of magnificent mountains covered with black looking woods, all together, forming the most beautiful outline, while the whole of the view is grand from its immensity. The descent from Mount Egebert to the town is terrific from its steepness, the road making very sharp turns and zigzags; we got down, however, very successfully, dragging two of our wheels, and on arriving in the town we met our *forebüd*, who told us that he had been unable to get rooms at Mrs. Werner's, where we wished to lodge, as that house was quite full; but that he had taken rooms at Carstang's, where we did *not* wish to go, but as there were no other inns in the town we had no option, and consequently went there. We found a very good apartment cleaned out for us, and were very comfortably established about seven o'clock, and at nine had an exceedingly good dinner.

*Saturday, 9th.*—I stayed at home all the morning. Belgrave went out to call on Count Wedel Jarlsberg, to whom we had five letters, and whom he saw in the middle of parliamentary business, as the Diet was sitting; he asked us to dine with him the next day at his house in the country, called Bokestadt. Belgrave then called on Count Sandels, (the Governor of Norway,) to whom we had also letters, and whom he found at home. We dined at four, and took a walk late in the evening on some high cliffs, looking down on the sea, where we saw both men and horses bathing; we then walked all about the town and on the piers, and called on Mr. Keyser, to whom Belgrave had a letter, but did not find him at home.

*Sunday 10th.*—We got up at half-past seven; tried at breakfast some of the chocolate with Iceland Moss, which we found very palatable. Belgrave went afterwards to the Norwegian Church, he came home about half-past eleven and read prayers with me; we had afterwards a visit from Monsieur Berg. At half-past one we set out, *en demi parure,* in a hired chariot and three, to dine at Bokestadt, Count Wedel's house, about eight English miles from Christiana. The road to it is, as usual, very pretty, lying by the water-side, and through fields, gardens, and forests. We arrived a little before three, and found most of the company, altogether amounting to about twenty-six, already assembled. We found Count Wedel exactly what he had been described to us, extremely frank, good-natured, friendly, and open-hearted; the house is very pretty, it seemed comfortable and nicely furnished, a large drawing-room full of pictures and furnished with green damask, a suite of several rooms and a very pleasant and cool dining-room. All the party, though so numerous, came, as Count Wedel said, uninvited, for he keeps a *table ouverte* with a large number of covers, which are generally most full on Sunday. After dinner we had coffee and tea in the garden, where we sat and walked. It is prettily placed on the borders of a clear little lake. We went to the kitchen garden, and to the stables, where we saw seven beautiful little Norwegian horses, dun or cream-coloured, with eel backs, and black manes and tails. Count Sandels, the Viceroy of Norway, and his wife, came in the evening, and when we returned from our walk, we

had a repast of tea, punch, porter, oranges, &c.
Count Sandels solaced himself with oranges and a
*glass of porter*, in which he inserted lumps of sugar !
We passed a very pleasant evening, were delighted
with Count and Countess Wedel, and returned home
between nine and ten o'clock.

*Monday* 11*th.*—We got up at seven, and breakfasted at half-past eight; soon after Mr. Myggind,
the English Vice-Consul, arrived, to assist Belgrave
in writing out the orders for horses, ' which the
*forebüd* was to leave at all the posts on the road to
Drontheim. This labour took up the whole of the
morning, and it was two o'clock when Hüberg was
enabled to set out on his journey.

We then went with Mr. Myggind to look at
some lodgings for me, when I was to return from
Count Wedel's at Bokestadt, which was to be on
the Sunday following. We got home to dress only
at half-past two, to go to dine at Count Sandels,
four English miles out of town. We arrived at
half-past three, and found a large party of above
thirty people, among whom were Count and
Countess Wedel, La Baronne Wedel, Madame
Folkt, &c., &c. There were present, besides several
ladies, Admiral Fabricius, several gentlemen and .
officers, and Mr. Myggind, who returned in our

E 2

carriage after dinner with us. Count Sandels' house is about half-way between Christiana and Bokestadt, and very prettily situated in a garden on the lake. The dinner was remarkably handsome, and would have been considered so anywhere, even in London. We stayed a short time after dinner and took coffee, and returned home by seven, as we had a great deal of packing and arrangements to get through for the next day. Mr. Myggind came again with the account that the lodging we had seen in the morning could not be had, but that he had seen another nearly opposite our hotel. I went with him to look at it, and found it very nice, but the people could not be sure of letting it till next Thursday. We left the negociation in the hands of Mr. Myggind, who then wished us good-night, after having been of the greatest use to us throughout the day. I forgot to say, that in coming home from dinner, we stopped with him at his house, which is small but very pretty, beautifully placed on the edge of the sea. We were well occupied in the evening in arranging the canteen, and all the preparations for Belgrave's journey to Dronthiem, which he was to begin the next day.

Christiana,
Monday, June 11th, 1827.

Dearest M——

Here we are living " habitually, like the angels,"
in the capital city of Norway, which I think sounds
very imposing and dazzling ; how you would like
this most beautiful of countries ! Shall I tell you
all that we have done since quitting Helsingborg ?
where, when I was writing to you, I had a strange
pain and swelling that came on in the muscle below
my knee, which in the course of an hour made
me quite lame. I could not, of course, tell what
it was, so I let it alone, and next day we set out
in the Swedish manner, having sent on an *avant
courier* the day before to order horses, six of them
to draw our carriage, and two to draw a little open
wicker carriage and part of our luggage. Ours are
harnessed four abreast, driven by the coachman,
the pair in front have a postillion, a great heavy
peasant without saddle or stirrups.

The horses are like a better sort of Scotch pony,
but in Sweden they are in bad condition this year ;
the intense heat last year having left them little or
no grass ; but they are sweet little beasts, and go
at a prodigious pace, supporting the carriage very

well about half way down the tremendous hills;
then they begin to trot, then gallop at full speed
over the inevitable bridge, which is sure to be found
at the bottom; then they rush straight up the next
hill at the same rate. They have no tricks, and
go as securely as possible. The stages are very
short, an arrangement which enables them to go
so fast.

At Gottenburg we found a Mr. Dickson, a rich
Scotch merchant, to whom we had been recommended, and who is married to a very agreeable
Swedish woman, who talks both French and English. They had been at Eaton in 1822, and
knew all about the place. They helped us to an
English physician, who prescribed rest for my leg,
and said I might put on leeches, which I did the
next day to the number of seven, and such voracious,
insatiable creatures I never saw; they did prodigious
execution. I remained quiet for two days, and by
Monday was perfectly well. Belgrave dined on
Saturday at Mr. Dickson's, and on Sunday at a
country place of a Mr. Wyk's, where he was taken
by Count Rosen, the Governor of Gottenburg. On
Monday, I was well enough to dine at three, at
Count Rosen's; we had about twenty-four people, a
mixture of merchants, aides-de-camp, and a curious

old Count Platen, the only *nobleman* who gives himself the least trouble to be useful in Sweden. He is much occupied with Mr. Telford* upon an enormous work, a canal to unite one of the lakes with the Northern Sea. He is about seventy, and talks English well. The dinner, like all Swedish ones, is composed of very good dishes carried round one after the other. The dinner itself is rather long, and the gentlemen drink a good deal of wine, of which they, during dinner, have every kind ; the dessert is very short, and both gentleman and ladies get up together ; then one has coffee, tea, &c. Some of the gentlemen sing beautifully ; they sung after dinner, with and without music, and we staid till late, as they made the *soirée* for us.

The way of living here is not splendid, but very easy and hospitable ; and nothing could be kinder than Mr. and Mrs. Dickson, and the Rosens, or more civil than everybody. We set out on Tuesday, and were three nights, making long days, on coming here. We saw, by the way, the Falls of Trolhälta, and the beautiful town and fortress of Friedericsthal, where Charles XII. was killed. We were not at all starved at the inns, as we

---

* The eminent English engineer.

were told would be the case; but have found
excellent dinners of salmon, black-cock, potatoes,
and our own bread and tea; and all the country
inns have excellent cream and eggs, so we live like
princes.

I cannot describe to you the beauty and charms
of this country, it is a succession of lakes, woods,
and rich fields, with rocks overhanging them, and
immense districts covered with forests. The road,
the whole of the way, is like going through a magnificent *Place;* the forests are covered with
bilberries, and full of lilies of the valley, wood
anemones, gentians, and a thousand beautiful sorts
of flowers, and the fields and rocks are purple
with heartsease, which grows wild. The magnificence and the charm of the views are not to be told;
so I need not try to do so; but I do wish you could
be here to see them.

From the moment we stepped into Sweden, we
heard of nothing but the praises of Count and
Countess Wedel Jarlsberg, who live eight English
miles from here; he is the greatest "Seigneur" of
Norway, and so universally popular among the
gentry as well as the peasants that at the time of the
troubles he had some votes for being chosen King.
He is married to the daughter and heiress of the

Minister Anker, a family who were, in these parts, what the Medici were in Florence; and an immense heiress she is! I never saw such taking people as they both are; he is the most open-hearted, good-natured, gay, and yet sensible man imaginable; and she is charming, very gentle and amiable, and excessively kind; both of them enjoy their delicious *Place*, with its forests, and their stud of horses, (seven beautiful cream colour with eel backs like one we once had at Trentham,)* and keeping *table ouverte* of twenty-six covers every day. We dined with him yesterday, the table was more than full; and nobody invited by a regular summons; but a very pleasant society. True, the dinner was at that horrid hour of three, which cuts up all one's day; but here it was very pleasant, as we spent all the evening in walking about the gardens, which are delightfully placed upon a little lake, with hills behind covered with wood like Switzer-land and Dunkeld. I shall write to you more about these people afterwards, as I am going to stay there some days while Belgrave goes to Dronthiem, which journey we find, upon examination, would be too fatiguing for me, as one must go on in little open carriages without springs, making very long

* The Duke of Sutherland's seat in Staffordshire.

daily journeys, (six days to Dronthiem only), and very bad sleeping places ; so I am to set out early with him to-morrow, when we are to meet Countess Wedel on the road ; and see something to be seen with her; then Belgrave goes on, and I come back with her and her ponies to her place at Bokestadt, where we dined yesterday. I stay with her till next Sunday, or Monday, when she is obliged to go to some warm baths for her health. I shall then return here, and remain in a lodging in a private house till Belgrave returns ; probably about a week. Then we set out immediately, and go by Danemora and to Fahlun, to see the mines, which will bring us to Stockholm about the first week in July. You would delight in Countess Wedel ; she is so natural and *prévenante*, and gentlewoman-like. To day we dine with Count Sandels, the Viceroy of Norway, a stupidish old man, with a frightful little wife, somewhat affected. The parliament is now sitting, at which Count Wedel is occupied generally from nine in the morning till late every evening. The Parliaments are held only once in three years, but they bring very hard work when they do come. Lord Bloomfield's coachman caught us up at Gottenburg, and a most valuable servant he is, as, besides being an excellent driver, he is a most useful, trusty, and intelligent servant, and talks English as well as the native languages. Our Helsingborg coachman is converted into an *avant courier*, so we are admirably provided. These two go on with Belgrave to Dronthiem, and Gartner, who is a very good cook as well as a good servant, remains with me. Perhaps Belgrave will see a Lapland tribe, as there is one between Dronthiem and Bergen, from whence those came who were to be seen with the reindeer at Balloch, two or three years ago. Perhaps he will see an elk too, for there are still some in the country ; and there are plenty of wolves and bears, but they do not come about till winter.

There is nothing to be seen or done in this town ; but that is lucky, as these three o'clock dinners—a few miles from town—leave one time for nothing. They seem to doat upon the King in this country ; the Crown Princess is expecting to be confined this month, which I am very sorry for, as we shall not see her, and everybody praises her highly. The women here dress horridly, like the English lower classes, with coloured prints, and they have a *mauvaise tournure*. The women, among the peasants, are hideous and dirty beyond description.

*Tuesday, June* 12*th.  At Carsten's Hotel, Christiana.*—We got up at half-past seven, and were busy
in arranging all Belgrave's things for his journey,
and also making other preparations to leave the
hotel, the master of which is a disagreeable cheat.
We left our carriage still at the blacksmith's, as it
was not quite mended, so Belgrave and I set out at
half-past seven in the little wicker open carriage and
pair, with his baggage, Zetterberg, the coachman,
following in a little one horse carriage. Belgrave
and I went (with one horse very lame) by a beautiful
road, full of superb views, to Barum, a house of
Count Wedel's, two posts from Christiana. It is
situated in a deep valley, with a rapid river and
some small iron works close to it; here we met
Countess Wedel, who took us first to see the cast-
ing of the iron in different moulds, and the making
of cauldrons, &c. We then went with her into
the house, which is spacious and one of the most
comfortable possible; the large room into which you
enter is in plan like an irregular L, full of nice
corners, and hung all over with prints and drawings.
She gave us an excellent breakfast of chocolate, cold
meat, wood pigeons, all kinds of bread, wine, &c.,
and after this we set forth to go a stage with Belgrave on his journey. Belgrave took Zetterberg,

and I went with Countess Wedel in a little open
chaise, her coachman driving a pair of her little
cream-coloured horses, with long tails ; it is wonderful how the animals go up and down the hills,
absolutely *climbing* up the steep ones, and almost
sitting down on their hind-quarters when they
descend. We changed horses about two or three
miles from Barum, Belgrave for two other post
horses, and Countess Wedel for a pair of her
Barum horses. We went through a magnificent
and enormous forest, with not a house to be seen
for miles, but surrounded with hills ; none, however,
were of great size, except one, till we came near to
Kingrede, which was much the most tremendous
we have seen ; all but perpendicular, and very long.
We had broken one of the shafts of Countess
Wedel's carriage ; this we left at the top to be repaired, and walked down the hill, which forms a
magnificent narrow defile, very precipitous and well
wooded, through which, as you descend, a splendid
view is gradually developed, of a very fine and
fertile valley, well wooded, and with several lakes ;
and at a distance are seen the glaciers covered with
snow. It is impossible to describe the scene, it
could only be rivalled by one that we had seen in
the morning from a great height ; as we looked.

down on Christiana, its bay full of islands, and surrounded by mountains. The hill was so steep that it was necessary to tie together two wheels of Belgrave's carriage, and it then required the united strength of Zetterberg and himself to prevent its running over the horses, who had great difficulty in scrambling down, and one of them tried by two immense jumps straight up in the air to get rid of the whole concern. We, at length, arrived at the bottom, but had before that been passed by Countess Wedel's carriage, which arrived cantering down the latter part of the hill, with the broken shaft perfectly repaired by the help of the stem of a young fir tree. We finally arrived at the inn where Belgrave changed horses; and after eating some oranges, he continued on' his way to Dronthiem, accompanied by Zetterberg.

Countess Wedel and I remained some time in the inn while our horses were baiting, and while we were sitting and talking in the best room were gratified by the view of an immense rat! We had the additional society of a very friendly puppy, who partook of some milk with us; and when our horses were ready, we set out again on our return, in the same carriage which had brought us. Our horses took us very steadily to the top of the hill, and then we exchanged them for a pair of little thin weasels, who could only gallop down the hills with us, but could hardly drag us up. At last, we arrived at Barum, and while the horses were changing we went to another manufactory to see an enormous iron hammer used for flattening iron. Our carriage and long-tailed dun horses then took us up, and conveyed us the latter part of the way by a cross, but still very beautiful, road to Boke-stadt, where we arrived after a delightful expedition of about forty miles, very tired and hungry, and well shaken, before nine. We found that Count Wedel had not returned from Christiana, and we made an excellent supper, at which were the tutor and the children. Soon after Count Wedel arrived as gay and *rayonnant* 'as usual; we talked for a little time in the drawing-room, and were very ready to go to our bed-rooms soon after ten.

*Wednesday, June 13th.*—We breakfasted about ten o'clock, Countess Wedel and Mr. Wolf, the children's tutor, her daughter of twelve, and her son Hermon, about nine years old, and Marie, a little girl also of nine, whom the Countess has adopted, her parents having been unfortunate. These children do their lessons in a small summer-house close to the house, where Mr. Wolf teaches them. After breakfast the Countess and I went in a little boat on the lake to try and catch some perch in a net, which was arranged by some men in another boat ; but our fishery only extended to seven, as the fish *would not* be caught. We then rowed across the lake to see the process of burning wood for charcoal ; then, as it was very hot, we came home, and sat in the drawing-room till three o'clock, when Madame Voght and her sister, Mademoiselle Frölich, came to dinner ; after dinner we went in the evening, in two little open carriages, to drink tea in a cottage belonging to the school-master of the district, about three or four miles from Bokestadt. We took our own provisions with us, but there was excellent cream at the cottage, which, though we were not expected, we found cleaner than most English ones. We drank tea in a large wooden room ; the cottage is in the most beautiful situation, on a sort of terrace which looks perpendicularly down into a valley with mountains covered with wood ; we came back about ten, and the ladies went home. Count Wedel did not come home to-day, on account of the Parliament at Christiana ; during its sitting, which lasts six months every third year, he is obliged to be in his place from eight every morning till eight or nine in the evening.

*Thursday* 14*th.*—We stayed at home all the morning working in the drawing-room ; after our three o'clock dinner we went to dress for Mr. Berg's concert at Christiana. We arrived there at about seven, and finding that the concert did not begin till eight, we remained at a small apartment which Count Wedel rents in the street of Skipper Garten, till it was time to go. We found the concert arranged in a small theatre, the orchestra consisted of about five and twenty, all amateurs, who performed very tolerably ; the singing was all by Mr. Berg, except one duet in which he was assisted by some gentleman who was inaudible. There was also a duet of violins. Mr. Berg sang some of Rossini's music, and ended with some Swedish national airs accompanied by himself on the pianoforte ; we returned to Bokestadt about half-past eleven, Count Wedel with us.

*Friday* 15*th.*—Count Wedel disappeared early for the Parliament ; the Countess and I sat in the drawing-room till dinner, when arrived a Monsieur Everlich, a secretary of the Viceroy, who brought Madame sa Mère and a stupid brother to dine at Bokestadt ; while walking in the garden the mamma

F

said to Madame Wedel, "Ah! Madame, si vous saviez comme j'adore mon fils—c'est-à-dire mon fils le secrétaire," to the evident detriment of the other *pauvre honteux*, of whom no notice was taken, except to give him the last taste of a stalk of rhubarb after it had made the round of the company. After these people went, Madame Wedel and I went in her close carriage-and-four to drink tea with Mr. Myggind, the British Vice-Consul, who has a house beautifully situated on the edge of the sea ; after tea, which we had in the garden, we walked about and rowed in a boat to the opposite land, to ascend a little height covered with strawberries and wild flowers, and from whence we had a magnificent view of all the surrounding country—the party consisted only of Monsieur and Madame Wedel, a brother of the Countess, and Mademoiselle Rosencrantz. We came home soon after ten o'clock.

*Saturday,* 16*th.*—We sat, as usual, in the drawing-room till dinner, and afterwards had five of the dun carriage-horses turned loose into the court to amuse themselves—and us. They galloped, kicked and rolled in the dust like furies, and when called, all rushed to the hall steps, to lick up salt and receive bread ; after a good romp, one was led into the stables, whither the rest, after a little more galloping and kicking, all ran of their own accord. We had a delightful quiet evening. The Count returned late; we had sent to him to make our excuse for not going to drink tea at Mr. Everlich's, which he had accordingly done. An amateur painter dined at Bokestadt to-day, and an incipient young painter, who was making a walking tour over the country, came in the evening to remain some days. The Countess was obliged to dispatch a *forebüd* this evening to order horses for our next day's expedition—fraught with the fate of the Viceroy and his *fête.*

*Sunday* 17*th.*—The Countess and I were obliged to get up at six, in order to breakfast and set out at half-past seven, leaving the Count in bed with the gout in his foot; we went in the Countess' barouche, with three of her horses, driven by Mathis, her coachman, to the post beyond Christiana, where we changed horses; at the next post we overtook their Excellencies, who were regaling themselves with bread and cheese, while they were changing; we went on about ten miles farther, when we arrived at the scene of festivity, Drebak, a very pretty little village on the sea-coast; here we found the Viceroy and Vice-reine, and about twenty of the company assembled; the Baronne de Wedel, Monsieur and

Madame Mausback, &c., in a private house which the owners had lent for the occasion; everybody looked very hot, and we did not particularly know what to do with ourselves, dinner being at two, while we had arrived before one. But we · were not first, for some of the company had been there already for two hours. *Les Conseillers d'Etat* and several others were all to come in a boat, which could not possibly get there in time, the wind being equally contrary. We waited about till two. *Point de bâteau.* Till three: *Encore moins!* To wait longer was by no means *convenable*, as the steam-packet on which we were all to be conveyed back to Christiana was expected about four; so down we sat to dinner in a large wooden room; the dinner had caught cold by waiting, all but the butter, which, by the excessive warmth of weather, had become rancid; the dishes were like "angels' visits," not "few," but very "far between," in order to give time for the scattered members of the flock to join us. But all to no purpose: it was not till we had got up from our laborious repast that they arrived, having walked two miles under a burning sun, because the adverse winds would not let them get nearer; some were very fat, some very thin, some with crosses, some with stars, but all were very dirty and very hot; all ate with their knives, and in no small quantity; the ladies followed suite. The steamboat or, in the language of the country, the *dampfschiffe*, happily did not arrive till past six, which was much later than usual ; we then made a noble procession through the assembled multitudes down to the pier, the poor Viceroy tottering with Countess Wedel and me, and a very large fat gentleman with old boots, all of a row; then followed the flower of the Norwegian nobility, who have much intrinsic merit, but are certainly not made for show ; the whole was closed with the band of music in a sort of green baize uniform. The more inactive of the party found some difficulty in choosing the right moment to skip in and out of the little boats, the wind being high and a *dancing* sea ; but we soon found ourselves safely disposed of on board the *dampfschiffe*, where our arrival must have been more splendidly dazzling than welcome, as we found that we added about thirty or forty to the three hundred and twenty souls already assembled there. There were many respectable persons but none so much so (or half so clean) as a very fine jet black English pointer, belonging to a Mr. Pelly, who was on board also. The band played a good deal; and by a desperate effort, Mademoiselle Wedel and I broke through a sort of "hunt the slipper" circle, in which the ladies of our party had been placed on our embarking, and in which we saw neither land or sea, nor anything but ourselves; but having already had more than enough of that sight, we went to amuse ourselves by looking out of the ship.

The sail up to Christiana is very fine, and the views are beautiful. We, at length, arrived about ten o'clock, and it would be ungrateful not to mention that the Viceroy had routed himself and all the State, and instituted this *fête* entirely for my amusement. Madame de Wedel was returning to Bokestadt, but I did not accompany her again, as she was to leave it in a day or two *pour les bains*. I therefore came to inhabit my new lodging, which I found a most delightfully comfortable one, consisting of an extremely clean staircase painted in marble, a very large drawing-room, a smaller one, where I dine and sit, an ante-room, where the servants dine, my bedroom, my maid's room, a lumber room, a kitchen, and lastly Gartner's room. I find a pianoforte in my room, and nothing can be more clean and comfortable than the whole place.

*Monday, June* 18*th.*—Got up between eight and nine, received letters which Mr. Bloomfield sent us from Stockholm ; breakfasted; then wrote letters for the evening's post; dined at three on a very good dinner, the soup, apparently, made of rice and cream. After dinner I read and worked, and played on the pianoforte. Madame Voght called about seven, and I took a walk with her about the town ; bought a blue and white striped *batiste* gown and some Norwegian music ; then came home to tea.

*Tuesday,* 19*th.*—Wrote letters. After breakfast, received a visit from Countess Sandels. At half-past twelve the Baronne Wedel called for me in her barouche and pair, to go to dine at Bokestadt. We stopped at a house belonging also to Countess Wedel, called Wechtereux, where she and the Baron live in the summer, to deposit cakes and comfits, as we were to have tea there in the evening. We then went on to Bokestadt, where we found Countess Wedel just sitting down to dinner, which she had begun alone, except with her children and the tutor, and a Mademoiselle Vich; but the party soon increased to six people more, besides ourselves. To show the simplicity of these family dinners, I will mention that the meals consisted only of soup, boiled beef, a large dish of fish of various kinds, and a large almond pudding. We saw the Count, whose gout was better; and after coffee was over, the

Baronne and I proceeded to Wechtereux, where preparations were made for a sumptuous *thé*. We waited for a time, which seemed ages, when at last arrived Count and Countess Sandels and Captain Sandels, Monsieur le Secrétaire Everlich, and Madame sa Mère and *voilà tout*. Mr. Myggind arrived at the conclusion of the feast. The evening was dreadfully tiresome, and I was delighted to come home, where I was deposited by the Baronne a little before ten.

*Wednesday*, 20*th*.—I amused myself with writing letters and drawing in the morning, and walked at two with Mr. Myggind, who came to fetch me to go to Madame Voght, where I dined *en famille;* nobody being there but herself, her husband (who is one of the *Conseillers d'Etat*), her sister, and Mr. Voght's children. I came home after coffee, early in the afternoon, and passed the remainder of the day " in peace and quiet."

*Thursday*, 21*st*.—I was to have got up at five, in order to go pleasuring with Madame Voght; but it had rained very much in the night, and luckily still rained so hard, that there was nothing to be gained by getting up till seven. She called for me at eight, in a little carriage and pair, driven by a man sitting behind us. The roads were very wet, and the car-

riage splashed the mud in one's face in the most
lively fashion. This manner of driving has the
*agrément* of rubbing the reins against your shoulder
the whole way, not to mention the whip, which after
admonishing the horses, generally recoils vehemently
in your face. We breakfasted on coffee and the
finest cream, with our own bread, at Ramsborg,
where we also changed horses, and went on through
the most beautiful country, abounding in the finest
views (though the day was very cloudy, but soft
and pleasant) to Drammen, a curious Norwegian
town, formerly of great opulence, but now much
sunk in wealth and importance; it is at the head of
a bay, quite encircled by the town, which consists of
merely one street, to the length of about a mile.
We turned back, and in walking up a long hill,
while the horses were eating some cut grass, we were
overtaken by the rain. I got wet through, but my
clothes dried naturally in process of time. The
carriage overtook us, and the rain continuing, Madame Voght took the reins, while the servant held
the umbrella over us. We stopped at a little inn,
to let the rain pass off, and there we dined, and then
got on to Ramsborg, where we again resumed Madame Voght's little brown horses, which came home
at a very quick pace. Sometimes it rained, some-

times not; but the air was delightfully soft and pleasant. When I got home, I found it was eleven o'clock, and being sleepy, I went to bed immediately, having taken no harm from my wetting.

*Friday*, 22*nd*.—Was not quite certain whether Countess Wedel might not come to breakfast here, on her way to *les bains*, so I sent early to inquire at her apartment in town, and found that her departure was again put off.

While I was at breakfast, Mr. Myggind called, and joined me. I had after that a visit from the Count's brother, General Wedel, who was just returned from Dronthiem, and had met Belgrave on his way. I wrote letters, and dined at home at three; after that Madame Voght called for me in her little carriage, where, as usual, the whip did *me* more harm than the horses. We went to see the Botanical Gardens, which are very pretty, and well arranged, and very flourishing; the gooseberries seemed pretty forward, and the currants also growing fat; the hedge roses just blowing, the others in young buds. It began to rain, so we drove to Madame Voght's, where I was to drink tea. I amused myself for some time in looking out of window, and watching one of the dragoons engaged in breaking horses, in a drenching rain, in an enclosure made for that purpose. He did not seem to me to do his work well, but pulled their mouths too sharply. After we had tea, the rain ceased a little, and I intended to walk·home; but Madame Voght would not hear of it, but insisted on conveying me home in her carriage.

Christiana,
Wednesday, June 20th, 1827.

My dearest M——,

I am very comfortably settled here in a most excellent, large, and clean apartment, where I arrived after that *fête* on Sunday, which I have described in C——'s letter. All last week I was at Bokestadt, with Count and Countess Wedel. She is a most efficient person, with very strong good sense, the most perfect *droiture*, the kindest heart, and the most taking manners I ever saw. She has, along with these, a sort of droll way of viewing things, which, added to great gentleness, makes her quite delightful ; and all this perfectly natural and uncultivated, as I do not believe she has any *talents acquis*, and never seemed to me to think of looking into a book ; but that is not the way of people here. The manner of living is so primitive, that, like the princesses of old, all the ladies are constantly occupied

with their *ménage* ; and Countess Wedel, who is the
first lady in Norway, takes it as a thing of course to
step into the kitchen to see how the dinner is proceeding, and if the fish is come. Nor is this all ;
she equally looks to the washing, orders what beasts
are to be killed and salted for the winter's provisions,
and so on ; makes all her own and her children's
clothes with her own hands, even to the gloves,
which she cuts out, and makes of reindeer skins.
And beautiful skins they are, but they have, as I
think, a nasty smell, though they all count it charming. She is also very fond of her horses ; they have
seven beauties, of the dun kind, with eel-backs and
and long black tails. It was our amusement of an
evening to turn all these creatures loose in a large
court before the house, where they scampered about,
rolled, galloped, and kicked like mad ; but the
moment they were called, they all rushed to the hall-
door, to eat salt and bread, and are as gentle as dogs.
In harness they go merely in a snaffle, and are quite
tractable and quiet. They have an excellent coachman, who can drive six in hand as easily as a pair,
which in these roads is no small merit, for though
the level roads are good enough, some of the hills
pass all imagination.

We went last week with Belgrave part of his

way on the road to Dronthiem, meeting Countess Wedel at another country-house of her own, where she has also iron foundries which supply the whole country. Our point was about five-and-twenty miles from here, and under the sun there cannot exist a more magnificent district than that which we went through, or more superb views over land and sea, rivers, lakes, and forests without end. The latter are quite like a dream of beauty, all carpeted with bilberries, strawberries, cranberries, (not ripe yet, of course,) lilies of the valley, and other beautiful little flowers. The sight that we went specially to see was a defile, and a view, which surpassed all we had seen before, with glaciers at a distance. The hill, down to the inn where Belgrave took leave of us, was the most tremendous we had seen yet, and that is *beaucoup dire ;* but the horses are very clever, and when they can no longer stand on their legs, they slide down almost in a sitting posture. We accomplished it all very well, and got home, *i.e.,* to Bokestadt, by about ten o'clock.

Every day at Bokestadt that we did not rigidly keep to ourselves in order to rest, there was some diversion in the way of drinking tea, or some expedition in the evening. A few people generally

dropped in to dinner at three o'clock, and it is the
fashion to go about again in the evening drinking
tea, or. eating at each other's houses; I wonder
they are not ill! I have more invitations of that
kind than I know how to get through, and I go
to as many as I can cram into the twenty-four
hours, not only out of civility, but because, as one
is here, it is best to see all that one can. Madame
Wedel has not yet been able to go to *les bains*, because the Count has the gout, so I went yesterday
with her sister-in-law, Baronne de Wedel, to dine
at Bokestadt. We found they had just begun
dinner, *i.e.*, the Countess, her children, and their
tutor, and six other people, who had all come in
anyhow, after she had sat down to her dinner,
which consisted of a very good soup, a large piece
of boiled beef, excellent fish of two or three kinds,
and a large almond pudding; and this is their usual
easy way of living. They are always delighted to
see you, and have not the folly of being *déconte-
nancée*, or of making excuses for not having more
dishes ; if you go in a friendly way without being
asked, you, of course, take your chance of what you
find, and they are very much pleased and flattered
at your coming. After that, we drove away in a
little barouche, to another house belonging to

Countess Wedel, where the Baron and Baronne live in the summer, to a *thé*, which, to say the truth, was a very tiresome affair, as there was only the Viceroy and his wife, a stupid little secretary and his mother, and my most useful friend, the Engglish Vice-Consul, Mr. Myggind, a German by birth. He is of the greatest service to me, arranges all my lodgings, and, in fact, does everything for me. He is a little old man who has been here eight years, sensible, straightforward, good-natured and *serviable* ; knows all the people and their ways, and is therefore very amusing ; they call him "Le bon Myggind."

When I dine at home, which is not often, I have a dinner supplied from a place near, consisting of soup, fish, meat, potatoes, and spinach, or asparagus, and sometimes more, and certainly much more of each than I can eat, and all for the *prix fixe* of *one shilling ;* moreover, all the things are extremely good. I believe the cheapness of living here in the summer is wonderful.

I forgot to mention that Count Wedel is collecting, for the King, a set of horses, larger than his own, of a pale cream colour, with very long black tails and manes ; they are beautiful animals, he has got four, but has to find five more. Unfortunately they are very rare, otherwise I should like some; but the trouble of sending them over is great, the expense none. One may have four (if one can find them) for less than four hundred écues, (each écu, or thaler, being three shillings and fourpence). To-day I am going to dine at two o'clock, with a Madame Voght, whose husband is a *Conseiller d'Etat*, but in point of pomp that means nothing. These people live in a house which looks like a better sort of cottage, within the citadel, and have perhaps one servant, and two maids, and dine as they can, children and all together, upon two or three dishes. The evening I have kept to myself, as I am to be up at three to-morrow morning to go on some party of pleasure, to which such early rising is a pretty beginning! Heaven knows where we are to go! but it will probably last till nine or ten in the evening. This life, if one were staying here for long, would be insupportable, for they are always pleasuring, drinking tea and dining in the summer, to make up, I suppose, for the long winter; but for a little while it is amusing to see how they live, and, indeed, it is wonderful they do live at all, considering the tremendous manner in which they eat all day. Three meals of meat, with lighter interludes of ale, porter, chocolate, salmon,

&c., and they regard me with pity for not joining
in these refections on a warm day, "et surtout,
Milady ne soupe jamais!" which, to any sober
Christian is really impossible, after a very good tea
at seven or eight o'clock, with plenty of bread and
butter, cakes, &c., to which they—sweet souls—
invariably add cheese as well as at breakfast. They
all eat with their knives, and nothing can be uglier
and coarser than the women, Madame Wedel
excepted. They have mostly horrid complexions,
and such hands, such feet, such ancles! all dressed
in coloured cotton prints, or old figured stuffs, the
worst *tenue* and the *plus mauvaise tournure* imaginable. Four of these lovely creatures are *dames
d'honneur* to La Reine when she comes here, of
which they are amazingly proud and *hautaines* to
the others. Then Madame La Baronne Wedel's
husband is Grand Chambellan de la Cour on like
occasions, and there is more jealousy and *tracasserie*
than could be imagined possible in such a distant
and remote place, and all for such nonsense. The
Baronne is a triumphant woman, with pink cheeks,
talking eternally, and is reckoned *très-jolie*. After
all this, it is but just to say that I never met such
good-natured, hospitable people; they *se mettent en
quatre* to amuse one, and would willingly never let

G

one be at home for half-an-hour. On Friday we are to have a *thé* at the Viceroy's, Saturday there are gardens to be seen, on Sunday there is a great ball at the Viceroy's, about four miles from town, in honour of the King's birth-day; and after that I hope Belgrave will be coming, as, at all events, I shall then have an excuse not to be taken out every day.

I tasted the other day at Bokestadt a piece of ham, made of a great brown bear, who was killed in the woods there in the winter. I hate all ham, but this was peculiarly bad. *Apropos* of it, you never saw anything like the enormous thick pieces of ham which the people gravely eat here at breakfast, dinner, and whenever they can find a chance.

It is very close to-day, and feels like thunder; some rain would do great good now, though the crops of grass have been fine hitherto, they expect three crops of hay this year, they have generally two, all in four months; the rapidity of the vegetation is something wonderful.

*Friday, 22nd.*—Fortunately it rained so bitterly yesterday morning that instead of at three or four, we could only set out at eight in the morning. We went through some twenty miles of exquisite country to a curious Norwegian town, called Drammen, and got back at eleven o'clock at night, after being wet through, and dry again.

There is nothing interesting from age or art in this country; all the houses are of wood, and to live as they best can in the winter, and to eat as much as they can in the summer seems the first object of the natives.

*Monday,* 25*th.*—Belgrave returned last night after twelve o'clock, very much pleased with his Dronthiem expedition, in which he found every sort of hospitality and kindness. He stayed there three nights, and has been excessively amused and entertained by his journey; but he was glad l did not go with him, as it is a journey of great fatigue, the road is in some places indescribable, and one seemed to climb over perpendicular masses of rock. On Saturday evening he encountered the most tremendous thunder-storm he ever saw or heard, with torrents of hail; but no mischief was done. On account of the Crown-Princess* having a second son, the Viceroy was obliged (luckily) to change his ball into a great dinner for the gentlemen only. We start again on Thursday.

* *Née* Princesse Josephine de Leuchtenberg ; this second son was Prince Francis, who died young.

*Saturday*, 23*rd*.—I had slept so badly, that I did not get up till nine. After breakfast, I went to call on La Baronne Wedel, whom I found at home. Came home and began to draw, when Madame Voght arrived to propose to me to walk to the Fort. I joined her, and we had a beautiful view from the top; then we went by some very pretty public walks by the sea-side; then to a small garden, belonging to the King, across the water; then I came home and dined. The soup was simply beer, sugar, spice, and lemon, with pieces of bread in it, exactly like the spiced ale in Cheshire, only this was quite cold. I dressed before six, to go to a *thé* at Laggersun (the Viceroy's). La Baronne Wedel called for me in a roofed *calèche*, in which were also her husband, her son, and her little girl. It rained very hard the whole way. The party at Laggersun was invited under the idea of seeing the servants, &c, dance round a May-pole, according to the Swedish custom, it being the *Veille du St. Jean*; however, the rain quite prevented everything of the kind. The party consisted only of ourselves, Monsieur and Madame Voght, Mr. Myggind, the Secretary and his mother, and a few more gentlemen. We went to tea, at which were also two large dishes of excellent wood-strawberries. Came home at about half-past nine.

*Sunday, 24th.*—Got up between eight and nine. After breakfast, read my prayers. At twelve the Baronne de Wedel called for me to go to church. We were in the Viceroy's pew, with himself and Countess Sandel and some of the Dames de la Cour, all *parées*, as the birth of the Crown Prince's second son was to be announced formally. There was first singing the Psalms, accompanied by the organ ; then a sermon ; then the priest read a letter announcing the Princess's confinement; then followed more singing, and the whole was concluded in about an hour. The Baronne brought me back home. Before I went to church, Hörburg arrived with a little note from Belgrave, announcing his arrival that evening ; he expected to be at Christiana about ten or eleven. I dined at home, and la Baronne Wedel called for me about five in her barouche and pair, to go to Bokestadt. On our way there we met Countess Wedel's servant, Chrétien, going as *forebüd* in a little cart with her luggage for the next day's journey. He gave me a note from the Countess, saying that she would breakfast with me next morning on her way. We found her and the Count at Bokestadt, with the other Baronne Wedel, Madame Lino, and Mademoiselle Vich. We had tea, stayed about an hour, and came home by nine. I prepared all things for Belgrave, who arrived at twelve, much pleased with his Dronthiem expedition.

*Monday, 25th.*—Got up at nine. Before I was half dressed, Countess Wedel and her party arrived, consisting of herself, her daughter Caroline, Madame Lino, and Mr. Wolfe. I dressed and finished breakfast as fast as I could, and with the help of Mr. Myggind's china, we did very well in a little time. They stayed about an hour, and then took leave. Belgrave, who was not dressed before, then breakfasted, and we passed the day at home. He had brought from Dronthiem a small jar of excellent fresh butter, given him by Mrs. Johnston, Mr. Knordrou's sister-in-law, and which, by pouring on it salt and water every night, and pouring it out every morning, was kept perfectly fresh and good. He also brought ten ermine skins, and eighteen dressed reindeers' skins for gloves.

*Tuesday, 25th.*—Got up about nine. After breakfast, we were busy arranging different matters all the morning. Mr. Myggind came at three to dine with us. After dinner we went in a hired open chariot and pair to the Botanical Gardens, where lives a most delightful good-natured monkey. From there we drove back to the town and to the Pier, and embarked on board a little boat to row to Lag-

gersun. The evening was delightful, though there
had been a good deal of thunder and lightning in
the afternoon. The town had escaped the storm,
which must have been violent somewhere ; but it
had all cleared off, and the weather was delicious.
We landed on a•little point of rock, and walked up
through some pretty fields to Mr. Kattenborn's, to en-
quire after Madame Kattenborn and leave our cards.
We then walked on to Laggersun, where we found
that Count and Countess Sandels were not arrived
from town, where they had been for the day. Walked
back to the boat, rowed across to Mr. Myggind's
house, to see the Kaegbar plant (*prunus patus*) and
his wolf-skin winter pelisse. Then had a delightful
row home, and landed on the other side from where
we had embarked. Walked through an inferior
part of the town, and got home by about nine. Mr.
Myggind drank tea with us, and then went away.

*Wednesday,* 27*th.*—I walked to Madame Voght's
to bid her good-bye ; it was very hot. At two
o'clock Mr. Myggind came, and took charge of
various parcels which we wished to send back to
England; he then assisted Belgrave in making out
the papers for the *forebüd* against our next day's
journey. He dined with us at four. We had the
beer-soup among other things. Mr. Kayser called

before the end of dinner ; after dinner he went away,
and Mr. Myggind walked with us to call on Count
Wedel, whom we found still in his apartment, not
being sufficiently recovered from his gout to go out.
He was in the middle of a committee, but came out
to see us. We then went to call on Le Baron and
La Baronne de Wedel, who were out. We came
home, and Mr. Myggind took leave, after being of
the greatest use to us.

*Thursday, 28th.*—We left Christiana at three by
an indifferent road, and a very hilly one. Crossed
three ferries, one of which was the stream that con-
veys the waters of the Mionne Lake into the River
Glommen, by the banks of which we drove for
several miles. It turned out a wet evening, and we
should have reached Ous, where we were to sleep, ·
in very good time, had we not been detained at the
last station upwards of two hours waiting for our
horses. We arrived at Ous, in a pouring rain, at
eleven, and found a very bad lodging near the inn,
which was too small to contain us.

*Friday, 29th.*—Went on at half-past eight. The
road still hilly, but pretty as usual, with forests and
lakes. Passed through Kouswinger, two posts from
the boundary, with a small fort upon a hill ; here
we were ferried over the wide and rapid Glommen.

At the post before Strand we entered Sweden, where the difference of the dress of the peasants is immediately apparent, being far more clean and neat than the Norwegians, who look very dirty. The men here almost all wear long dark-coloured coats, without buttons, and gathered in straight plaits behind ; their hair divided on the forehead, and combed straight down on each side, and all cut round at the same length, much like the pictures of the Puritans. The women wear straw bonnets, but look usually very coarse. We got to Strand in good time, and found a good inn in a pretty situation on the edge of a lake.

*Saturday, 30th.*—We left Strand early, and between the second and third stations, Leer and Kommap, we crossed a lake in a very small boat, in which the carriage was obliged to be put lengthways in order to be ferried over. At almost all the stations children bring baskets-full of strawberries to sell, the woods and sides of the road being covered with them, and they are now quite ripe and very good ; it is also very easy to get milk and sugar to eat with them. Before reaching Jylberg we passed a pretty place, something like an English village, with a large wood of birch trees ; after that the country is flat and ugly, till we come to Carlsttadt, where we found a very tolerable inn at the post; took a little walk to the church and came home to dinner.

*Sunday, July 1st.*—A very hot day. About two or three posts before Philipstadt we turned out of the regular road to Stockholm, and went by a narrow cross-road, which, according to annual custom, was undergoing the process of mending; but as the said process was only just begun, the road was rendered rather uneven by having all along one side in a regular row heaps of gravel, which was not yet spread, and the road itself was too narrow to allow of the carriage avoiding them. We arrived at Philipstadt in good time, and found a passable inn.

*Monday, July 2nd.*—A very wet morning; the road, just as usual, very pretty, rocky and wild, with plenty of strawberries. We got to Laxbro about six o'clock, and found the inn tolerable, but not so good as we had been led to expect. Belgrave and I lodged in a room in a sort of pavilion on one side of the house, the servants were in the centre, and there was a large clean kitchen. Opposite the inn was rather a handsome church, the whole covered with a sort of thatch of pieces of wood; the steeple had a cupola, and a very prettily-shaped spire; there was also near it a singular edifice of the same wooden thatch, containing three large bells. Almost all the houses here, and all over this part of the country, are of wood, painted an ugly reddish-brown, with white edges to the windows. Belgrave and I took a walk after dinner to a very pretty little wood behind the church, and went to bed between nine and ten. We passed through some beautiful old forests to-day and yesterday. Belgrave saw a hen capercailzie.

*Tuesday, July 3rd.*—Having a long day before us, twelve Swedish miles, we got up at four and set out at half-past six, and found the road very hilly, sometimes very beautiful; saw a hen capercailzie, also a blackcock walking in the wood, but he flew away at sight of us. At Bomarsbo we saw the Dalecarlians for the first time in the dress of the country. The men are in general very tall and fine-looking people; they wear their hair very long and bushy at the sides, and very broad-brimmed hats with round crowns, long-waisted, blue waistcoats, with stiff leather apron, and knives hanging from their belts, white shirt-sleeves, and remarkably thick-soled shoes. The women seemed all hideous, with their hair untidy; sometimes they had little close, dark-coloured caps at the back of their heads, short waistcoats with buttons, and very full, short petticoats of striped c oarse stuff; the whole *contour* very clumsy and ugly.

For the last stage or two the country became dreary and less pretty ; we passed several smelting works, and on approaching Fahlun, the country becomes a sort of desert covered with stones above the mines. The approach to the town is most gloomy, the place itself being most wretched, and covered with smoke smelling strongly of sulphur. We arrived about ten at a bad, small lodging, and could get nothing to eat but some fried fish like chub, full of bones, and some pancakes; our floors, though, were clean, and we soon went to bed. I had my own, and Belgrave another, which we constructed on a sofa, and we slept very comfortably.

*Wednesday, July 4th.*—Got up and breakfasted, and we did not go out till about one to call on the Governor, to whom we had a letter. He had not come to town, as he lives in the country, but arrived immediately after, when Belgrave saw him, and he came to our lodging with his brother-in-law, whom he deputed to show us about the mines. He also left us his little open carriage with a pretty pair of chesnut horses to convey us to them. They are about a quarter of an English mile from the town. When we arrived we went into a sort of warehouse, where we put on mining dresses, *i.e.*, loose, coarse cloth coats, and hats with wide brims ; we had as guides a tall, good-natured miner, with a loud voice, and a superintendent, besides a man who carried a provision of laths of wood for torches, a bundle of which ready lighted was also carried by each of the other guides. We then went into a building opposite the warehouse, and descended for a long way a wooden staircase, out of which we came into open air towards the middle of the great chasm; we then descended some external staircases, all of which, both external and internal, are made with thick stems of trees for the steps, which serves very well, and is not slippery; we then entered an opening and descended endless staircases through subterranean passages, which traverse the mines in all directions, and which are distinguishable by different names, such as "Nuna Louisa," "Gustaf Adolph," &c. The passages are carried sometimes like balconies over tremendous chasms, and on a stone being thrown down up comes a sound like thunder. These chasms have rails, so that you may look over them. We came to one without rails, which we could not pass, and which is the most tremendous looking object imaginable; the gallery leads to the edge of the abyss, where it terminates, and there is a corresponding one on the opposite side. One of the most striking effects is produced by looking down the staircase to the lowest mine, which is large and rather wide, and seems, as it is seen by the light of the torches only, to go down for ever and ever, like the staircase to the Hall of Eblis at the conclusion of "Vathek." Some of the galleries are very wet from continual drippings; there are two or three *salles*, or large spaces, in one of which the King and his sister dined when they came to Fahlun. The staircases are very easy throughout, and the whole place may be seen with very little trouble. The men were not working while we were there, but we saw a gallery lately begun, but which they had just left; they only hew out the stone, which is full of copper, and wheel it away in barrows. It is afterwards drawn in buckets up a perpendicular chasm, which is used for that purpose alone. The air in all the passages was perfectly fresh; in many places the vitroil had formed itself into green icicles.

We came up again by an internal staircase the whole way, and after taking off our dresses, went with the Governor's brother-in-law, who had waited for us above, to see a small collection of minerals in the warehouse, and visited also some rooms where business is transacted. The appearance of the external mine is that of an immense gravel pit, about an English mile in circumference, with some lines of wooden staircase climbing over its cliffs. There is, unfortunately, no direct way of disposing wholesale of the copper; most of it is sold to the farmers who smelt it themselves, and a good deal is smelted in Fahlun itself.

We went afterwards to see the vitriol made; this is done by letting the water run from the copper into a large tank, which afterwards flows into a quantity of receptacles like small wells, with machines like gigantic combs with the teeth downwards standing in them. The vitriol collects itself round these teeth in beautiful green crystals, which have the most extraordinary effect.

We took leave of our friend and came home to our lodging just in time to avoid a violent shower of hail, and Belgrave then wrote the *forebüd's* papers. We had ordered dinner at seven, but none appeared till eight; it was a better one than yesterday, as it came from a restaurateur's, where we were provoked to find, when too late, we might have had a very good apartment, and have been much better established than in our detestable lodging.

*Thursday 5th.*—We got up at five and left Fahlun without regret at seven, as a more forlorn, wretched, ugly place cannot be seen. As we proceeded we passed through a prettier country, and went over two floating bridges, supported upon rafts and resting on the water, which flowed over the bridge as the carriage drove along. We met quantities of little carts coming from Gifte, where there appeared to have been a fair or market. We arrived at Gifte at eight, and found it a remarkably pretty and neat town, on the mouth of a river, and close to the Baltic. In the middle of the town, the town is spanned by a beautiful small bridge of granite, with a very good and substantial pavement over it. On each side of the water there are handsome piers with neat steps for the people to fetch water. We walked out for some time and went down to a sort of boulevard formed by a long avenue of trees stretching out to the sea, and into a dockyard where ships were building behind the warehouses. Hardly a creature was to be seen about, and the evening was rather cold. We came home to our inn and had an excellent supper.

*Friday, 6th.*—At Elfkarleby, the first post from Gifte, we had a great row with the peasants, who were all half drunk and very insolent; under the pretence that a rope was broken in the harness, they wanted to prevent our setting out, and ran after the carriage, and a furious clamour ensued. They took two of the horses from the carriage, and finally they all fell to fighting one another—men and women—in which lively state we left them; we stopped two miles further on, and quitted the carriage in order to see a beautiful waterfall, composed of three separate ones, two of which are magnificent. The waters all unite just above a large bridge which crosses the road, under which they rush with tremendous force; it is a beautiful waterfall, and nearly equal to Schaffhausen. The country to-day was almost all forest, with excellent roads, and we arrived at a very pretty village (Osterby) where is a foundry and a large house belonging to Monsieur de Ham. We found the nicest little inn possible, very clean; and we took a walk before supper in a pretty wood close by, and went to bed soon afterwards. The gnats were great troubles.

*Saturday, 7th.*—We rose at eight, and went soon after in the little carriage which Belgrave drove, Setterberg with us; it was drawn by two little horses exactly alike, (a mare and her son), both bays, with black tails and manes, white faces, white legs, and white eyes, with which they looked back as they went along in the wildest manner. They trotted like lightning up hill and down. The road was very pretty and very good, and we soon arrived at the house of Monsieur Barouins, close to the mine of Danemora, to whom we had a letter of

H

recommendation. He received us very civilly, showed us a plan and model, and maps of the mine, and then walked there with us. The mine itself is much more striking than at Fahlun, being completely open to the bottom, whereas that at Fahlun is worked underground. The chasm down which you look is tremendous, and of immense depth; we saw the people at work below and a quantity of snow lying in the bottom. The whole is so perfectly seen from the top that we thought it useless to take the trouble of going down in a bucket. The rock, which is detached by blasting, is composed of iron, lime, and manganese. On each side of this iron stratum, which runs from north-east to south-west, is a stratum of the white feldspar granite; a considerable quantity of asbestos is found with the iron, and small portions of silver and copper. We were shown some petrified wood, and we took away several specimens of little pieces of iron stone, crystals of garnet, and asbestos. The iron stone is drawn up in buckets and taken away to be melted. The mine is very interesting and beautiful, and we heard several explosions like thunder from the blasting.

We departed after two o'clock, and came four posts and a half to Upsala, where is one of the oldest churches in existence; the walls are of large rough pieces of granite, and are said to have been certainly used in former times for Pagan worship. Close to it is a row of very large tumuli, supposed to be the burying-place of old Swedish kings; a subterranean passage is said to lead from one of them to the modern Upsala, about three English miles distant, just like the tradition in regard to many, if not most, monastic buildings in England. Nothing can be uglier than the country about here, it is a dead flat, without a tree, though it is not far distant from forests; but with fine crops of wheat and rye. We arrived at Upsala, at Jetman's, a good hotel, at seven; had tea, and took a walk up to the palace —a frightful building, consisting of a long flat front, with a round tower at each end, all covered with red plaster, and perched upon the top of a hill overlooking the town. The old palace, begun by Gustaf Vasa was burnt down; only an old gateway, and a few lumps of bricks are now remaining.

*Sunday,* 8*th.*—We got up about eight and breakfasted; after which we read prayers. Belgrave went to the Cathedral for a short time while service was being performed, and at half-past three we went there again, Setterberg serving as interpreter to the clerk who showed us over it. It is a large brick building with two towers, surmounted by cupolas covered with copper ; there is nothing very remarkable outside ; within it is lined with white plaster, and the nave and choirs are all in one. The communion-table is surmounted with plaster figures as large as life, and within a gilded grating on one side of it, is the silver coffin of Eric VII.,* there is a circular row of burying-places like chapels all round the east end of the church ; in the one immediately behind the altar is a handsome monument to Gustaf Vasa and his two wives, all carved in full length in marble ; at each corner of the tomb is an obelisk ; the body of it, which supports the figures is decorated with the coloured coats of arms of the different Swedish provinces. On the other sides are vaults containing some handsome tombs of the Oxenstierns, de Goers, Brâhès, and other families. At the other end of the church is a plain handsome monument of porphyry erected to the memory of Linnæus by his friends and scholars ; his body is buried at a short distance off. There is a monument of the family of Stures who were massacred by Eric XIV.,† and one of that of the Baron de

---

* He was King of Sweden in the thirteenth century.

† King of Sweden in 1560-68.

Banner executed by Christian II. some quarter of a
century earlier. In a room enclosed by an iron
door are some curious relics, an old wooden effigy
supposed to be that of Thor, a bit of a standard of
Margaret of the North, some fine cups given by
different kings or queens to the Cathedral, and one
taken in the time of Christina, (1632—54) from
Prague, encrusted with pearls and precious stones ;
among them one of the finest turquoises I ever
saw; two little enamelled crosses found in Steno
Sture's tomb, and several other curious articles.
Upstairs we went into a room containing a great
many magnificent dresses of the priests, and a glass
case holding the shirt, trousers, and doublet worn
by Sture at the time of his murder, and still stained
with blood ; a piece of Christina's riding habit, &c.
From the Cathedral we went to Linnæus' Garden ;
but unfortunately it has nothing remarkable in it.
There is on one side a line of building, which looks
like a decayed green-house, and contains two or
three rooms, in one of which the great botanist used
to give his lectures ; his desk, the table and chairs
still remain.

We came home and dined at six ; rested for some
time after dinner, when, animated by Setterberg's
description, we set out to see the garden, which

contains the Museum of Natural History. It is in front of the palace below the hill, the descent of which was formerly cut in terraces, and must have been very handsome. The middle alley of the garden is bordered with cut spruce firs, which are very tall and excessively thick, and have a very good effect on each side of a broad green walk. We met with a very intelligent gardener, who was waiting for us, though he let us knock repeatedly at the outer door without speaking to us, till we called him; he then took us over the garden, and into the orangery, which is superb as to space and height, though being summer, it contained very few plants, except a magnificent tree of *laurus nobilis* in a large tub in the centre. In a division at one end were some very fine Indian plants, bananas and palms; and the whole seemed extremely well taken care of, though the smaller plants were allowed to run up too much, and become stringy. This orangery forms one wing of the building; the centre of it consists of the museum, which was locked up before we got there, though the whole is open to the public at certain hours; but we saw through the windows stuffed elks, wild dogs, ourang-outangs, &c. The hill under the castle is covered with beautiful purple wild larkspur, of which we afterwards saw a great deal on the road to Stockholm. Yesterday was very windy, as was to day, but the evening grew very close and sultry. It being the time of the vacation we saw none of the scholars, nor did we see the inside of the University, there being, as we were told, little or nothing remarkable there. Upsala is on the whole a clean but melancholy looking town.

*Monday, 9th.*—We got up before six, and set out at half-past eight. From the first post we walked about half a mile down to the edge of a lake, over which we were to go in a boat, to see Skocloster, a seat of Count de Brâhès. There never was a more decrepit boat than the one in which we embarked— our two selves, Setterberg, and my maid, with two boatmen, whose knowledge of navigation was not, or did not seem to be, a remarkable feature of their character. They chattered incessantly (as do all the Swedes), entangled their oars, and did all but upset us. Belgrave scolded in vain; they only answered by "Ya, ya," and a sound between a groan and a sigh. We made three miles, after one hour's rowing against wind and tide, across the lake to the foot of Skocloster—a square white house, with nine windows in front, and four large towers, one at each corner, with a cupola at the top of each. It was formerly a monastery, and stands round a square court, the cloisters still remaining, with white marble columns. In that part through which you enter there is a large gallery round each story looking into the court. It is full of curious old family pictures and others of all kinds, and the walls are besides painted over with mottoes in Latin, French, and Italian; the staircases, which are very wide, are also full of pictures.

The rooms are endless as to number. In the first which we entered there is a cabinet full of objects of curiosity and beauty, in the way of cups, boxes of stones, jasper, &c., finely set, nautilus shells, beautifully mounted, amber caskets, and cabinets of ebony and ivory, and many other things of that sort. In the room adjoining there is a strange ceiling in plaster, representing all sorts of creatures, men, animals, birds, particularly large fat swans, very coarse and coarsely coloured, but so much *en relief* as to seem as if they must tumble down on the floor. Every room is full of pictures of the Brâhès and all their connections;* Field-Marshal Wrangel, who built the house, and whose bed is there; remarkable people of all times and nations, French, Swedish, and German, some very bad, others curious; particularly

* The Brâhès are the oldest family in Sweden.

two very pretty little ones of La Duchesse de Bouillon and La Duchesse de la Ferté on horseback; and quantities of Kings of Denmark and Sweden, &c., but infinite as to number. There are several rooms full of old armour, firelocks, swords, sabres, extremely old and curious, some of them having belonged personally to kings and remarkable people. One rifle had been used by Gustaf Adolphus in Germany, and there were many other trophies of the Thirty Years' War. Altogether the finest collection that exists in the north of Europe; a great number of ancient saddles, bridles, bits, and Queen Christina's slippers, and those of Eric XIV. These are arranged in rooms on the third floor, at the top of the house; several other apartments were occupied by a great quantity of books of all languages, which if arranged would make a fine library; other rooms also on the same floor, and never used, had their bare walls covered with some of the most magnificent tapestry we ever saw, and in great profusion. The subjects were mostly figures of the most vivid colours, with magnificent rich borders, such as would fetch any price in England. The house is altogether very curious, and well worth seeing; but to do so thoroughly would take much more time than we had to spare. We had not time to go into the church,

where there is a tomb of the founder of the family ;
but in passing we looked through five grated windows down into a most extraordinary vault, which
is now closed up, and has no other opening. All
the coffins of the family are there arranged in rows,
some like large trunks, and highly decorated. We
then returned into our frail bark, and came back far
quicker than we went, the wind being in our favour.
We had a very hot walk through a meadow, full of
long grass and all sorts of flowers and dragon flies,
and some corn fields ; we then got into the carriage,
and found a great deal of dust the remaining three
posts, all the way to Stockholm, passing by Rosen-
berg and Haga—both of them palaces of the kings.

The approach to Stockholm on this side does not
at all appear like that to a large town; in fact,
nothing is seen of it, or of the water either ; and we
found ourselves in the Drotting Gasse before we
thought we were in the town, except for the barrier
where we gave up our passport. We came to Lord
Bloomfield's* house in the Drotting Gasse, where he
had very kindly invited us to lodge, though he and
Lady Bloomfield were in England ; we accordingly
found a very nice suite of apartments, and servants,
and supper, and everything ready for us. Mr.

* See page 107.

Bloomfield* did not expect us so soon, our Fahlun letter not having arrived in time, so was absent on a fishing expedition; but the servant found the letters from England which were waiting for us here.

*Tuesday, 10th.*—Got up and breakfasted at ten o'clock. Had soon afterwards a visit from Mr. MacMahon, who was then acting as Secretary of Legation; and we passed the rest of the day in arranging our concerns. We dined at five; Mr. MacMahon came to dinner. After coffee we went out for a walk. We went down the Drotting Gasse, which is the principal street of Stockholm, but very narrow, and composed of great hotels and miserable-looking shops; we walked down to the water's edge. The combination of fine buildings with the water and rocks is very singular. The wind was tremendous, and carried away Mr. MacMahon's hat into the kennel; the dust was also detestable. We then walked over the bridge to the Palace, the exterior of which is very handsome; it is a long building, perfectly flat and simple, with a balustrade at the top, and two wings, all in very good taste. The wind and rain made it too disagreeable to walk any further, so we came home. Mr. MacMahon went

* The second Lord Bloomfield, G.C.B., afterwards British Minister at Berlin, then Secretary of Legation at Stockholm. He died in August, 1879.

away after dinner, and we had tea, and passed the rest of the evening in reading.

*Wednesday, 11th.*—A very stormy, rainy, windy day. We stayed in our room all the morning, writing letters and reading. Dined at half-past four. Mr. MacMahon dined; Belgrave took a long walk with him after dinner, but it was so stormy, that I did not go out.

Stockholm,
Wednesday, July 11th, 1827.

My dearest M——,

We have had a very pleasant journey for the last ten days from Christiana, through a beautiful country, full of forests and lakes, and with excellent roads; but I will spare you the description of it. We saw the copper mine at Fahlun by torch-light —all subterraneous passages and staircases, but very easy to go over, and interesting and imposing, with tremendous abysses. Then we went to Danemora, a beautiful mine, of tremendous depth; but happily it was not necessary to embark in a bucket, as by looking over from the top you see the whole mine at once, and all the people at work, with a quantity of snow lying in the bottom, where, from the perpetual shade I believe, it never melts. They find in

the mine quantities of asbestos, of which I picked
up a bit. We stayed the whole of Sunday in Upsala
to see the Cathedral, which is full of curious things
—the tombs of Gustavus Vasa and other Swedish
Kings, and of sundry great families, Linnæus, &c.
There are also cups given by Kings and Queens to
the Cathedral; one very fine one, covered with jewels,
taken from Prague in Christina's time, and a ward-
robe of curious old clothes, the shirt and dress worn
by Steno Sture when he was murdered by Eric II.,
and stained with blood ; a piece of Christina's riding-
habit, an old wooden effigy of Thor, a bit of a
standard of Margaret of the North, &c., &c., St.
Eric* in a silver coffin. I like the old clothes; they
are like bits of the real people to whom they belonged. Then we saw Linnæus' house and garden,
and a very well-kept botanical garden and museum ;
this last was the garden of the Palace at the time
when the great Archbishops lived there and made
war with the Kings of Denmark. There is in the
middle a broad alley, bordered with cut spruce firs
of great height and thickness, which grow faster
than yews, and look quite as well. This I throw out
as a useful hint for anybody making an old-fashioned
garden; they look like well-dressed company.

* He was one of the earliest Kings of Sweden ; he died in 1161.

We came here on Monday, seeing on our way Skocloster,* an old house belonging to the Count de Brâhè. It is a handsome, square, white house, full of windows, with a large round tower and cupola at each corner ; it was formerly a convent, and there still remain old cloisters round a square court within. There are three stories, with a large staircase, and in each a broad gallery all round looking down into the court. The galleries, besides their ornaments of pictures, have panels painted with pithy mottoes in every division, and under every picture there is a motto in French, Latin, or Italian ; there are numbets of rooms, and the quantity of pictures, principally portraits, exceeds anything I ever saw. Many of them are bad enough, but some very curious. Portraits of all the Brâhès and other connections, Marshal Wrangel who built the house, kings and queens of Sweden, and of other countries, two very pretty little pictures of the Duchesse de Bouillon, and the Duchesse de la Ferté on horseback, strange pictures of people dead and laid out for burial ; and there are besides fine and curious objects, in cabinets of ebony, ivory, &c., of crystal, jasper, amber, and all those sort of things, all which shows that the people had sense and discernment. There

* See ante, p. 103.

are also several rooms full of suits of armour, and the finest collection of guns, pistols, sabres, and every kind of arms from the very oldest, many of them having once belonged to famous people. Of shields, saddles, &c., there is a magnificent collection, and to crown all, several large empty rooms at the top of the house are hung with large pieces of the most splendid Gobelin tapestry, finer than any I ever saw in England, and such as would fetch any price if brought to London. It is a great pity that this is not done, for here it remains in these uninhabited rooms, in a house little lived in, though well taken care of. The house itself is perched on the edge of a lake and surrounded by woods. In the church there is a curious vault now shut up, but you can see in through five grated windows, where all the Brâhès are buried, in strongly-shaped and much decorated coffins. It is altogether a very interesting place, and would be delightful to live in if better furnished, as the rooms are large and endless in number, and not inconvenient.

We came here yesterday evening, first read our letters, then had an excellent dinner; we are in a comfortable apartment, and in one room there is a book-case, containing, fortunately among other things, the "Cabinet des Fées."

There are but few people in Stockholm now, as
they all live "in the country " in the summer, but
that means in little *campagnes* close to the town.
To-morrow we dine with the Ministre d'Etat, Count
Wetterstedt, and I have just been with Mr. Bloomfield to the only milliners, to try and get a decent
evening cap, but the thing is impossible. I am
obliged to buy separate articles and have them made
up by my maid, and the articles themselves are but
bad at the best. Never was such a destitute town
in every respect, literally the people cannot get a
book if they want it, which is not often. There is
nothing to be had but reindeer-skin gloves, which
have nice insides. We shall go in about a week,
hiring a vessel, to Abo. The passage is in general
good, and there are few or no difficulties in Finland.
We mean to be at St. Petersburg about the 28th.
Our weather is not very fine just now.

*Thursday,* '1 2*th.*—It poured with rain all day.
Belgrave went out after breakfast with Mr. Bloomfield to make some visits, calling on Count Wetterstedt and others. Count Vogna called here. I
wrote, read, and drew till dinner at half-past four.
Monsieur Bodisko, the Russian Chargé d'Affairs, an
amusing little man, dined with us, as did also Mr.
MacMahon. We went a little before eight to our own

room to read till tea-time, but were summoned forth again to see Monsieur Krabbe, the Danish Minister, who had come to pay us a visit. He is very gentleman-like and agreeable. We had tea and sat some time conversing, and went to bed about twelve.

*Friday,* 13*th.*—Breakfasted as usual about ten with Mr. Bloomfield. As it was still raining we did not go out in the morning, but finished our letters for the post, which was to go that evening. We dined at half-past four. Mr. Crabbe dined, and also Mr. Foy the English Consul. At seven we set out in the britshka, Mr. Bloomfield, Belgrave, and I, and drove to Haga, through a very pretty park to the palace, where the Crown Prince and Princess were living, to call on Mademoiselle Sophie Anker, one of the Princess's *dames d'honneur* to whom I had a letter from Countess Wedel; she was not visible, being with the Princess, so we drove on to call on Countess Suchterlens and General Suchterlens, the Russian Minister. He and his son were both absent, being gone to St. Petersburg, but we found the Countess walking with Monsieur Brockhausen, the Russian Chargé d'Affaires, and Monsieur Bodisco. We sat on a balcony and had tea, then walked in the garden, where are a quantity of animals, reindeer, fallow

I

deer, owls, doves, storks, &c. We walked through an adjoining garden belonging to *les Invalides*, who inhabit a large white château close by, and also close to the water. The house was built by Christina for her favourite, the Comte de la Gardie. After a very pleasant walk we sat a little while in the house, where there are some beautiful drawings of horses, droshkies, &c., by Orloffski, a Russian artist, and then came home; the evening was very pleasant, but as cool as September.

*Saturday, 14th.*—After breakfast we walked all over the house with Mr. Bloomfield. We had hardly finished when Countess Suchterlens came to bring me her Court gowns- for patterns. Those for town are black, and for the country grey silk. She also wanted to take me to Madame Fibbis, and to a shop for some more things that I wanted, after which she deposited me at the Ridderholm Church, where Mr. Bloomfield and Monsieur Brockhausen soon arrived. We waited a little while for Belgrave, who was gone with Mr. Foy to look at the vessel which was to convey us to Abo. The church is now employed merely as a burial-place ; there are to be seen here the tombs of several of the Kings of Sweden, particularly that of Charles XII., who reposes in a very handsome black marble sarcophagus, which is spoiled by some poor gilded decorations; his sword is hung up at one end, and a standard which he himself took in Poland is placed by the tomb, which is overhung with a quantity of other standards taken by him; the swords of others of the Kings are also suspended by their tombs.

We descended into two vaults which were open, and full of the coffins of the kings and queens, mostly of strange shapes, and with extraordinary decorations. All the Knights of the Seraphim* who can afford it are buried here; and the church walls in several places are covered with their escutcheons; that of each knight being placed at his death. Napoleon's escutcheon was among them.

From here we proceeded in Mr. Bloomfield's britshka to call on Madame Tascher, Lady to the Queen, at her apartments at Bellevue, where the Queen was then pleased to reside. It is a mere mass of small wooden houses, in one of which we found Madame Tascher at home. The American and Spanish Ministers arrived at the same time with ourselves. Madame Tascher was a large, fat woman, with a handsome face, something like Lady W——, and talking incessantly.

We then came home to dress for dinner at Count

---

* Another Swedish Order of Knighthood; founded in A.D. 1280.

Wetterstedt's; we went at four. It is about an
English mile from town in "the Park;" we found
a party consisting of Count and Countess Wetterstedt, Countess Tascher, and two other ladies, one,
the *belle fille* of the Count; Mr. Krabbe, Count
Voyna, and an infinite number more; we dined in a
*salle* which was only just large enough to hold us;
and had a very handsome dinner. Madame Wetterstedt is very handsome, and she seemed very good-
natured. Count Wetterstedt looks pale and ill; but
is particularly amiable and gentle in his manner.
Count C. de Löwenholm arrived before we left the
dining-room, when we went upstairs we had ice
first, and then coffee; the whole of the evening was
very pleasant, and we stayed some time before we
came home in a pouring rain. We there found the
English mail just arrived, and regaled ourselves with
tea, bread and butter, and the newspaper till eleven
o'clock.

*Sunday,* 1 *5th.*—Very wet morning so we did not
go out; breakfasted with Mr. Bloomfield at eleven;
after breakfast we read prayers and wrote letters in
our room till it was time to dress in order to go to
dine at Countess Suchterlens. At four we went in
the britshka, and found the Countess and Madame de
Suchterlens, Monsieur Bodisco, Monsieur Krabbe,

Monsieur Brockhausen, Mr. MacMahon, Baron Hozznier, and one or two more friends ; after dinner it was too wet to go out, so we stayed in the house, and looked at albums, prints, &c. Monsieur Hozznier and the other gentlemen sang, and after we had stayed some time, there arrived a Monsieur and Madame Acunha, and Madame Montgomeri's mother ; then Mr. Bloomfield, Belgrave and I went away, and drove through Haga, and thence, as the evening had grown very fine, to Carlberg, a military college, with a beautiful garden, where we walked for some time ; then came home, and had tea as usual.

Stockholm,
July 15th, 1827.

My dearest M——

We amuse ourselves very much, and go about with Mr. Bloomfield, who shows us everything and everybody. We sat down to a magnificent dinner at the house of Count Wetterstedt, the Minister ; there were twenty-four people, in a very small *campagne* close to the town ; he is an amiable, gentle person, with great kindness. Countess Wetterstedt put off her departure *pour ses terres* for some days in order to receive us. She is a strange woman, but

extremely civil and *prévenante*; I believe she has
been very handsome; the whole thing was pleasant
and entertaining.   The evening was excessively wet,
so we came home to our tea, and bread and butter,
in which Mr. Bloomfield, Belgrave and I indulged
largely.   It rained all this morning, so we did not
go out, but the mornings are dreadfully short, as all
these dinners are at four o'clock; and to-day we
have been dining with Countess Suchterlens, a
Russian, she is a nice, pleasing little person, and
helps me about my Court dress, as for the country
they *must* be all grey or lilac, with sleeves of a
particular kind; for town they are black.   But,
thanks to her, I am all prepared, so we are to be
presented to-morrow.

Madame Tascher de la Pagerie is the Queen's
great Lady, who presents most foreigners.   I called
on her yesterday, and found her a great, good-
natured, fat woman, with a handsome face.   She is
now living at a place close to the town where the
Queen and her suite are all encamped in a set of
wooden huts, surrounded with "flowery rocks,"
called Bellevue.   There are a few gentlemen-like
men here also—Count Voyno, and a Prussian Baron
Brockhausen; both agreeable people; breakfast here
to-morrow, after which we go on a round of sights,

the Palace, &c.; which will take all the day till it is time to wait on His Majesty.

On Tuesday Count C. de Löwenholm (brother of the Count who was in England), gives us a break-fast at the Palace at Drottingholm, where I am to call on the Countess; the latter is the most agreeable and excellent person here, but unluckily has been ill; then we dine in town at Count Voyna's, and I believe we shall sail on Wednesday for Abo. This town is very singular, some part of it handsome, and the Palace beautiful; but the whole style of society is limited and *borné*. All the foreign diplomatists hate it; the native people are so uncultivated; it is *à la longue* so dull. The difficulty of getting one's common wants supplied is great; so that one can well understand that for those who know better it must be a *triste séjour* for ten years; but to see it *en passant* as we do is very pleasant. I like the great dinners; and in this weather the environs and the drives through them are beautiful. We were to have had a great riding party, as there are horses here enough and to spare; but perpetual rain has prevented it. We have Lord Bloomfield's carriages, coachman, and horses at our command, and Mr. Bloomfield's britshka; plenty of servants and an excellent cook, and above all a nice house with some pretty pictures bought by Lord Bloomfield himself. You see we abound in luxury and dissipation, and now I *will* go to bed.

*Wednesday morning,* 18*th.*—I have got up early, being awakened by a fly who comes regularly to torment me; so I will take the opportunity of finishing this letter, which I have never yet had time to do. We made our expedition on Monday to the Palace, which is full of fine apartments. The Garde Meuble contains a great many interesting things, and the clothes of the different Kings. At five o'clock we went to Rosendahl, a little place of the King's, to dine, after being presented. It was all very pleasant, and we were charmed with the King himself,* who has better manners than anybody I ever saw, a great deal of tact and intelligence, with a particular *douceur* and a most agreeable voice, perfectly easy and well bred, with a pleasant *façon de raconter*, and extremely civil and *prévenant*. There is something remarkably *distingué* about him, from his fine head, good figure, and perfectly black hair. He said all sorts of good-natured and kind things, and was struck with a resemblance between Belgrave

---

* This King was Charles XIV., (Bernardotte,) the ablest of Napoleon's marshals. He was elected Crown Prince in 1810, and succeeded to the kingdom in 1818, on his predecessor's death.

and the Prince Eugène Beauharnais, and also Count Flahault.*

The Queen† is the most good-natured creature possible, and was very kind to us, admiring my dress and my hair, which certainly showed good taste. She and the King walked into dinner together; then Prince Oscar,‡ by whom I sat, with Le Grand Chambellan, and so on—a party of about twenty·; no ladies but the Queen's own. Prince Oscar is a little like Lord Graham,§ but better looking, very civil, talks very low, and a good deal, but is rather too stiff and *guindé*, not nearly as fascinating as the King. We sat a long time after dinner, talking with the King and Queen, who showed us a little apartment which is being prepared for her upstairs. About nine o'clock they took leave to go home, after the Queen had engaged us to remain to-day for a breakfast which Madame Tascher is to give us, in order that the Queen herself may show us Bellevue; so accordingly we remain.

---

* Auguste Charles Joseph, Comte Flahault, sometime Minister from the Court of the Tuileries to that of St. James's. He married the Baroness Keith and Nairn. He died in 1870.

† Bernadine Desirée de Clary, died December 17th, 1860.

‡ Afterwards Oscar I.; he began to reign in 1844.

§ Then M.P. for Cambridge, afterwards fourth Duke of Montrose; he died in December, 1874.

Yesterday we had a delightful expedition to Drottingholm (about eight English miles from here), much the handsomest palace they have. We arrived there about a quarter past twelve, and found Count and Countess C. de Löwenholm (she is a charming person) and about sixteen other persons; among them an agreeable Count and Countess Bjelsjoina— I believe that is the way to spell the name. He knew all about the pictures at Cleveland* House, which he had seen six or seven years ago. We began by going over the Palace itself; then we took a beautiful walk to a Chinese pavilion, where we found a pretty breakfast laid out, with every sort of delicacy. After being there for some little time, we all went, in open carriages, a little way off, through fine woods, to Count Bjelsjoina's. There, among other things, we saw a real Caucasian horse, who, when he is too hot, bleeds himself by opening a vein in his neck with his teeth, and is consequently all over scars. After walking about, we set out on our way home, we three making an *écart* by the way in order to see a beautiful view. To effect this we climbed up some rocks almost perpendicular. We met at the breakfast a Mademoiselle Oxenstierna, a

* Cleveland House stood on the site of Bridgewater House; the town residence of the Earl of Ellesmere.

good-natured person, a *dame-d'honneur*, daughter.to
one whom you know. We ended the day by a very
agreeable dinner at Count Voyno's, and in the evening there was a heavy storm of thunder and lightning. This morning, however, it is quite fine again ;
but I have no time to write more, as it is our last
day, and we shall be out the whole of it, and if one
is at home, people are constantly dropping in, beginning even, I believe, by breakfast at ten o'clock this
morning. To-morrow morning we embark. I believe Mr. Bloomfield intends sailing a little way
with us, and then we go on to Abo. Our *séjour*
here has been very pleasant and entertaining; we
have "done" and seen all that we possibly could do
or see.

*Monday,* 16*th.*—We breakfasted at ten, and went
afterwards—Mr. Bloomfield, Belgrave, and I—in the
britshka by the quay to the Moussbachen Hill,
where we got out, and went up it. The view from
it over Stockholm is the most beautiful panorama
imaginable. Thence we went to the Palace, and
sent the carriage away. Baron de Klingspöre, the
Governor, showed us over the Queen's apartments,
which are very handsome ; as also over the Museum
of Antiques and the Royal Library, where are some
very curious treasures; among others, an enormous

Bible, said to have been executed in one night, with the assistance of the Devil !

After that Mr. Schulzenheim went with us to the Garde Meuble, which is full of interesting objects, such as the cradle of Charles XII., &c., and a room full of clothes of former Sovereigns ; among them is the dress in which Gustavus was shot at Lutzen, those which Charles XII. wore when he was shot, and those in which Gustavus was stabbed by Ankerstrown. The latter were all over blood. From this, which is all well kept, we went to see the *Salle des Nobles*, all hung with their escutcheons. We then came home, rested a little, and dressed to go to dine with the King and Queen at Rosendahl. Belgrave was in uniform, and I had the usual courtdress for the country, of *grey* silk.

Rosendahl is about two English miles from here, and a pretty little place it is. We arrived in good time, and found Count Wetterstedt and one or two others ; more soon arrived, and then came in the King and Queen and Prince Oscar. They came to speak to us without any ceremonial of presentation. The Queen had with her Madame Tascher, who came in before, and three other ladies; the party altogether numbered about twenty. Dinner was soon announced, and confirmed by the King, " *Mes-*

*sieurs et Mesdames, vous êtes servis."* He then went in first with the Queen, and Prince Oscar followed ; I followed with Le Grand Chambellan; then came the others. The Queen sat and talked a long time after dinner in the drawing-room, which is furnished with chairs and sofas worked by her hands and those of her ladies. The King went about the room, and talked to everybody. At nine the King took leave, saying everything that was kind and civil. Prince Oscar followed him. The Queen stayed a little while to settle about a breakfast at Madame Tascher's, at Bellevue, on Wednesday, for which she wished her to keep us; so of course we agreed to stay. She then took leave very kindly, and went away with her ladies in an open carriage. We all, of course, followed. There is a magnificent, enormous porphyry vase in the garden before the windows. We then came home and had our tea with Mr. Bloomfield, who, by some form of etiquette, was not invited to this dinner.

*Tuesday, July* 17*th.*—We had breakfast as usual, and at half-past eleven Belgrave, Mr. Bloomfield, and I set out in the britshka for Drottingholm, eight English miles from Stockholm. We went by a very pretty road, and across two floating bridges. We made our way to the Palace, where we were received by Count and Countess Charles de Löwenholm (he is the Govenor of the Castle), and found there Count and Countess de Bjelsjoina, Mademoiselle Oxenstierna, Monsieur Brockhausen, Monsieur Krabbe, Count Voyno, Count Adolf Rosen, Baron Hozznier, and Baron de Geer. We first went over the Palace, which is handsome, and stands in a beautiful situation on a lake. In the hall, among others, was a good picture of a Laplander driving a reindeer in a sledge. There are many handsome apartments, some of them a good deal out of repair. In one were pictures of Charles XII. and all his generals ; in another, all the Ladies of the time of Louis XIV., a picture of Charles XI., and his hat, in a glass case. There is also a pretty library, and a small gallery of antique busts. After seeing the Palace, we walked in the gardens, where it was very hot. The gardens are beautiful, with magnificent alleys of fine trees and wild walks through woods. We came to a place called La Chine, being composed of a large Chinese pavilion in the centre, and several smaller ones. There is in the drawing-room a book-case, containing, among other books, "Le Cabinet des Fées." There are several apartments fitted up with Chinese furniture, and in the largest of these we had a beautiful breakfast; we then walked about the other rooms. In the floor above is one with silken walls, where a whisper on one side is heard on the other. We then all drove in several open carriages to Count Bjelsjoina's, about a mile distant through the wood. Here we found a very pretty place, and, among other things, saw a white horse from the Caucasus, very ugly, but the characteristic of whose breed is to bleed himself when too hot by opening a vein in his neck with his teeth, and this creature was covered with scars accordingly. From here we all returned to the Palace, Madame de Löwenholm and Mademoiselle Bjelsjoina going in the britshka with me. We then took leave of our frieuds, from whom we had met with every possible kindness, and returned as we came. We made an *écart* to turn out of the road to see Marienburg, a military college, where we climbed up some " perpendicular rocks " to see a magnificent view of Stockholm across the lake. We descended by an easier path, and then returned home by six, after a delightful expedition. Belgrave and I then walked to some shops in the town, and at seven we walked to dinner at Count Voyno's, close by. There we met Mrs. and Miss Baker, and Mademoiselle Krabbe, Monsieur Bodisco, and Count Rosen. After dinner Count Voyno told us some tremendous ghost stories, during which we had a most furious and most appropriate storm of thunder, lightning, and rain.

*Wednesday* 18*th.*—Being as usual awakened by the flies, I got up long before I was called, and accomplished several letters. We breakfasted about half-past ten, to which came Count Voyno and Count Rosen, and soon after twelve we set out to go to Bellevue, Belgrave in his morning dress, and Mr. Bloomfield in uniform. We went first to Madame Tascher's; we found her sitting in her room, so we sat a little while with her, looking at her albums, and were just going to the Queen's apartment, when Her Majesty arrived. She came and sat very good-naturedly with us; we then dawdled about in a very hot sun, waiting for the Prince Royal, who did not arrive till after the Queen had taken a *bouillon*; in despair we then went to breakfast in a square pavilion, our party con- sisting only of ourselves, the Queen, the Prince Royal, Madame Tascher, Countess de Löwenholm, Monsieur Hamilton and a few more gentlemen of the Court, the Queen's Chambellan, &c. The party was to have consisted of fourteen, but one being prevented coming, the poor Chambellan was obliged to retire, the Queen having a prejudice against sitting down thirteen at table. After breakfast we went to see the Queen's habitation, which consists of half-a-dozen of the smallest rooms imaginable, very nicely furnished. Madame Tascher has a small hut of three or four rooms to herself; but the other ladies are miserably lodged. We passed a long time in sauntering about, and *dans des indécisions* as to whether the Queen would have courage to go on the water or not, after a great deal of lingering, we at length all embarked in the Queen's boat, a very pretty one, like a gilded monster, with red morocco seats enclosed in the middle. We remained on the water but for a very short time, and then landed, and walked on by a very pretty wall close to the water, till we met the carriages. The Prince Royal then took leave, and, as the Queen wished to show us more of Bellevue, she took me in her barouche and four white horses, with her two ladies; Belgrave went in a barouche and four black ones along with Mr. Bloomfield and the Chambellan; we went by a beautiful drive to a pretty place belonging to a silk merchant, called, I believe, Sweden. Here we got out, and walked through a beautiful shrubbery up to a hill, where we feasted our eyes with a wonderful view, and then walked back to the carriage and drove back to Bellevue. There we took leave

K

of the Queen, after passing six hours in her company, during which nothing could exceed her good-nature and kindness, and anxiety to show us everything worth seeing. She gave me two little porphyry candlesticks ; we came home rather tired, and dined at seven. While we were at dinner, Count Wetterstedt very kindly came to bid us goodbye, and sat with us during the whole time that we were at dinner, and brought us two iron medals of the King, *de la part de la Comtesse.* Count Voyno also came; and after they were gone, the door opened and in walked Countess C. de Löwenholm, who was just come from the Princess. She stayed a little while, and was, as usual, very agreeable. We had afterwards coffee, and then tea, and then went to bed, as soon as we could finish packing our things for our next day's departure.

*Thursday July 19th.*—Count Voyno and Mr. MacMahon came to breakfast at eight. We collected all our goods and chattels together and went down soon after nine with Mr. Bloomfield in his britschka to the quay, in order to embark in the packet which was to convey us to Abo. Count Voyno came into the packet, and then took leave of us. Mr. Bloomfield and Mr. MacMahon sailed a little way with us, and then returned in a boat. We found the packet very comfortable ; we had engaged a cabin with four beds for Belgrave and me, another with two, where Davidson slept, and two other sleeping-places for Gartner and Zetterberg, whom we took on with us to drive us through Finland, as the travelling there is performed in exactly the same manner as in Sweden. Our fellow passengers were only a few gentlemen, a Monsieur Hamfeldt and Monsieur Leuche, both traders, who were going up to near Torneo, and thence to St. Petersburg, and two or three officers, all very civil, quiet, gentleman-like people. The weather was very pleasant and perfectly calm, and the little wind that blew was in our favour. The sail from Stockholm to Abo is perfectly beautiful, the appearance of the town from the sea, and the Palace, which is always most conspicuous, is like enchantment, as, indeed, is the whole voyage, amidst a labyrinth of little wooded islands, for the most part uninhabited, but exhibiting the prettiest mixture of rock and wood that can be imagined. We had a slight thunderstorm about four o'clock, while we were in our cabin at dinner, a repast which we made on some beef that Gartner boiled, and new potatoes, which formed a small part of a collection of provisions given us by Mr. Bloomfield. These provisions consisted of a roast turkey, and an enormous blackcock pie, bread, cherries, wine and brandy.. We came up on deck again, and stayed there till dark, when we had tea in our cabin, and went to bed; we slept very satisfactorily for nine hours, during which we unconsciously passed through the only space of open sea (about twelve Swedish miles) which occurs in the whole voyage, unornamented with islands.

*Friday, July 20th.*—We rose between eight and nine, and found ourselves at anchor close to the Island of Aland. The morning was delightful, and Belgrave was tempted by the beauty of the sea to take a dip, which he achieved from some neighbouring rocks. When he returned we immediately put out to sea, with a very favourable wind, which, without causing the least roughness on the water, carried us through a continuation of the beautiful scenery of the day before, at the rate of twelve English miles an hour. Nothing could be more delightful or more lovely than the whole of the passage. Towards evening we had our first sight of Abo, which looked extremely pretty at the head of an intricate bay ; a sort of road is marked out in the water with piles of wood, and called "the Channel." It leads straight up to the town, and you sail for a considerable way up a line of river or canal with houses on each side, very like a Dutch town.

We arrived at seven, and disembarked soon after with perfect ease, close to the inn where we intended to lodge; both the carriages were got out before nine, and we found tolerable rooms at "La Société." After we had settled ourselves in them, we went out to walk, and by means of wooden steps mounted a high hill overhanging the town, and crowned by the Observatory. Though it was nearly dark, the view over the town was very fine, and we found Abo much more considerable and much handsomer than we had expected.

*Saturday* 21*st.*—After breakfast Belgrave received visits from the Vice-Consul, and a merchant, who assisted him in changing some Swedish money into Russian, and we set out at eleven along a very bad sandy road. We stopped at ten o'clock in the evening at Ofwerby, to eat some supper, which Gartner prepared for us; we then continued our journey till two o'clock the next morning.

*Sunday* 22*nd.*—We arrived about two in the morning at Bjorsby, where we stopped for about four hours. The servants slept in the house,

Belgrave and I got such rest as we could in the carriage, and at six we went into the inn to dress and eat some breakfast. We were again on our way at seven, and proceeded by rather a better road, but still very heavy; the country is very like that of Sweden, with rocks and low forests, but not so pretty. We reached Helsingfors at eight, and went to a Mademoiselle Washlund's hotel, where we found tolerable rooms. We went out to walk in the town, which is beautiful, very clean-looking, with very handsome houses and a fine *Place*.

*Monday,* 23*rd.*—We got up early. Belgrave had a letter to a Mr. Alftan, whom we found living in the inn; and he went with us at nine to see us on board a little vessel which carried us about half a mile across the sea to the fortress of Sweaborg. This vessel is employed by the Crown, and worked by soldiers; it goes backwards and forwards three times a day, another crossing alternately with it. It was quite full of people, and we went quickly across, passing by the fortress. Sweaborg is a place of extraordinary strength, and considered quite impregnable, there being only a very narrow channel completely commanded by the fortress, by which it can be approached; all the surrounding part of the sea being so filled with rocks as to render it unsafe for ships. There are walls without end, and cannon in proportion. When we saw it we were told it contained two thousand soldiers; their pay is two copecs a day,* and their food, black bread, onions and salt! We saw several curious subterranean passages in the walls, for the soldiers to hide in, during the time of siege. There are also docks where ships were building; we walked about till eleven, at which precise time the vessel again sailed, quite full of passengers. The wind being in our favour, we were again at Helsingfors in ten minutes; and after Mr. Alftan had changed some money for Belgrave, we set out again at one. Nothing particular happened on the road, and we arrived at Borgo at seven in the evening. Here we found a very comfortable inn, with an enormous large ball-room for a sitting-room.

*Tuesday,* 24*th.*—Started at half-past six, and went by an excellent road at a very quick pace, Belgrave driving part of the way. We went through Lovisa and Gudinshanen to Hevenick, which we reached about eight, and where we found a very small inn. The floors were all over sand—and fleas, &c., into the bargain. There was very little to be got to eat; but, as we had our own provisions, that did not signify much.

* One hundred and twenty copecs make an English shilling.

*Wednesday*, 25*th*.—We got up at four, and set out at half-past six, and were edified by seeing a Russian merchant, who had arrived two or three hours before, fast asleep on a Persian carpet, and wrapped up in a fur cloak on the wooden bench in the porch ; a little Russian boy, his servant, sleeping on the steps.   We set out as soon as we had done breakfast; the road continued to be very good to Wiborg where we arrived at four.   Here we were detained for two hours, *i.e.*, till six, by the particularities about our passport.   We found at Wiborg the first decided symptoms of Russian life, the men with long beards and loose Eastern dresses.   We went on till ten, and then stopped at Hotake, where we supped upon the blackcock pie.   Started again at eleven, Belgrave driving, and my maid inside. He drove half the night, and remained outside till morning.

About three stages after Wiborg, that is to say about one in the morning, I was awoke by finding ourselves entangled with some carts, which Belgrave thought he could pass without rousing their drivers, who were all asleep on the top of their loads. Gartner rushed up from behind the carriage, and begun beating the man in the foremost cart, forgetting that the ropes of our harness, and their long projecting axles were fast entangled.

*Thursday*, 26th.—The stage to Belog Ostrow, is a horrid road, and our horses refused to pull us up hill, and broke the hind pole by kicking. This is two stages from St. Petersburg ; here we left off the Swedish way of travelling, and changed our harness, and entrusted ourselves to a Russian coach-man with a long beard, and six reins for four horses. The road was still very sandy ; we were again detained here by some little difficulties about our passport, and left it about eight, and proceeded by a very sandy road, through some long and pretty Russian villages in a very flat country, till we approached St. Petersburg. The road was long and perfectly straight.

It is impossible to describe the magnificence and striking effect of this most beautiful city, where all the streets, which are very wide, seem rows of palaces, with fine gardens, and magnificent bridges over the Neva, a very wide and superb river. Indeed the whole place, with all the people in Eastern costume, is more like a scene in the Arabian Nights than anything else, and much surpassed any-thing I had before imagined. We found a letter from Mr. Disbrowe,* the English Chargé d'Affaires,

* Afterwards Sir Edward Cromwell Disbrowe ; he died in 1851.

at the *barrière*, telling us that he had taken
apartments for us at Demuth's, whither we went
accordingly. We arrived at noon, and found a
most excellent set of eight rooms, one of which was
a very large dining-room with a parquetrie floor.
Some of the others consisted of bed-rooms, drawing-
rooms, and a nice little boudoir surrounded by
sofas had also floors of parquetrie. Our first
proceeding was that of washing and dressing, and
we were tolerably hungry and ready for a good
dinner even at three o'clock. In the evening we
rested and had a visit from Mr. Disbrowe.

*Friday, 27th.*—We were to have called on Mr.
Disbrowe about noon; but, as there was then a
thunderstorm, we did not go till two. We walked
to his house on the Quay in a beautiful situation,
but at a considerable distance from our lodgings.
We found him and Mrs. Disbrowe, and Mr.
Kennedy, Mrs. Disbrowe's brother. They gave us
much useful information on various topics, and
asked us to dine with them the next day. After
staying there some time, we took leave and walked
across the bridge, down the Quay as far as the
Commercial Hall, which like all the other buildings
in St. Petersburg is very handsome. We then came
back over the same bridge, and walked round by the

Palace, and home again by the *Perspective*, a very long and beautiful street full of shops. This walk was extremely entertaining, from the beauty of the city, the extraordinary appearance of the inhabitants, and the variety of carriages, some of which are drawn by very fine thorough-bred horses. We dined at six, and did not feel disposed to go out again.

*Saturday*, 28*th.*—It had rained a great deal in the night, and continued to pour in torrents all the morning till about noon. We passed the morning in writing letters, and at half-past twelve Mrs. Disbrowe called to take me out; we went to the English " magazine," which is a collection of many shops in one, something in the way of Howell and James', but smaller. We went also to some other shops, and made some more purchases at Corbvière's, some more at Anthoni's, and some other places for working materials and patterns. Mrs. Disbrowe brought me home at four. Belgrave, who had been out walking, came home at half-past four, and at five we went to dine (in a carriage which we have hired for our stay here) at Mr. Disbrowe's.

Like all other carriages used here, it has four horses, which are driven as an Irish set, with an immense distance between the wheeler and leaders ; and the little boy who acts as postillion drives on the wrong side. At Mr. Disbrowe's we had a very pleasant dinner, of only themselves and Mr. Kennedy, and after dinner we looked at Russian prints. The Spanish Minister, and Mr. Fontenay, the French Chargé d'Affaires, called in after coffee ; and at about eight we set out with Mr. and Mrs. Disbrowe in their carriage (a landau) to call first on Count and Countess Nesselrode\*, who lives out in the country, but who was not at home, and then to go to the French play. The theatre is about two English miles distant, being *dans les isles*, where all the great people have their villas surrounded with gardens.

We found a very pretty little theatre which had been constructed in the space of two months ; saw two vaudevilles, and then set out again for a *soirée* at Princess Galitzin's. This lady is *belle fille* to the Governor of Moscow. We found her and two other ladies, and several gentlemen. There was one whist party, and a table prepared for *mouche*, the fashionable game here ; however nobody played at it. We arrived at half-past ten, and

---

\* Count Nesselrode was for many years the Minister for Foreign Affairs at the Court of St. Petersburgh.

found two pretty rooms, one circular with a dome, but no windows; the other with a large bow-window full of flowers, in which we sat. We were visited by Countess Potemkin, whose brother is gone for life to Siberia, having been a ring-leader in the late conspiracy; at half-past eleven we sat down to tea. There was a little dwarf among the servants. After tea, Princess Galitzin sung some very pretty airs, with a beautiful voice, her husband accompanying her on the pianoforte. After all this we set out about one to return home. In the middle of one of the streets, however, we were admonished by a gentle descent forwards of the coach, that it was time to give up our places, which we did with composure and dignity; on examination it was found that the pin of one of the wheels had broken; it was necessary to take off the horses, but before they were free, one of them was frightened by one of the servants flapping a cloak in his eyes; he jumped forwards, and in so doing separated the still adhering wheels from the coach, which conse-quently descended abruptly on the ground, and the horse set off straight home, the other three remaining quiet spectators.

Mr. and Mrs. Disbrowe, Belgrave, and I then

walked back along the streets; it luckily was very
fine; and we fortunately escaped being taken by
the *patrole* who walk about with hatchets on long
stalks. We found an empty *calèche* going by, in
which Mr. and Mrs. Disbrowe put themselves, close
to our hotel, where we arrived in perfect safety at
two in the morning.

Demuth's Hotel,

St. Petersburg.

Saturday, July 28th, 1827.

My dearest M——,

Here we are, in the most beautiful city ever be-
held, well worth coming twice the journey to see;
and we are all as well as possible. I will take up
our history where I left it. Our last day in Sweden
we passed at Bellevue, where we went soon after
noon. We walked about in a burning sun with the
good-natured Queen, and at two sat down to breakfast with her, the Prince Royal, and about ten other
people. Then we walked in and out of the house,
which is extremely small, through the pleasure-
grounds, and then went in a boat, much to Her
Majesty's affright; after which the Prince Royal
took leave, and the Queen proposed a drive. Accordingly she took me in her barouche, with her

ladies ; Belgrave followed in another with Mr. Bloomfield. We had a lovely drive, and more walking, for the Queen, although very fat, is always walking, to the despair of her ladies. We did not get back to Bellevue till half-past six. The Queen was very sorry to take leave of us, and nearly cried, saying all sorts of kind things, how she wished we could have stayed longer, and that she almost wished not to have seen us, so great was her regret at parting with us. I believe she sees but few *civilized people*, and evidently rather regrets Paris, and said, among other things, that, though nobody would believe it, " *C'était une triste chose que de changer de destinée.*" She gave me a pair of little porphyry candlesticks, that I might not forget her ; nothing could be more kind and cordial, and if we had not said we were going in the evening to see a *bal de la bourgeoisie*, she would have kept us *pour le dîner et ensuite pour toute la soirée*, which is no joke, as she sits up working and talking till two or three o'clock in the morning. The Prince Royal does not look so well out of uniform, and does not seem " thorough-bred," though they all think him perfectly beautiful. He is very accomplished, sings very well, and draws with a great deal of taste.

Well, to return, we came home to our dinner,
during which we had parting visits from our friends,
and Count Wetterstedt sat with us all the time.
We were so tired with our morning, and so comfortable at home, that after all we did not go to the
ball.   Next morning Count Voyno came to breakfast with us at eight o'clock ; went on board our
ship with us, and then wished us good-bye.   Mr.
Bloomfield and Mr. MacMahon sailed a little way
with us, and then returned in a boat.   Nothing
could be kinder or more anxious to make everything
pleasant than Mr. Bloomfield; he gave us a collection of provisions, enough, as our servant expressed
it, " *pour approvisionner fifty thousand russes.*"   Our
sail from Stockholm was quite beautiful ; we had a
good wind, delicious weather, a blue sea without a
wave, and our whole way lay through a labyrinth of
little wooded islands, like a scene in a fairy tale.
We embarked at ten in the morning ; slept very
comfortably all night in our cabin, and when we got
up found ourselves at anchor off the Island of
Aland.   Belgrave took a dip in the sea, and we
immediately sailed again, making way at the rate of
twelve miles an hour, the sea smooth as a lake, till
we reached Abo at seven in the evening of Friday,
having had a very good passage of thirty-three

hours. We set out again next morning, and got here on Thursday, at noon, having stopped half a day at Helsingfors, to see the wonderfully strong fortress of Sweaborg. Some of the Russian conspirators were found confined in a part of it, but they were suddenly taken away one morning about two months ago, and nobody knows where they are sent to. The Polish conspirators are not yet tried, but no more are to be executed.

We travelled for two nights without stopping, and arrived here, as I have said, on Thursday, in perfect health and prosperity.

We are superbly lodged in a large set of apartments at this hotel, where there is also a very good French cook. Mr. and Mrs. Disbrowe are here, and we dine with them to-day ; if it will but be fine (it is now pouring in torrents), I am going out first with her to some shops. We are in hopes of the Woronzows* coming to-morrow in the steam-packet. The old Madame de Lievent† has been very ill, but I daresay we shall see her.

---

* Simon, Count Woronzow, was a great Russian noble, who owned a large property in the Crimea. His only sister married, in 1808, George Augustus, eleventh Earl of Pembroke.

† Russian Ambassadress in England for many years. The old Princess, then in St. Petersburg, had been governess to the Emperor Nicholas and the Imperial family.

L

The Emperor is now at the camp, about eighteen miles from here. I believe we shall go to see it on Wednesday, when the Empress is going; there are forty thousand men under arms; we shall be presented, in due time, to them all. The Dowager-Empress* is already aware of our arrival, and is charmed that anyone should come so far to see St. Petersburg. One sight of the fair city, however, is well worth all the trouble. Beautiful and extraordinary it is! The streets are all palaces; the river magnificent; the people in Oriental dresses; and I never saw anything to equal the beauty of the horses, who all seem thorough-bred, and are certainly most magnificent creatures. We shall stay here till about Wednesday week; then we go to Moscow, and thence to the fair at Nisnei; after that, are uncertain whether to return by this place and the Riga road, or to go from Moscow to Warsaw. . . . The only idea that I can give you of this city, is that it is like the finest scenes of cities and palaces at Covent Garden Theatre. I am going to have a carriage and four horses, as that is the way in which people *comme il faut* go about here.

*Sunday, 29th.*—We went at eleven to the English chapel, which is a handsome building. It rained in

* Born Princess Mary of Wurtemberg, mother of the Emperor.

torrents when we came out, so we came straight
home, and wrote till four, when we walked out and
went to the Kasan Church, which is externally very
magnificent, with a semicircular row of double
pillars; the inside is equally beautiful, with a profusion of enormous granite columns, the capitals and
bases of which are gilt, producing a remarkably fine
effect. In the church is the tomb of Kutusoff, one
of the most celebrated of the Russian generals at
the time of Napoleon's invasion; a simple stone,
surrounded by iron railing, with trophies at each
corner. Inserted in the wall there is a flat bust,
somewhat black, of the Virgin Mary, decorated with
diamonds and jewels, with panels of wood under-
neath it, which are devoutly kissed by the people.
The altar is finely decorated; standing before it are
enormous candelabra of silver, and the surrounding
balustrade is of solid silver also. In front, there was
still remaining the platform on which the body of
the Emperor Alexander, and subsequently that of
Miloradowitch,* had lain in state. We then came
home, dined at six, and in the evening took a drive
in our carriage and four to Les Isles, and walked in
the garden of the Emperor's Palace of Irlagen,
which is full of beautiful flowers.

---

* Another Russian general of the same time.

*Monday, 30th.*—We went with Mrs. Disbrowe to the malachite manufactory, in the Rue des Pois, where we saw some very pretty things, and among others a magnificent vase and pedestal, entirely of malachite, for which they asked fifteen thousand roubles. After that, we went to see the Winter Palace, containing l'Hermitage, in which are all the pictures and treasures of every kind collected by Catharine II. The pictures are innumerable, and of every school; some very fine ones among them. The collection of jewels is beyond estimation, and all are extremely well arranged. There are a Paul Potter and a Murillo, both exquisite; a very pretty little picture of monkies, by Teniers, and hundreds of others, of every master; rooms full of Wouvermans, with the inevitable white horses; one of Rembrandt, and a large collection of beautiful little Dutch pictures; there is also a complete room of the French school, and one also of the Russian. Upstairs is a very fine collection of medals and coins, and a very pretty garden opening from rooms on the second floor.

We also saw the Winter Palace, which is all in the same building, and perfectly magnificent; nothing can be finer, or more splendid in every respect; and the arrangement of the rooms seems, at the same time, to be perfectly convenient and comfortable.

After this, Belgrave and I went to Anthoni's, a jeweller's, and then came home to dress, in order to dine at five at Mr. Disbrowe's, where we met Prince and Princess Soltikoff, Madame and Mademoiselle Vassiliwitch, Count Nesselrode, Count Zichy, and the Countess de Bombelles. After dinner, Madame Vassiliwitch wrote to her brother-in-law, General Leverschoff, respecting our going to see the camp next day. After the dinner company were gone, Mrs. Disbrowe, Mr. Kennedy, and I went in the carriage and four to drive to Irlagen, and saw the inside of the Palace. The Dowager-Empress's rooms are below; those of the Emperor and Empress above. It is a small house, but containing a good many rooms, very prettily furnished. We then met Belgrave and Mr. Disbrowe at Princess Dolgorouki's. She is an old, sensible-looking, civil woman, who had been a favourite of Potemkin's; she is mother to Princess Soltikoff, whom we found there; no other ladies, except a Princess Zuboff, and Princess Dolgorouki, one of the great ladies of the Court, who was playing at whist. There was also a mouche-table, at which Mrs. Disbrowe and five others played; a few gentle-

men sat about and chatted, among them Prince
Dolgorouki, the son of the house. I was never so
bored in my life, and considerably relieved by the
appearance of supper about twelve o'clock, at which
we did not sit down regularly, but each person had
a plate, &c., given him, or her, wherever they were
sitting, the dishes being carried round by the
servants. We got home about one o'clock, nearly
tired to death.

*Tuesday* 31*st.*—We wrote letters in the morning for the *courier,* who was to set out at three ;
we then dressed and went to Mr. Disbrowe's to go
with them to the camp. I went with Mrs. Disbrowe in one chariot and four, and Belgrave went
with Mr. Disbrowe in another. We waited a little
while for Mr. Disbrowe to finish his despatches, and
then departed after four, we arrived at our quarters
about half-past five, the distance about twenty-one
versts ; we drove to General Lewerschoff's habitation, which was in the middle of a wooden village,
and consisted of two or three of the peasants'
houses, (all made of wood,) united together and
made tolerably comfortable by papering the walls,
and putting in a little furniture. We were very
kindly received by General Lewerschoff, who introduced his two aides-de-camp, Count Suvalow and

another; we soon went to dinner, at which were
two other aides-de-camp. The dinner was the most
*recherché* and excellent that was possible, served on
very handsome plate; there were a great many
different wines, and among other dishes one of the
red mushrooms, which were excellent. We had
coffee simultaneously with dessert, and set out very
soon after to see the camp. Mrs. Disbrowe and I
went in a drosky drawn by two magnificent horses,
the one in the shafts black, and the one for show
grey. General Lewerschoff himself rode a beautiful
English horse, and mounted Belgrave on a very nice
chestnut, and Mr. Disbrowe on an equally good
bay. All these horses were very highly trained,
and went very superbly. The view of the tents
over the plain was very fine, there being between
thirty and forty thousand men encamped. We passed
first along the centre, in the middle of which is the
Emperor's tent; the men were at their evening
exercise; we then made a long round by a lake, and
returned by the tents of the *avant-garde*, where we
stopped some time, got out of the carriage and
walked among the tents; went into one of the
kitchens, which are like pyramids made of turf:
the perfect order and neatness of the whole arrangement is wonderful, and the walks between the tents

and the divisions and sub-divisions are as perfectly clean and neat as a flower garden. We heared the *retraite* played, which begins by a march, and is ended by a beautiful hymn, which they played admirably; after which, at a given signal, every soldier takes off his hat and says a prayer in a sort of chant; the effect of this, when performed by so large a body of men, at the same moment, is most striking and impressive, and the whole sight, on an immense plain, in a beautiful evening, was at once touching and splendid. After passing some time here, we returned to General Lewerschoff's house, had tea, and returned home after a most delightful evening arriving about half-past ten.

*Wednesday, August 1st.*—Belgrave and I set out at noon, and went to the English "magazine," to the banker's and to the Museum, where is a large collection of Natural History, a very fine skeleton of a mammoth, a stuffed servant of Peter the Great, of great height, &c. In the rooms above is a figure of Peter, dressed in his best costume, the instruments he worked with, an ivory lustre he made; his horse and dogs—these all wretchedly ill-stuffed—an amber looking-glass, belonging once to Charles XII., &c. Then to the Commercial Hall. Belgrave went in to look at it; then to two booksellers, a shop for the shawls which the Russian coachmen wear as sashes, and of which we bought two beautiful specimens; then we went in to look at a church close by, it was the Day of Elias, and there were many people crossing themselves and bowing to their favourite Saints, whose shrines were covered with gold and silver and precious stones, while lamps were burning before them, &c. We then came home, dined at home, and drove after dinner several versts, though not out of town, to see the Tauride, a palace built by Potemkin for Catharine, and now only used to shelter some old maids of honour, and for the Imperial *fêtes*. The dwelling-rooms are very pleasant, but the *grande salle* is beyond all description. It is of enormous size, supported on each side by a double row of white columns. Each column, surrounded by mock silver wreaths, out of which proceed hundreds of candles which, when lighted, produce an effect like magic. On one side of this large room is an enormous semi-circular green-house with gravel walks, though all roofed in, and with very large windows; it is divided into beds for flowers, and the trees are made of framework, supporting quantities of coloured lamps; the pendant to this on the other side, is a very large and beautiful circular room, joined on by an arch to the large central *salle*, containing some very pretty antiques, the busts placed on consoles on the walls, and lighted in the same way with the hall in the centre. Among the statues there is a particularly fine Egyptian one in grey marble. After going all through the house, we walked in the gardens, which are very pretty, and the evening was delightful. When we came near home, Belgrave got out and walked, whilst I went to call on Mrs. Disbrowe, who not having been quite well, would not, I found, be able to go to see the parade next morning at the camp. I then came home.

*Thursday, August 2nd.*—We got up at five, breakfasted, and set off at half-past seven in Mr. Disbrowe's travelling chaise (which he lent us) and four horses, with his *chasseur*, to go to see the *grande parade* before the Emperor at the camp. We drove first to General Lewerschoff's, and were told that if we went on we should find his carriage; this we did, and accordingly got into it and proceeded to the scene of action. We placed ourselves, with a few other carriages, in a very good place, near where the Empress was stationed, accompanied by the Grand Duke Michael,* and surrounded by their staff. We had the choice also of General Lewer-

---

* Younger brother of the late Emperor Nicholas.

schoft's drosky; but as it was broiling hot, I remained in the close carriage, while Belgrave got out and walked about with Mr. Kennedy.

The number of men who passed twice before the Emperor was forty-two thousand; the infantry came first; the first the Corps de Cadets, which was composed entirely of noblemen's sons, among whom the young Grand Duke Alexander,* was marching in the ranks, he appeared something like his uncle, the late Emperor, fair, with a round face, he was dressed in the uniform of the Paulofsky Regiment, with a high cap, of red, white and gold, without the least shade to the face. The Foot Guards followed, and then came the cavalry. The Cuirassiers (the Emperor's) in white uniforms with black helmets and cuirasses, mounted on very fine chestnut horses; heavy dragoons on bay and black horses; red hussars, on grey horses; lancers, &c., the rear being brought up by a troop of Cossacks. The first time they passed at a slow trot, the second time the cavalry went by at a slow canter; but the Cossacks trotted, not possessing any other pace but a trot or a gallop. The artillery, which was very finely appointed, with cannon, and portable bridges, had magnificent horses; but, in fact, they were all

* The present Emperor of Russia; born in April 1818, then in his tenth year.

fine, particularly the chestnuts. Each regiment
had a full band, which played as they went past.
The Emperor said to each regiment in Russian,
" I am contented," to which they answered in
a sort of scream, " we are glad to do our en-
deavour." The whole sight was beautiful. After
all was over, the Emperor thanked the men, and they
retreated in long files to their respective destinations.

We returned to General Lewerschoff's habitation,
where we remained while our post-horses were putting to our carriage, as they had baited there while
we were at the Camp. General Lewerschoff's two
aides-de-camp joined us, and we went to see the
General's horses in his stable. We declined an
invitation to go to a *déjeuner* at Princess A. Galitzin's,
as we were in a hurry to reach home. We called at
Mr. Disbrowe's; found them all out. Belgrave then
went to the banker's, meaning to walk home. Soon
after I came home, Mr. and Mrs. Disbrowe called,
and we settled our plans for the next day. We dined
at half-past five; at half-past seven Mrs. Disbrowe
called for me, and we visited at Mrs. Middleton's,
the Portuguese Minister's, and Princess Kourakin's,
and found nobody at home. Returned home; Mrs.
Disbrowe stayed a little while, and went away. We
had tea, and received a letter from Madame de

Lieven, appointing us to pass next Sunday at Paul-offsky, with the Dowager-Empress.

*Friday, August 3rd.*—We went soon after break-fast to see the model for the scaffolding of the out-side colonnade of the Eglise Isaac, and a beautiful model it is. The architect, Monsieur de Montfer-rand, then went with us to the place itself. The church was originally begun by Catharine II., in marble; finished by Paul, in brick. It is now pulled down, all but a very small part, which, in a church, must always be left, to begin an entirely new one. The columns for the colonnade, by which it is to be entirely surrounded, are magnificent; each of a single block of granite fifty-five feet in length, and sixteen feet in diameter. The machinery and method of raising and placing each pillar on its base is very curious. The capitals and bases are of bronze, and it is to take, at least, ten years in building. After this, Belgrave went with Mr. Disbrowe to look at some pictures, and I went with Mrs. Disbrowe to a quantity of shops, including milliner's, to arrange about my Court-dress for Sunday; we also went to the English " magazine" (Mr. Jackson's) for hand-kerchiefs, embroidered with costumes, &c.; and we ended by a visit to a confectioner's. I set Mrs. Disbrowe down at home, and met Belgrave close by her house ; he came home in the carriage with me, and we then dressed for dinner immediately. Dined at Mr. Disbrowe's ; met Monsieur aud Madame Segnaven; after dinner they went home to go to the Promenade aux Isles for the *fête* of the Empress-mother, where Belgrave and I went with Mr. and Mrs. Disbrowe in their landau. We found crowds of people on foot in all sorts of dresses; the number of carriages too was immense; we were obliged to go in a regular line round and round the islands, the order of march being rigidly enforced by gens-d'armes, who were stationed at different places. We got out to walk, in order to hear the band of horn music, which was stationed exactly in front of the Palace at Irlagen, and in which each performer plays one note. They played the overture to " Lodoiska"—the effect is very pretty, with rather too much sameness, and sounds very like an immense musical box ; the horns are in a gradation of sizes, from very small to quite . large. We came away about ten, as the fireworks were not to begin till eleven. The night was beautiful, and the yachts on the river, with lamps lit along the rigging, looked very pretty.

*Saturday August 4th.*—Belgrave went out after

breakfast to see about the passports, Mr. Kennedy came here, and I walked with him to several shops; bought patterns at a French one ; went to some Persian shops, and then to some Russian ones in the bazaar; bought two chains of sea-horse bone from Archangel. A very hot day. I went to Madame Turin's to accelerate the arrival of my gown for the next day, as we were to be presented to the Emperor and Empress at Tsarskoe-Selo, before going to the Dowager-Empress's at Pauloffsky. Belgrave too went to some shops. We dined with Mr. Middleton, the American Minister; besides Mrs. and Miss Middleton, there were Mr. and Mrs. Disbrowe, Monsieur and Madame Segnaven, Monsieur and Madame Guerreino, of Portugal; Count de St. Germain, and several others ; after that we went *aux Isles* to call on Madame Vassilikoff, who was out ; so we came straight home.

*Sunday, August 5th.*—We got up at half-past six, and were off at half-past eight, in our travelling carriage and four for Tsarskoe-Selo, about eighteen miles from St. Petersburg; we arrived there soon after ten, and were shown to a very pretty apartment in the Great Palace, where we dressed. Belgrave, of course, in his uniform; we were ready

by half-past eleven, the time appointed, when the
Count de Modena came to tell us that we should be
received at a quarter past twelve, when he would call
for us. We had therefore time to eat some luncheon,
which was prepared for us; a little after the time
fixed, he returned and took us in a royal coach to a
smaller palace, Le Palais Alexandre, a few hundred
yards from the other. We walked across a terrace
into the house, into a large *salle*, with servants in
Turkish dresses, here we waited a little while; when
old Princess Volkonsky, whom I remembered perfectly in England with the Grand Duchess Catharine,*
came in; and after a little while the Chamberlain
came to say that the Empress was ready to receive
me, and that Belgrave was to go to the Emperor.
I was then shown with my old Princess into the
Empress's private sitting-room, a beautiful and large
apartment, full of books, music, and flowers, and
opening to a delightful garden; the Empress was
there with two little Princesses, her children, the
Grand Duchess Marie and Olga.† She received me
very kindly, kissing me on both cheeks, but

---

* Sister of the Emperor Alexander; her first husband was the Prince
of Holstein-Oldenberg; she married secondly, in 1816, the late King
of Wurtemberg.

† The present Queen of Wurtemberg.

did not let me kiss her hand. She looked very handsome and was prettily dressed in light blue, with a light blue hat and feathers, and a necklace of three rows of enormous pearls. She made me sit down with her, and talked very agreeably, and a great deal about Gower,* whom she remembered perfectly at Memel. In the middle of this chat the Emperor came in without being announced, and sat down with us, and talked for a long time very cordially and good-naturedly. After he went, the Empress sent for Belgrave, who came and kissed her hand; she remained for some time talking to him standing, and then said, she would keep us no longer, as we were going to Pauloffsky, but hoped to see us on our return; she then kissed me again, and took leave of us; and we returned to the other Palace, over the whole of which we were shown by Count Modena; it is immense and magnificent, comprising long suites of rooms, with beautiful floors and covered with gilding. We saw the private apartments of Catharine II. and those of the late Emperor† and Empress, which are delightful and comfortable. In the Emperor Alex-

---

* My eldest brother, afterwards the second Duke of Sutherland.

† The Emperor Alexander I., who died in 1801.

M

ander's room all the things were as he had left
them, his slippers by his bed, his clothes, brushes,
boots, &c., all scattered about, and his books,
pencils, &c., were still on the tables. I forgot to
mention that a room, forming one of a long
suite, is famous as being lined entirely with amber,
which, however, has only the effect of a heavy
yellow marble. Countess Modena and her
daughters came for a moment to see us in our
rooms, and we then set out ready dressed for
Pauloffsky, about three miles off.

On our arrival we were shown to a very
handsome apartment; and immediately the *maître
des cérémonies* came to conduct me to visit the
Dowager Princess de Lieven, who was governess
to all the Imperial family, except Alexander—she
is now eighty-five years of age. We reached her
rooms by a long suite of passages and staircases. I was very kindly received by her: she
had the most charming manners, and was dressed
in perfect good taste for her age. She asked
many questions about Count and Countess Lieven,
in London; but we were soon unwillingly obliged
to take leave of her, as it was time to go to
the Empress-mother. We were then taken to
*La Salle Grecque,* a very handsome room, where

we waited a short time, with some of the
Court people, till the Empress* appeared; she is
very tall, and *bien conservée* for her age (sixty-
eight), with remarkably good manners, and very
handsomely dressed in white, and with a magnificent set of turquoises and diamonds; her face
is large and rather flat, but with a very pleasing expression; she walks slowly and with some
difficulty, but with great dignity. She kissed me
on both cheeks, like the other Empress, and
received us both with the greatest kindness; afrer
talking a little while, she retired, saying she
hoped to see us at dinner, and we were then
conducted to a semi-circular gallery; soon after
which the Empress arrived, and at three o'clock
we went to dinner. The dinner was magnificent and superbly *monté;* at dessert, the Empress
cut up an apple of the celebrated transparent
kind, and gave me some seeds to take home
to plant in England.† When dinner was over,
we went back to the *Salle Grecque,* when the Empress took me out on the balcony and talked
for some time. I asked her leave to see her
Institut des Dames Nobles, this she gave readily,

* The Empress-mother was the widow of the Emperor Paul.

† This I did carefully, but they never succeeded.

and said she would give immediate orders for
us to see both that and the Convent de St.
Catharine. She then invited everybody to drink
tea at Le Pavillon des Roses, and forthwith retired ; we were immediately taken in a coach
to another small palace, a few hundred yards
distant to the Grand Duchess Helen, a daughter
of Prince Paul of Wurtemberg,* who is fair and
pretty, talked very fast, and asked a great number
of questions. I was presented to her first, and
then Belgrave, and we then returned to the
Dowager Empress's Palace, where Belgrave took off
his uniform and put on an ordinary evening dress.

We were to have driven out *en ligne*, a sort of
open carriage like two benches, joined back to back,
which had just come to the door with six horses,
when it began to rain, which of course put an end
to our expedition, so I went and found Princess
Kourakin in the passage, and we went together and
paid a visit to one of the *dames d'honneur*, whose
rooms were just opposite to ours, across the passage ;
a message then came that the Empress wished us
to see her private rooms, which open into an
exquisite flower garden, to which nobody has access
but the Empress herself. We were rather hurried

* Brother of the then King of Wurtemberg.

here, as she was already gone to the *salon*, whither we followed, and found that she had kept a place at her table for me to play at *mouche* with her, and a party of Princess Dolgorouki and Prince Volkonski, and several more. All this time, during supper, the windows which were open down to the ground, were full of the populace who were looking in. After supper, about half past ten, the Empress went round her circle and took leave of us, saying that she should see us again on our return from Moscow. She then retired, and every-body of course separated; we went to our rooms, and dressed for our journey home, about twenty miles, where we arrived very tired soon after one in the morning. It rained in torrents during the latter part of the way.

*Monday, August 6th.*—Belgrave and I went out soon after breakfast on a shopping tour, to buy books, maps, &c., and to see the Convent and Church of Alexander Neffsky, who lies buried in a great silver frittered-away shrine in the church; this shrine was erected in his honour by Catharine II. There was service going on, performed by the monks, who are dressed in black with high caps, and black veils hanging down behind them; the dress is handsome. Their singing in the church

without music, had a very fine effect. After that
we saw a strange ceremony of the priest blessing a
book for a woman. We dined at home at seven,
and did not go out in the evening.

*Tuesday, August 7th.*—Belgrave went to call on
Mr. Boulgakoff, the ·Directeur des Postes, and soon
after eleven we went to see the Convent of St.
Catharine, and the Institut for the education of
three hundred *dames nobles*, founded by the
Dowager Empress. The different classes have
different coloured stuff dresses, white aprons with
bodies, extremely well made, and long gloves; they
are all exceedingly well behaved; the Directeur
and the Supérieure· and several subordinate
officers went over the place with us, they asked
the children many questions, and particularly
in subtle metaphysics, which they answered very
glibly.

We stayed here some time, and then went to
see the church in the Citadel, on each side of the
altar are the coffins of some of the last Emperors ; on
the right are those of the late Emperor Alexander and
his Empress, that of Anne Paulowna, his sister, and
that of Paul, all covered with palls of dark green
cloth edged with· gold, and the cypher of each on
the top, also in gold ; on the other side are the

coffins of Peter I., his wife, and daughter; and that of Catharine II., all similarly covered and decorated.

The church is lined with standards taken from the Turks and Persians; on one is the mark of a hand in two places, clearly defined in blood. From here we went to the Palace of the Grand Duke Michael, where we found, by his orders, an aide-de-camp ready to receive us, a servant in almost every room, and sentinels in every corner. The house both outside and inside is magnificent; it contains quantities of delightful rooms, beautifully furnished, some with Lyons silk, all of different colours, and some with *faux marbre* beautifully painted; the house besides is one of the best arranged and most convenient that I ever saw. We also saw the Grand Duke's private apartments, in which are several good pictures and drawings of soldiers, horses, &c.; also his armoury, which is very fine and varied, and contains besides the ancient armour, specimens of all the modern uniforms of different countries. There are three glass cases, entirely filled with clothes which had been worn by the late Emperor. There is a delightful garden belonging to this Palace, which was given to the Grand Duke (*i.e.* the Palace) by

Alexander; and the whole thing is perfectly superb.
We then came home to dress for dinner. Belgrave
dined at a large banquet under orange trees at
Count Bloom's, the Danish Minister; and I dined
with Mrs. Disbrowe; we were only ourselves
and Mr. Kennedy, as Mr. Disbrowe dined also
at Count Bloom's. In the evening I was going
to set down Mrs. Disbrowe at Mrs. Middleton's;
but as we met Mr. Disbrowe and Belgrave
coming back from dinner, she went with Mr.
Disbrowe, and I came home with Belgrave, and
wrote letters till near twelve, when I went to bed
dreadfully tired.                    .

St. Petersburg.<br>Tuesday Morning, August 7th, 1827.

Dearest M——

I want so much to write, and have so little
time that it is quite terrible! There is so much
to be done here both morning and evening,
that one never has a moment to one's self,
and I begin this whilst waiting for the carriage,
to go to see the Dowager Empress's Institut de
St. Catharine, and the other Institut of Les Dames
Nobles, which we do by her particular permission.
Last Tuesday we had a charming treat, which

was, going to the camp, about eighteen miles from the capital. We went with the Disbrowes, and dined with General Lewerschoff, at his quarters; these occupy two or three wooden cottages in a Russian village, where all the officers live; we were only ourselves, himself, and his four aides-de-camp; he has made his rooms very nice, and gave us a dinner as good and as *recherché* as one could have in Paris, served on very handsome plate. Among other things was a dish of scarlet mushrooms, which we were inclined to vote poisonous, but we found them, on trial, excellent. After dinner he put Mrs. Disbrowe and me in a drosky, with two magnificent horses; he and Belgrave, and Mr. Disbrowe were mounted on the finest horses I ever saw. We went all over the camp, which being placed on an immense plain, with tents for forty thousand men, was a beautiful sight; the Emperor's tent was in the middle. The whole thing is kept in the most perfect order; at nine o'clock we heard them play the *retraite* which is followed by a magnificent hymn; then at a signal all the soldiers take their hats off and recite a prayer, which closes the scene; but the effect of this, when performed by forty thousand people in their different regiments all at

the same moment, is the most striking thing
possible. On Wednesday morning we "did" a
number of shops and visits, and in the evening
went to see La Tauride, built by Potemkin for
Catharine, in which there is a *salle*, and a covered
garden, and a *chef-d'œuvre* of magnificence ! On
Thursday we got up at five and started again to
the camp to see *la grande parade*, *i.e.*, all the
troops passing in review twice before the Emperor
Nicholas, which finished this year's campaign. It
was quite a beautiful scene ; the regiments are
splendid, and so are the artillery ; the cavalry too,
are admirably mounted. We saw many celebrated
people. The young Grand Duke,* just nine
years old, is a very nice boy ; does his duty in the
ranks like a common soldier, and is extremely well
brought up, being inured to all sorts of fatigue,
exercise and discipline.

We saw all the proceedings from General
Lewerschoff's carriage, the driver of which knew
just what to do and where to go. (General Lewerschoff commands the heavy cavalry.) We came
home to dinner, and made visits in the evening.
Next day we went to see the foundations of a
new church which is in the course of building,

* The present Emperor, Alexander II.

and which is to be surrounded by granite columns like Persepolis, fifty-five feet high, and sixteen in diameter, and exquisitely polished. We dined with the Disbrowes, and in the evening drove to a Promenade aux Isles, where there were bands of music, illuminations, and thousands of people, it being the *fête* of the Empress-mother. In the evening I found a very kind note from the old Princess de Lieven, appointing us to pass Sunday with the Dowager Empress at Pauloffsky. Saturday morning I walked with Mr. Kennedy (Mrs. Disbrowe's brother), to a quantity of Persian and Russian shops, which was in itself very entertaining; and I received a notice that the Emperor and Empress would receive us on Sunday, at half-past eleven at Tsarskoe-Selo—twenty miles from here— before going to the Dowager Empress. I had much to do in order to get my dress in time; however, it all came punctually to a moment. It was very pretty, of a canary-bird colour, trimmed with blonde, and a large hat with white feathers.

We dined that day, Saturday, at Mr. Middleton's, the American Minister, and met among others Signor Guerreino, Portuguese Minister, who was in England some time ago. On Saturday we had to

get up at half-past six for our presentations in the
country. We got to Tsarskoe-Selo in very good
time, and found a pretty apartment ready for us
to dress in, and the Count de Modena came to tell
us that the Emperor and Empress would receive
us soon after twelve. We had, therefore, time to
eat some luncheon which they gave us; and in
due time the Count de Modena came to fetch us
in a royal coach, as the palace where they live
is a few hundred yards from the great one. We
were shown into a beautiful *salle*, opening into
an exquisite garden, by which all these palaces
are surrounded, with a profusion of orange trees,
&c. In a short time came old Princess Volkonsky,
uglier than ever, and covered with orders and
diamonds; she remembered all about us in England, and told me, certainly without much senti-
ment, that Princess Aladensky, the other old
fright, was dead. In a little while the Count de
Modena, and the Ministre des Cérémonies, came to
tell us that the Empress* was ready for me,
and the Emperor for Belgrave. Accordingly I
went with Princess Volkonsky to the Empress,
and found her in a nice large room, full of
furniture, books, music, flowers, &c., in short,

* Born Princess Charlotte Alexandra of Prussia.

her private sitting-room, with two of her daughters. She received me very kindly; she is a very interesting person, very handsome, but pale and *souffrante*; she has very good manners and great amiability; she seemed rather nervous, and is, I should think, a person of much feeling. She made me sit down with her, and talked for some time, and a great deal about Gower,* whom she desired we would ask to come to Russia, *avant que nous sommes tous trop vieux;* she sent one of her children to look for a pair of scissors that he gave her at Memel, and which she always uses for her work, but the children could not find them, though she says they are always kept with her *métier*.

In the middle of this the Emperor came in without being announced, and talked for a long time much about his regiments and horses, and went to look for his youngest child to show me, but it was asleep. He then sent for the young Grand Duke, but he, too, was out bathing. The Emperor is very cordial and good-natured in his manner, and said that he hoped to see us again when we came back, as he was then obliged to go and visit his mother, and went away. The Empress

* My brother, the late Duke of Sutherland, then Lord Gower.

talked for a little while longer, and then said, "Nous excuserons l'étiquette, et je m'en vais envoyer chercher votre mari." Belgrave came and kissed her hand, she remained a little while talking to him, standing all the while, and then said that she must not keep us, as we were going to Pauloffsky, and so took leave, adding she must see us again on our return. We then went back to Tsarskoe-Selo, where the Count de Modena showed us all over the Palace, which is enormous and magnificent; we saw the private apartment of the old Catharine, and also of the late Emperor and Empress—delicious rooms—all the Emperor Alexander's things were left about as he had left them, some of his clothes, slippers, &c., pencils, knives, books—nothing had been touched. From the windows of a long gallery we saw Princess Mary of Wurtemburg,* a niece of the Duchess of Kent, sitting out working with her ladies; and from another we saw three Princesses of Georgia, then residing at St. Petersburg as hostages, or prisoners on parole, and just returning from a drive.

After seeing all this, and much more, we drove

---

* Daughter of Prince Paul; married, as Helena Paulowna, to the Grand Duke Michael of Russia.

off to Pauloffsky, about three miles; we had a beautiful apartment given us for the day, and immediately after a chamberlain came to take me to see the old Princesse de Lieven, who has been dangerously ill. She is eighty-five, and the nicest, cleanest, best dressed person (suitably to her age) I ever saw; her manners are a charming mixture of *douceur* and *noblesse*, full of kindness and thoroughly *bien élevée*. After I had been with her a minute, the Emperor was announced ; of course, my conductor and I retired to an ante-room, where we thought we were safe; but contrary to our expectation the Emperor came through that room, expressed himself excessively shocked that we should have run away from him, and gave me his arm to accompany him to Madame de Lieven, and made me stay through the whole of his visit. He shows, as they all do, the greatest respect and affection for Madame de Lieven, and kissed her most tenderly both on coming and on going. After he went away, Belgrave was admitted ; she was very good-natured to us both, and we liked and admired her extremely. We left her soon, as it was near time for our visit to the Dowager Empress. Madame de Lieven had with her her two sons, one whom she introduced as her eldest son, and the other looked older than the Monsieur de Lieven* who was in England. We were taken through a suite of rooms and galleries to a large *salle,* with a few chamberlains about, where the Empress appeared soon after. Neither she nor the young Empress would let me kiss their hand, but kissed me on both cheeks. She received us with great good-nature, and after a little conversation, she said that she hoped to see us again at dinner, and so retired. We were then taken to a semi-circular gallery were we found about twenty-six ladies magnificently dressed, and still more gentle-men ; my friend, the old Princess Dolgorouki, whom I had thought quite decrepit at her own house, came out gay and youthful, in an apricot coloured gown, trimmed with bunches of violets— like a fashion book—and with the help of rouge, still looking very handsome. The Nesselrodes all civility, but as they are still in the country we are to dine with them on our return.

Well, to go back to the Court. After we had been there a short time the Empress appeared, and as soon as she had done the honours of her circle, we all went to dinner. She of course went first and alone, as the Grand Duke Michael, who was to have come, had not arrived ; after her went all the ladies

* Afterwards Ambassador in England for many years, both before and after 1827.

separately, and then all the gentlemen. The places
of the guests were all settled beforehand. The
Empress in the middle of the great table; next to
her the Grand Duke Michael, who came in soon
after; then her first lady; then I, then the *grande
maîtresse* of the Grand Duchesse Helen, and so on.
All the great ladies were arranged on the same side
with the Empress, and opposite were all the gentlemen, among others Belgrave, who sat by Count
Nesselrode. The other gentlemen and *dames
d'honneur* were at the two other tables. The dinner
was handsome and magnificently *monté*. After
dinner we returned to the *Salle Grecque*, where the
Empress took me on the balcony and talked for
some time, and gave us permission to see her two
Institutes, des Dames Nobles and St. Catharine,
then invited all the company to drink tea " dans le
Pavillon des Roses, mais à condition qu'elles
mettront des robes fermées et de grands manteaux."
The men were to take off their uniforms at all
events for the evening; and by great good luck I
had taken with me a white *gros de Naples* gown
with long sleeves, which was just right. One of
the ladies was desired to take us for a promenade in
an open carriage before tea, to show us the gardens ;
but just when the carriage appeared with six

N

horses, it began to rain, so we could not go, and
the Pavillon des Roses was out of the question.
But I quite forgot to mention, that before we
undressed we were taken in a carriage to the
Grand Duke Michael's habitation, about one mile
and a half off, to be presented to the Grand Duchess
Helen, who not being well, did not come to dinner ;
she is pretty, with very fair light hair, talks very fast,
and asks innumerable questions; we were presented
to her one after the other. That done, we returned to
the other Palace, and were soon called by one of the
ladies to see the Empress's cabinet, at her desire.

This cabinet consists of a suite of small rooms,
furnished in the most perfect way, entirely in
beautiful *broderies de tapissaries*, like ours, and
with everything imaginable of refinement, *recherché*,
beauty, ease, and comfort, opening into a delicious
flower-garden, into which nobody ever has access,
except herself; she is very fond of flowers, and the
rooms were filled with the finest and rarest flowers,
she had plenty of canary birds also, and a very
handsome poodle. From this apartment we were
called in a hurry, and on going up-stairs again to
the great room, I found, to my dismay, the Empress
was waiting for me to begin her game at
*mouche*, of which I did not know one bit. But,

however, a young Prince Hohenloe,* the Wurtemburg Minister, undertook to teach and help me; and succeeded so well as to make me win. The Empress also helped me herself occasionally, talking very agreeably the whole time. She played the whole evening, except for about twenty minutes, when the Grand Duchess Helen came and took her place; but she stayed a very short time, and the Empress took her cards again, and played till she had done supper. This meal is served round, like tea, each person has a knife, plate, fork, &c., if he or she likes; this people put on their knees, or where they can. In the meantime, the Empress sent Belgrave to see her pictures, her library, &c., with which he was delighted, and he then joined the young gentlemen and ladies who were dancing in the outer room, and danced for some time. The Empress then sent the Grand Duke Michael to fetch him, and talked to him about pictures, &c., She made me a great *éloge* of Lord Granville† and Lord St. Helens,‡ and finally took

* The same Prince whose reputed miracles afterwards caused so much sensation both in England and on the Continent.

† Half-brother of the first Duke of Sutherland; afterwards Earl Granville.

‡ A celebrated diplomatist, many years British Minister and Ambassador at various foreign courts; he died in 1841.

N 2

leave of me, saying, she depended on seeing us
on our return. Nothing could be kinder than she
was to us, as well as to everybody else : she said besides, she would write immediately to some friend of
hers—I do not know who—to take care of us at
Moscow, and gave me orders for us to see her
Institutes. We have been at one of these Institutes
to-day, and saw three hundred young ladies like
Madame de Lieven, and all just as well behaved.
To-morrow we are to see seven hundred more.
After going there this morning, we went to see
the church of the Citadel, where the late Emperor and Empress are buried; thence to the
Grand Duke Michael's Palace, which both inside and out is the most completly magnificent
and comfortable house I ever saw. It is only
just finished, and was given him by Alexander;
the furniture too, is quite beautiful, and in the
best taste. He had very good-naturedly ordered
an aide-de-camp to show us everything, so we
saw all his private apartments, and a superb
armoury, with several cases of clothes of the late
Emperor, and a complete collection of armour
and uniforms of all nations. Belgrave has just
been dining at a great dinner of Count Zichy's
(the Austrian Minister), and I with Mrs Dis-

browe and her brother. I am writing in great haste, for I have more letters to write, one to Lord Granville, full of royal messages, from the King of Sweden, which I have never yet had time to despatch.

To-morrow we have a thousand things to do, and to pack up (for we start next day for Moscow), and to dine with the Disbrowe's at a great dinner. We expect to get to Moscow on Monday or Tuesday, then to rest a day, then go on to Nisnei, where rooms are taken for us; to stay there three or four days, come back to Moscow for five or six days more, and then here again for about a week; till then I do not expect to have time to write again.

*Wednesday, 8th.*—Got up soon after seven. Belgrave went after breakfast again to Monsieur Bulgakow's about his *courier*, and at ten we went to the other Institut des Dames Nobles, for which purpose a man in uniform was told off to conduct us, by order of the Empress; we were received by the Inspecteur des Etudes, and by Madame d'Aglebert, the Supérieure, who was the governess to the present Emperor Nicholas, and is a Dame de Portrait, and of the Order of St. Catharine. She was very kind to us, and we saw the whole in detail; there are here seven hnndred and twelve pupils, two hundred of whom are *bourgeoises*, the rest nobles. The education is perfect as to accomplishments, and comprises besides all the usual branches, geometry, metaphysics, drawing, music, &c. We went to see them all at dinner, previouslv to which they said a prayer, and then sung a hymn, the effect of which was extremely pretty, they then sat down to table; to-day being a *jour maigre*, the dinner consisted of a soup of gruel with raisins, a dish of fish, and one of rice; on other days there are also three dishes, one of soup, one of meat, and one of vegetables, or something sweet. While they were at their dinner, the Supérieure gave us luncheon, and we then took leave of her. The maid-servants of the institution are all educated here. The sleeping rooms are very large, and contain a great number of small beds arranged in two dormitories; the school-rooms are also large, and look horribly dull, being destitute of any furniture save benches and desks. The children come as early as six years old, and stay six years more, during which time they never leave the establishment, and never go out, except twice a day, for an hour each time, in a dull garden. The house is very spacious, the passages immensely wide and long, the rooms all very large and high, the children all hold themselves upright and stiff, like Madame de Lieven; there were not many pretty ones. The Empress-mother comes very often to see them, and sometimes for the whole day. She has a handsome apartment reserved entirely to herself.

We went away soon after one o'clock, and went to the malachite manufactory—Maderni's—where Belgrave bought a magnificent malachite vase (for fourteen thousand roubles) and two small ones, and a large *cassette*, and a square *presse-papier* of lapis lazuli for two thousand more. We then went to the bankers, and I went to the English " magazine" and some more shops, and then came home; we packed up some of our St. Petersburg purchases for Mr. Kennedy to send by the *courier* by Saturday's steamboat, and made many arrangements for our next day's journey, when we were to set out for Moscow; then dressed and arrived tolerably late for dinner at Mr. Disbrowe's, where was a party of five-and-twenty: Mr., Mrs. and Miss Middleton, General de Suchterlens, a nice old man, who had taken Swea-borg from the Swedes, his son, Count Suchterlens,*

* Who they say, afterwards, actually sold his wife.

Monsieur Bodisco, General Dausebach, the Hano-
verian Minister, Count Palma Stiernend, the
Swedish Minister, and several others. Monsieur
and Madame Segnavine, Monsieur de Bombelles, and Count Zichy, came in the evening.
We sat out on the balcony after dinner till our
return home, when we arranged our affairs, wrote
letters, paid bills, " did" this journal, and I hope I
may soon say, " had tea and went to bed."

*Thursday, 9th.*—We got up at six, and were busy
in attending to our packages ; Mr. Kennedy came
just after breakfast to receive our last words and
execute our commissions, and to bring us letters for
Moscow. I walked with him to leave some orders
at the English " magazine ;" just before we set out, I
received a letter from Princess Lieven, enclosing
another from the Empress-mother to the Governor
of Moscow, as she had promised us. We set out
at eleven, ourselves in our own carriage, and the
little carriage going before with a *courier* and our two
beds, for Belgrave had also made the acquisition of
an iron one at St. Petersburg. We had a good
road, and found ourselves at Pomerania at seven,
but could not get there so many rooms as we should
have liked, as they were all preparing for the
Emperor, who was expected there somewhere in

the morning; however, those we had were very clean, the inn was excellent, and so was our dinner.

*Friday,* 10*th.*—We set out at six; the country all along was flat and desolate looking. We got to Novogorod about three, and stopped at a *traiteur allemand's* to dine; we had a good dinner, but the inn was very dirty. Novogorod is a large straggling town surrounded with old walls, and looks altogether like a wreck of former greatness. As soon as we had dined we went on again; at Bronnita, the stage beyond Novogorod, the good road ends, and it continues very bad, occasionally made of trees laid across, sometimes of deep sand, and for long distances it consists only of a hundred different tracks over a vast extent of sand. We arrived at Crelsi at one on the morning of Saturday, 11th, and found a room for my maid in the inn, where she had a bed made up on one of our mattresses. Belgrave and I slept in the carriage, and were called at half-past four, when we went into the inn, a wretched place, to wash and dress and breakfast (we had our own bread and tea), and were off again at half-past six. We arrived at Zimagore about three, and dined extremely well at a German *traiteur's,* went on again immediately and overtook our *courier* at eleven at Khotilovo, where, as we found the inn very clean, having been just built, we decided on remaining for the night. We had tea and went to sleep in our own beds. This night, like the last, was extremely dark; our road was occasionally through deep sand, and sometimes at full gallop over the grass without any road; our drivers, the wildest-looking creatures imaginable, with long beards, and most often in sheep-skin pelisses, the wool inside, which in the middle of the day must be rather warm; they encourage their horses, who go at a wonderful pace, by the strangest screams and cries, and keep singing a great part of the way. The stages are very long, generally above thirty versts, some even thirty-eight, a verst being three-quarters of an English mile. From the stage before Zimagore to-day we had six horses.

*Sunday,* 12*th.*—We left Khotilovo a little before nine; had a tolerable road. We came to the last stage with seven horses and sometimes more, and performed it, though it consists of thirty-eight versts, in three hours. Got to Torjök at seven; found a good inn. After we had arranged our beds, we went into the shop (which is within the inn) for the gold and silver embroideries on leather for which Torjok is celebrated We bought fourteen large sashes and thirteen small ones, a pocket-book,

and a good many shoes, and ordered four large
reticules, two of red and two of green leather, embroidered with gold, and two yellow portefeuilles
with silver, and Belgrave ordered six pairs of boots,
two red, two maroon with gold, and two yellow with
silver all of different patterns ; this took us till nine
o'clock, when we dined and then went to bed.

*Monday,* 13*th.*—We left Torjok at eight, and got
about two to Tver, where we stopped at a large,
rambling, dirty inn, also kept by a German, to dine ;
it began to rain while we were here, and continued
in torrents the whole of the day and evening. We
set out as soon as we had done dinner, Belgrave went
outside, so as to enable my maid to go within on
account of the rain. It grew very dark, and the
rain continued to inundate the roads, over which we
went at a furious pace, till we reached Savidoro, a
miserable place, at half-past eleven. Here Belgrave
arranged himself in the inn upon one of our mattresses, and my maid and I slept in the carriage till
five, when Belgrave was called, and on awaking we
found that the rain had ceased and the morning was
fine.

*Tuesday,* 14*th.*—We continued our course at six,
and stopped at the next place, Klin, to dress and
breakfast ; then we set off again ; the road im-

proving, we soon arrived on the regular new *chaussée*, parts of which are practicable at present only between St. Petersburg and Moscow. The last stage the road was excellent—a hard, good Macadam—and we got to Moscow at seven. Rooms had been taken for us in Koppe's Hotel, only moderately clean. The country round Moscow is, as usual in Russia, a dead flat, and the approach to the town on this side has nothing striking. We arranged ourselves in our apartments, dined and went to bed.

*Wednesday,* 15*th.*—Got up at eight; had very good bread and butter for breakfast. Belgrave went out to look for Mr. Gillibrand and to call on the Governor, and then sent back the *courier* we had brought from St. Petersburg—the Directeur des Postes here having promised him a better one. It rained all the morning, and I did not go out, but wrote letters. Mr. Gillibrand called at five and went out with Belgrave to look for a carriage to hire to convey us to Nisnei ; he was out for two hours and more, employed in going to all the coachmakers' shops before he could find one which would suit us, but at last he succeeded and found a blue barouche.

*Thursday, August* 16*th.*—We were busy the whole of the morning in arranging our things and packing up for our journey. We took lodgings at an Englishwoman's (Mrs. Debaire) for my maid, whom I intended to leave at Moscow while we went to Nisnei. At one o'clock, Belgrave went to call on the Governor, who gave him a letter for Nisnei. We had luncheon before we set off, and at five in the evening we embarked in a lapis lazuli coloured *calèche*, which carried all our things (of which we took very few) in bags under the seats, and thereby left us room to put up our feet at length on the opposite seat, which was very convenient for night. Belgrave's servant went on the seat with the driver; and in this guise we departed with four horses abreast; we travelled through the whole of the night, and slept very comfortably, though the road was very rough.

*Friday,* 17*th.*—We arrived about seven in the morning at Pokroo, where we got out to breakfast, and then wished we had stayed in the carriage, the inn being most hopelessly dirty and horrible; so we went on as soon as we had swallowed our tea. Nothing particular happened through the day; the road generally very rough and sandy, and the country quite flat, we reached Vladimir at seven; it is a curious old town, full of churches with minarets, and bells continually ringing. The inn

here is tolerable. We took a short walk before
dinner, and looked into a church, where a service
was going on ; then came home, dined, and slept
in our own beds. It is vain to expect any such
article in a Russian inn, a sofa being. the only
thing approaching to it. Vladimir was formerly
the residence of the " Grand Prince," of whose
old château there are a few remaining walls,
like those around the Kremlin, and an old cathedral
adjoining.

*Saturday*, 18*th*.—Got up soon after four, and
were off at seven ; the road sandy the whole way ;
dined in the carriage on our own provisions. We
saw at night, between Deatches and Mourom, a
village burning at some distance. We were fast
asleep, when we were suddenly awakened by the
splash of water, and found ourselves embarked in
a ferry-boat, crossing a large river, having just
changed horses at Mourom, about two o'clock in
the morning.

*Sunday*, 19*th*.—Having crossed the river, we were
taken by a twisting cross road ; and began by
sticking fast in a sand-hill, out of which the horses
could not pull us. We should probably have
remained there for days, or perhaps for years, had it
not been for the Siberian post, which was passing

by in five light carts, with numerous horses; the people gave our carriage a push, which helped us up the hill, and also gave us an additional horse to the five we had before; and with this wide *attelage* we went through meandering tracks, and through copse woods, where the road was sometimes hardly wide enough for a pair. We came to a brook, which it was necesary to cross, and which was simply a deep bog, aided by a few rotten planks placed across with wide intervals. In the midst of this, the middle horse contrived very naturally to fall down; so we were compelled to stop, with black mud up to our axles, till he could be pulled up again; we were then pulled out with a desperate jerk on to the opposite bank. Our carriage was fortunately as strong as a piece of artillery, or it never could have stood a mile of this extraordinary road. As we went along we met constantly long lines of carts, returning with merchandise from Nisnei, and also large flocks of fine-looking oxen; and passed several times parties of prisoners going off to Siberia, strongly guarded.

The morning broke with a thick fog, and the road became pretty enough, through a country covered with corn, and occasionally green turf, over which, we galloped at a prodigious rate; some

versts further on we came to the top of a deep
dell, with a regular quagmire full of holes at the
bottom, through which lay our way.   There was
no road apparently; but we had an indication of
the track, that we had better *not* take, by seeing
some carts struggling through the bottom of this
ravine, though nearly absorbed in the mud.   We
descended a very steep place, straight into this bed
of mud, through which our driver very dexterously
guided us, just avoiding some tremendous holes;
we then went on prosperously, and found a better
road.   We stopped about eleven o'clock to breakfast at Osiabjovo, where we found a fairly clean
room, though full of flies; and also our little
carriage which contained the *courier* and beds; it
was undergoing repairs, having been overturned in
the night, and the front wheels broken; this done,
we set forth again; the stage began by a very
steep hill, upon which the horses ran back, instead
of forwards, and were got up with great difficulty;
there were three other hills which we climbed,
without any particular danger.   The next inn was
a much better one, but we did not stop at it, the
road being very good from Yarimovo to Alexovo,
where there is another good house.   After this the
road was again very sandy; the dust rose and

remained hanging over the road like a fog all the way from here to Nisnei, the road was covered with long lines of carts returning from the fair and market; there must have been some hundreds. We did not arrive at Nisnei till after dark, and descended a very steep hill through the town to lodgings, which had been taken for us in a house near the bridge ; we found a very good apartment of six rooms, and tolerably clean, but not abounding in comfort, there being nothing in it but tables, chairs, and sofas ; we, however, soon put up our-beds, got dinner and a supper of our own provisions, and portable soup, &c., and went to bed at twelve, having arrived about ten.

*Monday,* 20*th.*—Had visits in the morning from Mr. Schöhl and Mr. Foottil. Belgrave went out with them, and walked afterwards with me about the fair till we came home to dinner at seven. The fair is the most amusing scene that can be conceived. It is about half a verst from the town on a peninsula, between the Rivers Oka and Volga, which meet immediately below it. There is a regular town built on purpose for the fair ; it consists of long rows of warehouses and shops, with piazzas before them, the whole forming a very large square with innumerable subdivisions; the part where the

o

tea magazines are placed is built in the Chinese manner, and there is a Tartan mosque near. Each sort of article has its separate quarter; there is one quarter for furs, which are very cheap, one for shoes, one for leather, one for all sorts of things used in dying, such as indigo, logwood, cochineal, &c., of which the Bokharians take a great deal in exchange for their merchandize. The shops from Moscow are the most showy, and every sort of thing is to be found, from the commonest, of a copek in price, to the most valuable. The people themselves are as entertaining as any part of the scene, as besides thousands of Russians, there are abundance of Tartars and Bokharians, and all kinds of tribes in different dresses; and some of them fine-looking people.

We were just thinking of going to bed, when Belgrave's servant told us there was a great fire near; we looked up and saw a great stream of light illuminating the entire street, so we put on our things and went out; the fire was at two or three versts distance, and on the opposite side of the river; but nevertheless it lighted up the whole of the quay, where we were walking, the river, and shipping, and the heights above the town. The blaze was terrific, and as there was just wind enough to fan it, the fire increased every instant. After we had walked about a mile, and stood some time on the quay watching it, we returned home, leaving it apparently still augmenting; some time after we heard the engines and machines for cutting away the wood-work pass by our windows, at full gallop, to assist in putting out the fire.

*Tuesday,* 21*st.*—We drove in one drosky, and Mr. Foottil in another, to the place where the fire had been the evening before; it was a great steel manufactory which had been burned down. There were large heaps of ashes still red hot, which the engines were endeavouring to put out, under the superintendance of an officer. After that we drove back again through long suburbs, and through the fair, where we stopped at a part we had not seen before, the quarter for the horses. We saw two or three Russian studs for sale; some pretty looking horses, but none very remarkable. We went on from here to the place on the Volga where the tea is disembarked, of which there was great quantities. The accommodations at the fair are calculated to provide for fifty thousand people, the whole is kept extremely clean, and in very good order. After walking up to the fortress we came home to dinner.

*Wednesday,* 22*nd,*—We wrote letters in the morning, and then went at one o'clock, in the same drosky we had the day before, to drive round the town. The old walls, which formerly protected the city from the Tartars, are very handsome, and descend the steep hill on which the fortress is built in a gradation of terraces, with wide flights of steps on the top. The view over the town, with the Volga winding slowly along, full of sandbanks, through an immense flat plain, is fine and striking. We drove entirely round the town, and then went to Mr. Foottil's to walk over the fair. Belgrave called on Monsieur Tschumaya, a Greek merchant, to whom he had a letter from Mr. Bulgakow at Petersburg, and who immediately came down to walk with us, and to go shopping. We went to look for shawls, and begun by a Bokharian, who, after some solicitation, took us mysteriously upstairs, to their living rooms, over the warehouses, and produced a beautiful white Cashmere shawl, with all possible borders and corners; for this they asked five thousand roubles. M. Tschumaya lifted up his hands and eyes, and begun to argue, and in five minutes the price was four thousand; that was still, however, much too dear, and M. Tschumaya continued bargaining, screaming and gesticulating for near an hour, when the price became near two thousand. We, however, went away, and before we had gone twenty yards, one of the Bokharians followed, asking if we would give two thousand one hundred ; but when we went back, the other had changed his mind, and would not take it. So away we went, and saw some others, which M. Tschumaya talked and reasoned over in the same manner; but as we intended to see more the next day, we concluded nothing. We begun, however, by going to a fur shop, where, with Monsieur Tschumaya's assistance, we bought eight parcels of ermine skins, made up ; each parcel of forty skins costing twelve roubles each. We also bought two parcels of squirrel skins for linings for pelisses. After passing a long time in looking after these purchases, we returned home to dinner. Mr. Foottil dined with us at seven. After the first day, Gartner cooked our dinner in the kitchen of the house. I should have mentioned that we saw again to-day, on the finger of a Bokharian, a beautiful turquoise ring. We had asked the owner what he would take for it the day before; he said two hundred roubles ; but Monsieur Tschumaya argued to-day till the price came down to fifty roubles, when Belgrave carried it off in triumph. We also bought, under Monsieur Tschumaya's auspices, some engraved cornelians, and some Turkish pastilles of different kinds.

Wednesday, August 22nd, 1827.

Nisnei Novogorod, on the Volga, three hundred and sixty miles from Moscow, and near the confines of Siberia, Tartary, Persia, &c.

This is certainly a fine and imposing date to begin with, and though I did not expect to write again before returning to St. Petersburg, I cannot let a few moments pass by this morning without giving myself the amusement of telling you some more of our history, which has been perfectly prosperous. We got to Moscow in six days, travelling through two nights, and sleeping the other three. The road is, in many places, marvellous, being the choice of one track amongst five hundred through deserts of sand, and going over this in a dark night often at full gallop, with the drivers shrieking and screaming to their horses, is the wildest scene that can be imagined. We stayed only one day in Moscow, and as that day was rainy, I did not go out, and therefore saw nothing; but we were in haste to get on to the fair here, and mean to stay at Moscow a week as we go back. The journey here from

Moscow is a most wild one of three hundred and sixty miles, which we accomplished in a nice lapis-lazuli coloured *calèche*, hired there to save our own. I left my maid in lodgings at an Englishwoman's house; this saves a great deal of trouble on the road, and I do very well for myself here. We slept only once, at Vladimir, a curious old place, formerly the residence of the Sovereigns, or "Grand Princes," before they were Czars, and while they were in some degree tributary to the "great horde" of the Tartars.

We travelled through two nights, which was rather pleasant, as the weather has been delightful; we sleep perfectly in the carriage, and without any great fatigue. The road is occasionally a mixture of deep sand and rotten · planks, to avoid which they sometimes go by a by-road, where one's horses, six abreast, are compelled to go along a road that would be narrow for a pair. We had some tremendous bogs to get through, in one of which we were nearly remaining, for one of the middle horses fell, and we were some time getting him up. At another place we stuck in a sand-hill till relieved by the Siberian post, which was going by in light carts with numerous horses, one of which it lent to help us; however, we got through it all very well, and without any accident. Our little carriage, containing our *courier* and our beds, was overturned; but they are all quite well, nevertheless. We arrived here on Saturday night, and are very well off, as we have the best apartments in the town. There is a fast going on now, it will last for a fortnight; during this time the natives eat no meat, but we do not observe it, and live richly, our servant being an excellent cook. The Russian bread is excellent everywhere, and all provisions are to be got here, beautiful fruit, and the best of tea. This town is very curious, 'built on a steep bank over the junction of the Oka and the Volga, with such fine old walls and gateways, erected by the Russians against the Tartars, surrounding a large space where the fortress is. The walls go down the hills in a sloping sort of way, with stairs on the top, and the arches are only recesses, like places for beds. There are several curious old mosques, &c., but the fair itself is delightful; it is held in a town built on purpose, about half-a-mile from the real town, but connected with it by bridges, and on a peninsula between the two rivers; there are warehouses and shops in regular rows, with piazzas before them, and each sort of thing has its separate quarter; one contains

a handsome row of saints to hang up in houses;
but the most curious part consists in the merchants
themselves. There are quantities of Tartars, not so
many Persians, on account of the war, Arabs,
Circassians, Georgians, Bokharians, who bring turquoises and shawls, but such magnificent shawls,
with such borders! The price, of course, is enormous in proportion. Then merchants from Moscow
with beautiful shops, fine pearls and precious
stones; in short, every sort of *article de luxe* that
can be conceived. The people are in all kinds of
dresses, some of them fine-looking people with
handsome countenances; nothing can be more
entertaining than the entire scene, and it is well
worth the trouble of coming to see it. There were
no Arabian horses this year, but some Russian
studs of not very fine ones. In one of them we
met an English groom belonging to one of the
Galitzins, who had formerly lived with Lord Yar-
borough. We had letters here to a little English
merchant, who goes about with us, and is of the
greatest use   In short, no one could get on better
than we do, with the exception of being plagued to
death by the common house-flies, whose impertinent
familiarity exceeds anything I ever saw; they
never leave one, but flock all over one's hands and

face, buzzing, biting, stinging, and tickling incessantly. One would never sleep, but for a handsome drapery of sky-blue patent net, which entirely
covers our beds. The country all the way from
St. Petersburg here is as ugly as possible, a dead
flat of deep sand, but covered with corn, all open,
without hedges or divisions, but all wild and
extensive, and the view from here towards Siberia
is still the same. It is very fine to look down
from the old Tartar fortress on the heights above
on to the town, and then over an immense plain,
with the Volga creeping slowly through it.

Moscow, Tuesday 28th.

Here we are again after a most prosperous
journey which we performed in three days and two
nights without stopping to sleep; considering the
nature of Russian inns, this is generally the best
way of travelling, and we arrived here yesterday
evening soon after past seven, without any detriment
to mind or body ; and delighted to have made our
expedition, which has proved in every respect a
most curious one. The miserable sketch of the
wall on my first page will give you no real idea of
the thing ; but I made two little drawings under a
broiling sun, which I will show you when I come

back. We made a very useful acquaintance at
Nisnei, in a Greek merchant, to whom we had
been recommended, and who spared no pains in
going with us everywhere. Clamouring, screaming
(like an Italian), and frightening the people out of
more than half the price asked for anything we
wanted to buy ; but it is the regular system with
all the sellers to ask twice, or more than twice, as
much as they mean to take for everything. Sometimes a negociation is a week pending — the
Bokharians are very subtle people, and very fond
of bargaining. In the middle of the second night
of our journey, in rain and darkness, bump went one
of the springs of our carriage, and we were two
miles from any help! They found that a great nail
had come out, so it was tied up, and lasted so
till we got to the next village, where a blacksmith
completed the work ; so we came on with perfect
success, and found our rooms quite ready, and my
maid expecting us : she had found friends from
Scotland who had taken great care of her, and
shown her all the sights in our absence. There
are here quantities of Scotch governesses, who are
much prized as being able to teach the children
English, which they must talk very prettily ; these
women come out originally as lady's maids and

talk broad Edinburgh or Aberdeen. . . . They have beautiful apples here, quite delicious, not the least like crude apples, and another kind with fruit-like jelly within.

*Thursday*, 23rd.—After breakfast we received a visit from Count Crapavinski, the Governor, who was very civil and wished us very much to dine with him next day ; but we declined his offer, saying as an excuse that we were obliged to go on, as we had no dress, &c., for dining out. He offered us every sort of facility for our journey, and after he was gone, we set out walking to make some drawings under a broiling sun. I made two drawings of the walls, and a view over the town, and one of the old fortress church ; and at three we returned by appointment to the fair, where in company with Mr. Tschumaya we laboured for between four or five hours arguing in all the Bokharian warehouses about shawls. We saw some magnificent ones ; but the merchants are rather reluctant to show them, and unfold them with great gravity and indolence. They always begin by asking twice as much as they really mean to take. The owners of the first shawl we had seen came after us to-day, to say that they would take two thousand one hundred roubles for the one for which they had asked five thousand ; but on looking at it again, we abandoned the bargain thinking the border too heavy for the fineness of the middle. While these negociations were pending, and very long they were, the Bokharians gave us excellent sweetmeats of pistachio nuts, done over with sugar; but a *négoce* for a shawl sometimes lasts here for a week or ten days. We, however, ended ours' to-day by buying a fine long white one, and a beautiful square one for Mamma; we also bought at a Persian shop two bottles of otto of roses, two little saints in brass, in frames, and returned home, completely tired with our day's work.

*Friday,* 24*th.*—We went after breakfast to Monsieur Tschumaya, who had got for our choice a very handsome brown fur pelisse which we bought; I wanted his opinion also as to some turquoises, with the assistance of Mr. Foottil and a little Bokharian broker, who had been our companion in all our purchases. We went to some other Bokharians, who showed us some turquoises, which we carried along with the owner to Monsieur Tschumaya. The turquoises were very fine ones ; but as the man asked too much for Mr. Tscuhmaya to approve, I was obliged to leave the negociation in his hands, to be terminated after our

departure, and bought then twelve others from
another man (an Armenian) for one hundred and
fifty roubles. The owner of the others produced,
from the interior of his sack, a few turquoises of the
most magnificent colour—dark blue—which he
would hardly let us look at, but immediately put up
again, saying he expected more than five hundred
roubles apiece for them. We then took leave of
Monsieur Tschumaya, to whom we had great
reason to be obliged, for the very great assistance
he had given us in making our purchases; returned
home, had dinner, and passed the evening in
packing up our things and preparing for our
departure next morning. Mr. Schöhl called in the
evening, and we had previously taken leave of Mr.
Foottil and his warehouse.

*Saturday*, 25*th*.—We got up at four, breakfasted,
and set out at seven, going down hill in the first
stage; the horses not being used to hold back, declined doing so altogether, and one of them fell, but
he soon got up again, and in the middle of the
second stage, we found our little carriage arrested in
its progress by the two fore-wheels having come to
pieces; we stayed there between three and four
hours while they were mending it, and when it was
nearly repaired, we set out again.

Before we left Nisnei, there was a police officer waiting, by order of the Governor, to escort us out of the town, but we declined his services. However, at our second stage, we were met by another (a captain) in a kibitka and three, equally ordered to place himself at our disposal, and to conduct us as far as the government of Nisnei extended; the Governor also had had all our horses ordered at each post. We went on all night.

*Sunday*, 26*th*.—Got to Mourom by the straight road, avoiding the by-road in which we had been nearly immersed in bogs in going to Nisnei; we breakfasted in the carriage at the next place, and arrived at seven o'clock at Vladimir, where we got out to dine, but did not stay longer, having previously determined on going on without sleeping; therefore, at eight o'clock we set out again; it soon grew dark, and we were speedily asleep, but we were awakened by a violent rain.

*Monday*, 27*th*.—At two a.m., we were still more unpleasantly disturbed by the spring of our carriage giving way; it was discovered to be occasioned by the absence of a great nail, which had abruptly taken its departure when it thought it could not be discovered in the middle of darkness and rain. We were more than two versts from any help; so they

tied up the injured spring as best they could, and
we made our way slowly to the nearest village, where
it was repaired by a blacksmith. The rain soon
cleared off, and we slept cheerfully through the whole
of the night, got at half-past seven to Lipnia, where
we breakfasted in the carriage, and set off again in an
hour. Stopped half an hour to eat cold meat in the
carriage at four o'clock at Novaga, and arrived at
Moscow at half-past seven in the evening. The
streets were full of people in gala dresses, on account
of being the eve of some great feast at one of the
churches. This also was the last day of a fortnight's
fast, which seemed duly celebrated by many people
being extremely intoxicated. We came to Koppe's
Hotel, where we found a very good apartment, and
Davidson already there.

*Tuesday,* 28*th.*—We were delighted to have a
thorough washing and dressing after our journey,
and were busy all day in writing our letters. We
dined at seven. We heard in the evening from the
Hamburg newspaper of Mr. Canning's death having
taken place at Chiswick on the 8th.

*Wednesday,* 29*th.*—After breakfast, we received a
visit from Mr. Gillibrand, who, to our great satisfaction brought us letters from home. Belgrave
wrote, and I finished my drawings till between three

and four, when we went out in a little rain, which soon cleared off, in a *calèche* and four, to call on the Governor and to pay some other visits; we found that Countess Potemkin and Countess Pouschkin were gone to the country, and in going to search for Princess Z. Volkonsky, we passed by the convent of Devitchi Pol, the exterior of which is beautiful, surrounded by fine old walls and towers; the centre church has an immense gold cupola, with four other minarets round it, these are of lapis lazuli colour, which produces a most beautiful and rich effect. We then drove round the Kremlin, to inquire at La Maison des Enfants Trouvés at what time Prince Serge Galitzin would be there next day; then went into the Kremlin through the holy gate, where everybody is obliged to take off their hat, on coming on the terrace. The view over Moscow with all its gilded domes and cupolas over vast extent of ground, is perfectly beautiful; and the *emplacement* of the Kremlin with all its rich and grotesque architecture is very fine. From here we drove home, and dined at seven; we ate to-day some of the extraordinary apples, with a peculiar kind of semi-transparent inside, which grow nowhere but at Moscow; the fruit is generally excellent, and the greengages are divine.

P

*Thursday, August 30th.*—Mr. Gillibrand called at eleven to go out with us ; we went in a carriage and four, which we hired by the day, and he in his droskey, to Negri's, and to several curiosity shops, but found nothing to tempt us, except three bits of lapis lazuli, which I bought for seals. At between one and two we went to La Maison des Enfants Trouvés, for Belgrave to see Prince Serge Galitzin, who was to be there at that time, and to whom we had a letter from the Dowager Empress. We saw him, and he invited us to dine with him on Sunday in the country. We then continued our course with Mr. Gillibrand, and went to the regular shops, which are all like our Burlington Arcade, enormously multiplied and increased, under cover, and very close and disagreeable. We bought some embroidered handkerchiefs and three tula boxes, and then went to the fruit market, which is very pretty ; the quantities of fruit, especially of apples, is wonderful, and particularly good. From thence, when Mr. Gillibrand departed, we went to the English "magazine," a wretched place, where we found nothing worth buying ; and then came home to dinner. In the evening we had a long and very pleasant visit from Prince Galitzin, the Governor.

*Friday, August 31st.*—We had before breakfast

a visit from the secretary of the French Consul, who had assisted Robert* in his purchases here last year. At eleven o'clock we went to La Maison des Enfants Trouvés by appointment, as Prince Serge Galitzin had ordered that the place should be shown to us. The poor children are taken in here as soon as they are born, or at any age, provided with nurses, &c., and educated in a useful manner for trades of different kinds. There are both boys and girls, and the establishment is very large. We saw them all at dinner, which was all arranged in the same way as those we had seen at Petersburg ; it being a *maigre* day, the soup was *chitche*—a sort of sour soup very much used in Russia, and very disagreeable. While we were there, Dr. Hammel arrived, having vainly sought us at our hotel. He had been sent by the Governor to take care of us, and shqw us anything we wished to see. He had been in England with the present Emperor† and the Grand Duke Michael, and spoke English perfectly. Finding when we went home that Prince Yusupoff had given orders that we should see the Kremlin, at two o'clock we accordingly went there, and Dr. Hammel with us. We went first to the

* Lord Robert Grosvenor, now Lord Ebury.
† The late Emperor Nicholas, who died in 1855.

treasury, which is much too full of riches for me
to attempt any description of it. We were received
by a general officer, who was appointed to show it
us. There were the coronation dresses of Paul and
the Empress Mary ; of Alexander and his Empress,
and of the present Emperor and Empress; also of
Peter I.; several thrones, thickly inlaid with gold,
turquoises, and rubies ; jewels beyond number,
belonging to the old Czars; the crowns of the
different subsidiary kingdoms, Siberia, Astracan,
Georgia, Casan, &c., &c., set with stones, which
must be quite inestimable in value ; dresses of the
Czars, inlaid with jewels; gold and silver dishes,
cups, vases, &c., of the most enormous size, and of
very fine workmanship; cups and dishes of agate,
pearls, crystal, &c. These are all arranged round
a large room ; the crowns upon pedestals; the other
articles under glass cases, each of which has a
separate attendant to watch over it, like a race-
horse in his stable. This room is joined by a large
gallery, with yellow marble pillars, and some bad
pictures of all the Sovereigns of Russia, from their
beginning, to the armoury, which contains a splendid
collection of arms of all kinds, and sceptres incrusted
with jewels. Along the walls are hung chains of
silver and also of gold, which, in time of any great

tumult, were hung before the places where the Czar stood, to keep off the crowds.   Quantities of saddles and horse-furniture are here; one set in particular, which was sent as a present by the· Sultan to Catharine II., and is covered with most magnificent jewels, diamonds, pearls, rubies, emeralds, sapphires, in short, of every kind; sledge furniture, embroidered in pearls; one covered with lapis-lazuli and coral and riches of all kinds, much too numerous to describe.   In the midst of all this splendour is a common wooden arm-chair, of the most simple construction, with an old cushion and four short poles on hinges, which served as a brancard to carry Charles XII. after he was wounded at Pultova. The chair was found on the field of battle after he fled to Bender, and  there are marks of fractures by a ball on the hind bars of the chair.   From these apartments we went to see a large model of the Kremlin, and of what the Empress Elizabeth intended to make it, but which was luckily never put in execution, as the first step would have been to throw down the old Kremlin walls, which form a principal part of the beauty of the whole.   From this we went to the adjoining Palace, to see the rooms of the Emperor and Empress, and those of the Dowager Empress ; all very pretty, but nothing

very remarkable. Then to the Church of Ivan
Vasiliki, where the coronation took place. It is
small, but superbly and richly decorated; full of
gold, and silver, and jewels, and pictures. Two
monks showed us the coffins of all the patriarchs
of Russia, which are arranged under crimson velvet
or black cloth all round the church. They then
took us to their treasury, which contains the most
wonderful riches—dresses of the old patriarchs—
among them those of Nicom; jewels of great value,
particularly two enormous carved onyxs, a great
many cups, &c., of silver, an immense silver boiler,
and several large silver vases for containing the oil
for extreme unction (one was half full), all the
sacred oil that is used all over Russia being boiled
previously here; and in a large room near is the
stove used for it, just like those for boiling the
dogs' food in a kennel. There were some very
curious MSS. also here—one said to be written by
Sophia, sister of Peter I, and another by a daughter
of Peter II. Passing on, we saw the room where
the Emperors dined after their coronation. It is
a very old room, with low ground arches, supported
by an enormous thick square pillar in the centre
of the room, carved over in all sorts of grotesque
old figures of animals, chimeras, &c. The relieved

parts are gilt, which has a very good effect; and
the room is done up in very good taste—the ceiling
gilded in the ribs of the arches, the walls hung
with crimson velvet with gold cyphers, eagles, &c.,
so that the whole has a magnificent effect. We
then went into another church close by; also
small, but equally rich in decoration with the other.
Round the walls here are arranged all the coffins
of the old Czars, covered with palls of crimson
velvet. The lamps here, as in the other, are very
large, and of solid silver. The pictures of the saints
are embellished with diamonds and jewels, and the
treasury is far richer, and must be worth millions
in precious stones alone. There is one cup all over
jewels, with two onyxs sculptured, each as large as
one's hand; one was cracked across in removing it
to secure it from the French; several others covered
with rubies, diamonds, &c.; some large gold plate,
given by Potemkin; a beautiful cup, with an ivory
stand, turned by the Empress-mother, and also
enriched with rubies and diamonds, given on the
occasion of the Emperor Paul's return from Sweden.
But the most extraordinary of all is an immense
Bible, bound in a thick mass of solid gold, and set
with stones, and in particular emeralds, whose size
exceeds all belief; the book is too heavy for one

man to lift.   There is also a small agate cup, with
the oil used at the Emperor's coronation, some of
which still remains in it.   It is impossible to describe
a quarter of the riches of this place, where there are
besides quantities of old coronation dresses.

I forgot to mention that in a corner of this
church there is a tomb containing the body of some
saint, enveloped in gold and silver drapery, with
one hand, perfectly black, exposed to view.   The
Russians declare that this remained untouched
by the French, though the railings, &c. of the
tomb are of silver.   There are many relics both
here and in the other church ; a bit of the true
cross, &c., &c.

After seeing these churches, which are all most
interesting, and have the richest appearance with a
sort of melancholy from their darkness, and lamps
constantly burning in different corners, we took
leave of Dr. Hammel and came home to dinner
soon after five, and at half-past six went to the
play, where we had a very good box ; as the play
and farce were Russian, we were not too much
agitated by our interest in the performance; but the
house is beautiful, we thought larger than Drury
Lane or Covent Garden, and the boxes so constructed as to be suspended one row over the

other without a single pillar or any other
impediments to seeing. The pit is divided into
two parts by a slight barrier through the centre;
the seats are all separate, and very handsome
arm-chairs; but there were very few people in the
house.

*Saturday, September* 1*st.*—Soon after breakfast we
had a visit from Mr. Patraine, secretary to the
French Consul, who brought us some turquoises to
look at: I bought several; and Belgrave gave me a
beautiful ring set with diamonds. It poured with
rain all morning, but as we had no time to lose, we
set out at noon, and went in quest of Princess Z.
Volkonsky, who was living for her health in a
*petit pavillon*, near the Devitchi Pol Convent;
after much search and inquiry we at length found
our way to her abode amidst mud and devious
tracks. She was living in a miserable-looking
wooden house, but not being well, was still in bed
and could not see us. We then drove to the
convent, the outside of which is beautiful, surrounded by fine old walls like a fortress. We
saw one of the churches which it contains; this is
small, beautiful, sombre, and gorgeous; like those
of the Kremlin, also with saints, books, and jewels,
and a handsome cloister round it outside; an

uninteresting, dirty-looking man showed it to us ; but we could not see the nuns' rooms ; however, as they were all living in little white-washed outbuildings, and from the specimen of some of them—little old women dressed in black—one had not much temptation to be curious. The rain began to clear off, and we drove from here to the Convent of St. Catharine—the Dames Nobles pay seven hundred roubles annually, and the bourgeoises five hundred—where we met by appointment Prince Serge Galitzin; he showed us first ·the· Institut of the Demoiselles Bourgeoises, which I need not describe here, as it is exactly on on the same plan as that at St. Petersburg; from there he took us to a great Hospital pour les Malades Pauvres, where we were received on the steps by a circle of physicians and surgeons covered with orders, and Les Dames de la Charité, who attend on the poor sick people ; we saw a great many of the latter in very airy, comfortable rooms, all kept as perfectly clean and in as good order as possible. It is a very fine institution and receives all sick people gratis, besides giving medicine and advice to those who do not wish to go into the house.

Thence we went to l'Institut des Dames Nobles,

where the Supérieure showed us over it all; it is
also just like that at St. Petersburg. There is a
new house building for it, which will be ready in .
three years. We came home, dined soon after
four; and after dinner Dr. Hammel called to see if
we would take a drive; accordingly he preceded us
in his drosky past Countess Orloff's villa, to a
garden lately bought by the Emperor, now rather
out of repair, from whence we had a beautiful view
of Moscow; but as the sun was setting, the ground
wet, and the evening very cold, we were not
tempted to go on farther to La Montague des
Moineaux. In returning we got out to look
into the Manège, which is much the largest room I
ever saw, and is the largest in the world, with a
roof unsupported by pillars. We walked some way
through the Kremlin Gardens at the foot of the
walls, which are extremely pretty and in beautiful
order, and occupy the place of what was formerly
a piece of dirty water, the present Governor Prince
Dimitri Galitzin having covered it over and
constructed these gardens. Illuminations were
preparing for Monday, the anniversary of the
coronation; we then came home.

*Sunday, 2nd.*—Belgrave's leg, which had plagued
him ever since we came to Moscow, being still

inflamed, we remained at home this morning in order to let it rest, and read prayers after breakfast. We had a visit from Monsieur Roussowsky, the Directeur des Postes; and at three we set out to dine with Prince Serge Galitzin, at his country house, seven versts beyond the gate. We went through a perfect flat, the road pleasingly diversified between bog and sand. We found him and two old sisters, his niece, Princess Trubetskoi, and her husband, Prince Dimitri Galitzin, the Governor, a Monsieur Narishkin, an old Prince Masolskv, Grand-Maître de la Cour, and a good many more people, and several old ladies ; and a large English setter dog. The house is very simple but with handsome rooms. We soon went to dinner, and walked afterwards in spite of the cold evening in the gardens, which are large and pretty, exactly like an English shrubbery, with gravel walks, a small river spreading into a lake, and many ponds. The orangery seems a good one, and there are some fine orange trees. This is reckoned the finest place in the neighbourhood, but would not be thought much of in England; it is however remarkably well kept, and in the highest order. We came home to the house, had tea, and set out at about eight o'clock to come home; the latter part of the way we had a beautiful moon, by which the town and particularly the old walls of the Kremlin looked magnificent. Belgrave, on account of his leg did not walk much at Prince Galitzin's, but went in a boat with Prince Trubetskoi, and met us at a temple in the garden built to contain a bronze statue of the Dowager Empress, which has been lately placed there.

*Monday, 3rd.*—After breakfast at eleven o'clock, an aide-de-camp of the Governor came to fetch us by appointment to go to the cathedral service in the Kremlin for the anniversary of the coronation; he preceded us in his drosky, and when we arrived we found the troops drawn up within the walls of the Kremlin, before the doors of the church, waiting for the Governor, who was not yet arrived, and a large concourse of people. The church was extremely crowded and perfectly full, and we made our way, with the help of the aide-de-camp, to the places reserved for us, which were immediately before the altar, which was surrounded by people in uniforms, among them Prince Serge Galitzin, Monsieur Narishkin, &c. The Archbishop of Moscow, who officiated, was assisted by the Archbishops of Georgia and several others—prelates and abbots. The sight was magnificent, all the lamps of the church being

lighted, and the dresses of the archbishops and priests
are splendid.   The Archbishop's was green and
gold, and differently coloured embroidery, and he
wore a blue velvet mitre covered with pearls.   The
dresses of the others were equally magnificent ;
some of the priests had velvet dresses of lapis lazuli
colour embroidered with gold ; the archbishops and
bishops were, besides, blazing with jewels.   Soon
after we were there the Governor arrived ; the service was high mass followed by prayers, the litany,
*Te Deum*, &c. ; part of it was chanted, and the singing
was very fine, during some parts of it the enormous
bell of Ivan Vasiliki was sounded, and seemed
exactly like the bass notes of an organ thrilling
through the building.   The Archbishop preached a
sermon from a blue velvet desk, which was placed
in front of the altar ; he seemed to perform with
much eloquence and in a mild, agreeable manner.
Throughout the prayer for the Emperor, during
which the archbishops and all the priests were in the
middle of the church, the whole of the congregation
knelt down ; some of the Bible was then read, and
the whole concluded with a *Te Deum*.   The service
was altogether very fine and well worth seeing.
Before leaving, the Governor invited us to his box
at the play for the evening, which we accepted.

After coming home for a short time, we set out again and drove first to visit Mr. and Mrs. Gillibrand, whom we found at home, and then to the Siminopky Monastery, about three versts from the town, where we got out and walked on high ground close to the convent, to see a fine general view of Moscow. We then returned home, driving round the Kremlin walls on our way. We dined at six, and at eight an aide-de-camp of the Governor's came to conduct us to the play, where we found the Governor, not in his crimson velvet box in the centre of the house, but in a very pleasant stage-box at one end of the orchestra. The play was ended, and we saw an indifferent ballet which ended about half-past eight; and we then drove about the streets to see the illuminations, our friend the aide-de-camp preceded us part of the way till he reached his own house, opposite the Kremlin, and we then continued in the file of carriages, which was a very long one, generally of carriages-and-fours, round the Kremlin walls, and then within them till we had seen everything that was to be seen, and then came home. The illuminations were not fine in themselves, but the effect was beautiful from the magnificence of the buildings, the Kremlin and churches which they brought out; a very long line of windows over the shops, which were only lighted by some lamps round each window, made a blaze of light, and the gardens were illuminated, and the walls and towers in part also. The Governor had had a dinner of about seventy to-day, to which Belgrave was not able to go, from the sting in his leg preventing his putting on his uniform—which said uniform was left behind at St. Petersburg!

*Tuesday, 4th.*—We passed the morning in packing up and set out at two from Moscow as heretofore, in our own carriage, which, as well as the little carriage, had undergone a thorough repair while we were at Nisnei; at the end of the first stage, however, our near front wheel became indisposed and went into a fever, which detained us for some time; at length the attack subsided, and we travelled on through the night, Belgrave going outside, in order that my maid might come in; the night was very cold.

*Wednesday, 5th.*—We breakfasted in the carriage, Gartner making tea in the inn, or post-house, and bringing it to us; we found this plan much the best, and we did the same thing every day, and dined also in the carriage on our own cold beef and bread and wine. Belgrave always went outside in the night, and came into the carriage in the morning.

This was the only night that we stopped to sleep between Moscow and St. Petersburg, and we arrived at Torjok between seven and eight. We first went to the shop to get the embroidered articles which 'we had ordered before, and found them all ready. We then dined and went to bed.

*Thursday, 6th.*—We got up before five, breakfasted and set forth; our wheel, which had been ailing before, again stopped us at the first stage, as the box within it had smashed; by great good luck the blacksmith·at Vidropous had one ready, which just fitted, and on we went again with great success; the day cold and rather rainy. We continued our journey all day and' all night, and dined in the carriage while we were stopping at Holilovo.

*Friday, 7th.*—We breakfasted in the carriage at Zagelligi, and had a pleasant journey all day as heretofore.

*Saturday, 8th.*—At one in the morning, we passed through Novogorod; breakfasted while we changed horses at Tchoudova; ate apples at Pomerania, and arrived, to our great satisfaction, at St. Petersburg at ten o'clock in the evening; found our old apartment at Demuth's ready for us, and very comfortable. We soon sat down to tea and an omelette, of which we stood much in need; found the sting

Q

in Belgrave's leg, which had pained him much this last day terribly irritated, swelled and inflamed; and never were we more happy than to go to bed after three days and two nights of incessant travelling.

*Sunday, 9th.*—We got up late, breakfasted, and sat in the little room lined with sofas, as Belgrave was obliged to keep his leg at rest. We read prayers, had a visit from Mr. Disbrowe, who announced, to our great joy, that he had a packet of letters for us, and told us that Lord Goderich* was made first Lord of the Treasury after Mr. Canning's death. After he went away, he sent us our letters and some newspapers; we remained reading these and talking till dinner at seven, after which we returned to our little room, and passed the evening most comfortably.

*Monday 10th.*—As Belgrave's leg still confined him to the sofa, after breakfast I walked out by myself to Corbiaux's, the English " magazine," and several other shops in the *Perspective ;* came home and wrote some letters. Mrs. Disbrowe called, and I went out with her, got some music, went to the English " magazine" and Anthoni's, and laid in a store of de-

* The Right Honourable Frederick Robinson, afterwards Lord Goderich, and eventually first Earl of Ripon ; he died in 1859.

licacies at the confectioners. I dined at five at Mr. and Mrs. Disbrowe's; met there Monsieur and Madame Guerrieno and their son, Miss Middleton, Monsieur de Bombelles, and Monsieur Fraser, Monsieur Custrin, and the Prussian Chargé d'Affaires. Some people came in the evening. As Belgrave's leg had not looked so well when I came out to dinner, I sent for Mr. Walker, the physician, to Mr. Disbrowe's, and took him home in the carriage to see the leg, which was very sore, and with a good deal of heat. Mr. Walker prescribed a linseed poultice, and stayed some time, after he went we had tea, and then went to bed.

*Tuesday,* 11*th.*—Before seven in the morning, and before I was well awake, I got a note from Mrs. Disbrowe, saying that if I liked she would call for me at nine, to go to the church of St. Alexander Neffsky to see high mass, and a great procession, &c., it being the saint's fête. I accordingly got up unwillingly, dressed myself, choked myself with my breakfast, and was ready by the time appointed. Belgrave could not go because of his leg. Mr. and Mrs. Disbrowe called for me soon after nine, and we found the streets full of people to see the procession of priests, who walk from the Kasan Church to St Alexander Neffsky, about three versts, and with-

out any breakfast, as they never eat till after they
have received the sacrament. We were obliged to
dismount at the outer gate, the carriages not being
allowed to come within the precinct, and walked to
the church, which was lined on one side with Cossacks
and soldiers, and a few of the diplomatic corps, who
had already arrived ; their station being on one side
of the altar, we arranged ourselves there. The
middle part was filled with officers and generals in
uniform, and the opposite side was reserved for the
Imperial family. We waited an hour and a half to
our despair ; at length the Emperor arrived with the
young Grand Duke Alexander* and the Grand
Duke Michael ; the service then proceeded, the usual
high mass, interspersed with various little attentions
to the shrine of Alexander Neffsky, in whose honour
the fête was held. A priest who offered incense before it, incensed the Emperor also, to whom he
always bowed three times, and once to the little Grand
Duke and to the Grand Duke Michael, they returning the salutation. At the conclusion of the mass,
the Emperor went to kiss the shrine, and lifted up
the young Alexander for the same purpose. Prince
Michael and many others also kissed it, and the
whole service was ended. The singing, which was

* The present Emperor.

performed by the choir of the Emperor's chapel, one hundred and twenty in number, beginning with very little boys, and ending with some fine bass voices, was most beautiful, and without any instrumental music of any sort, which made the effect quite perfect. We did not reach home till one, having gone to the church at half-past nine, and remained standing the whole time. I then came home, dressed for the morning, and went first with Belgrave to Corbiaux's, where we made some purchases in malachite. I then brought him home and went on *aux isles* to call on Madame Nesselrode and Madame Dolgorouki, neither of whom were at home. I then came back to Belgrave.

*Wednesday*, 12*th.*—Dr. Walker came just as we were sitting down to breakfast, and pronounced Belgrave's leg much better. After breakfast we went out in the carriage to the banker's, to Mrs. Disbrowe's, and to Monsieur Boulgaloff's and drove round by the great theatre. I then brought Belgrave home, and went to call for Mrs. Disbrowe, with whom I visited Madame Elmdt, Grande Maîtresse to the Grand Duchess Helen, at Kamien Ostroff. We found her at home, and saw a very pretty Persian carpet, which she had been working; we then called on Mrs. Middleton, who was at home; Countess

Modena whom we found at home, with Count
Modena and their daughters, one of whom is going
to be married to a Prince Zuboff; we then called on
old Princess Volkonsky, but did not find her within.
I then set down Mrs. Disbrowe at her own house,
and went to a French shop in the *Perspective*, then
to the English " magazine" and then to Mr. Jackson,
the *lingère*, and so home.

*Thursday*, 13th.—Belgrave and I went out in the
carriage soon after breakfast to the Hermitage where
we walked about for some time looking at the
pictures, especially admiring some by Rubens, and
a landscape by Murillo, a landscape and a large dog
by Paul Potter; a Titian, and a little picture of
monkeys by Teniers; these last four all being in the
same room. We came home at three, and I then
went with Mrs. Disbrowe a long round among the
Russian shops, where I bought some Archangel
chains, a pin and ear-rings of Siberian stones, and a
Siberian topaz seal; came home at half-past five, and
Belgrave and I dined alone together; drove afterwards out to Kamien Ostroff and back. We came
home to tea and found a note from the Count de
Nesselrode, begging us to put off our dinner with
him, which was to have been the next day (Friday),
till the Saturday.

*Friday*, 14*th.*—We received an early notification from Count Nesselrode that we were to dine to-day at three with the Empress-mother. We went out after breakfast, and Belgrave called on Monsieur Boulgaloff, and then we went to the Disbrowe's. Belgrave's leg was luckily to-day almost recovered, and we were ready dressed in time; but our carriage which we had ordered to come at two, did not appear till near three, and we therefore set out in the certainty of being too late for Her Majesty, whose habitation was a very small one close to Kamien Ostroff, which she had given up to the Grand Duchess Helen, for a time; however, on arriving, we found to our great relief that the Empress had not yet appeared. The party consisted of about twenty,—Princess Dolgorouki, and her daughter-in-law, Prince and Princess Soltikoff Prince Radzivil, Countess Elmdt, and some of the ladies of honour, General Suchterlins, &c., and Mr. Fisher, the head of the Botanical Garden. The dinner was very agreeable, and the Empress, as usual, extremely civil and good-natured; she was accompanied by a large white poodle, for whom she made many apologies. After dinner she talked for a short time to everybody, and then took leave of the whole party, embracing me, Belgrave

kissing her hand on our final taking leave; we saw
the Empress' youngest child, the little Grand
Duchess Olga,* walking in the garden; and we
then went by the Dowager Empress's recommendation, preceded by Mr. Fisher, to see the Botanical
Garden, which is a splendid establishment; it has
existed for only two years, but the luxuriance and
growth of plants from all quarters of the globe is
quite astonishing. There is one verst and thirty-
two fathom of hot-houses and conservatories, containing everything that is most rare and extraordinary, and all in the most perfect order. After
travelling over this in our full dress, we came home
and had tea. After breakfast we had despatched
three trunks to go by sea to England, one of clothes
which we no longer wanted, one of malachite ornaments, &c, and one of furs.

*Saturday,* 15*th.*—Belgrave and I went at noon
with Mr. Disbrowe to one of the educational institutes to hear the Emperor's singers practice; there
were some very fine voices among them, particularly
a bass and a tenor. The effect of the whole is
wonderful and magnificent. After that, Belgrave
and I went to see Princess Lieven, whom we found

* Born in 1822, and married in 1846 to Prince Karl, then heir-
apparent to the King of Wurtemberg, and now King.

in her apartments, the Palais d'Hiver, having just
finished her dinner; the passage to her rooms being
perfectly dark is lighted with lamps; we paid her
a long visit and then went to leave Belgrave's card
at Prince Volkonsky's and Prince Dolgorouki's, then
to the English " magazine" and to pay my bill at Mr.
Jackson's; then home to finish our letters and dress
for dinner at the Nesselrode's at five. We found
them in a small *campagne* near Kamien Ostroff; there
were there the Disbrowes, Prince and Princess Soltikoff, Count and Countess Laval, Count Bloom,
Prince Dolgorouki, Prince Hohenloe, Monsieur
Fontenay, Monsieur de la Rochefoucault, and the
Dutch Minister, whose name I forget. The dinner
was of the most *recherché* description, and very
pleasant; but in the middle of dinner, a thunder-
clap burst upon the society by Belgrave asking
generally if anything had been heard of the result
of the trial of the conspirators. A dead silence and
universal consternation ensued, and it was afterwards
explained that such a subject was unheard of and
never allowed to be mentioned; it was too sacred,
too mysterious and too awful to be permitted in
conversation !

After dinner, Countess Nesselrode asked us if we
would like to go to the French play; we accepted

her offer, and accordingly we and the Disbrowes
went with her to the small theatre in town, where
we saw a sort of translation of " The School 'for
Scandal," called " Les Deux Cousins," very well
acted, and an amusing farce, " Monsieur et Madame
Denis." After that we came home. The play was
all over by ten. The theatre is a nice little one ;
Madame Bras, who acted a kind of *concierge* in the
first piece, is a very good actress.

*Sunday,* 16*th.*—We received a note early from the
Count de Nesselrode, saying that the Emperor and
Empress would receive us in the Palais d'Hiver at
noon. So we dressed ourselves accordingly, and
were there at the right time ; after we had remained
a short time in one of the rooms which look upon
the Quay, with one of the chamberlains, the Count
de Modena came to say that the Empress was ready
to see me ; we went through two or three rooms,
and found her in her private apartment, a beautiful
large sitting-room ; being a corner room, it commanded two separate views of the Neva ; it was
most comfortably and exquisitely furnished in green
satin, and full of pretty things of all sorts ; in one
corner a statue of a nymph by Canova, and in
another part of the room, a sitting figure by a Prussian artist, Chandes, I believe. The Empress, though

expecting her confinement immediately, was looking remarkably well and in great spirits, and very merry, talking a great deal; she showed me her rooms, the bed-room where she is to be confined, and her dressing-room. After some time, the ·Emperor came in and stayed a little while, and then went out again, saying that he must go and see Belgrave. The Empress continued to talk, and said a great many kind things about my eldest brother, Gower, and gave me messages for her family at Berlin, the Duchess of Cumberland,* &c. After some time the Emperor returned and talked a little while, and then took leave, saying that he was going to the Grand Duke Michael, and that he hoped that some time or other we should return to Russia. The Empress then remarked that she was not " en état de recevoir Lord Belgrave," but still said she would receive him; he came accordingly, she talked to him for some time, and then we took our leave, she begging us not to forget her. She was dressed in a cap and lilac merino gown, with a long lace scarf, and wore an enormous pearl necklace; nothing could

---

* The Princess Frederica Caroline Sophia of Mecklenburg-Strelitz; she married, as her third husband, Ernest, Duke of Cumberland, and eventually King of Hanover, who died in 1851. Her first husband was Prince Louis of Prussia; her second the Prince of Solms.

be more amiable or agreeable than the Empress.
The old Princess Volkonsky was there, but nobody
else.    After this we drove to Mr. Disbrowe's, to
settle about dining with them to-day ; we then came
home, made up our letters and parcels for the bag
that was going by the steamboat, and went at five
to dine at Mr. Disbrowe's.    Nobody was there but
themselves,    ourselves,    and    a    young   Monsieur
Malorti, aide-de-camp to General Dunnbach.    At
seven, Belgrave and I, and Mr. Disbrowe went to
evening service at the English church, but Mrs.
Disbrowe could not go, having a toothache ; we
went back to drink tea with her, where also Mr.
Beckford came.

Demuth's,

St. Petersburg.

Monday, September 10th,     .

Here we are again much contented with all we
have seen and done, in spite of the rain, cold
winds, and hail-storms of Moscow.    I certainly
cannot say that it is very warm here ; it looks
gloomy, and suspicions are afloat of an early
winter, but we shall not be caught, though we are
not sorry to have got so far back again.    Our last
day at Moscow was the anniversary of the Corona-

tion; and the Governor, Prince Dimitri Galitzin, who was most kind to us, gave us places for High Mass in the Kremlin Cathedral, where the service and singing was magnificent. Archbishops were there, covered with pearls and jewels, among others the Archbishop of Georgia. In the evening we went with the Governor to the play, where we sat in his box, and then drove about to see the illuminations which were very pretty; a beautiful moon rose over the Kremlin, which is unique in itself; and the treasures it contains and the riches of its churches are quite inestimable. We made a rapid journey from Moscow to St. Petersburg, sleeping one night only on the road, and travelling through three others. This morning we received a sudden intimation that we were to dine at three with the Dowager Empress, at a very small *campagne* just out of town, where she goes now to stay, as she has given up her regular house at Kamien Ostroff for the present to the Grand Duchess Helen who has just got a third daughter, and wanted a boy. So accordingly we went, and found a party of about twenty, among them the old Princess Dolgorouki, of whom I spoke before, and who always comes out dressed like a primrose, and looking handsomer than you can imagine, and Princess Soltikoff, her

daughter, and many others. The Empress was
the perfection of kindness and good-nature; and
gave me "sweets and sugar-comfits;" we had
a very pleasant dinner, after which she took leave
of us, promising me a letter for the Grand Duchess
of Weimar;* then we all went our different ways;
we, by her desire, to see a splendid Botanical
Garden, with more than three quarters of a mile
of hot-houses and conservatories, very high, and
full of fine, rare, luxuriant plants. They do everything here on such a gigantic scale. Some of their
windows, though enormously large, are made of
single panes of glass; sometimes they are double,
and opening like French windows. I have been
highly amused here with shops and visits; and we
have been again to the Hermitage to look at
the pictures, some of which are exquisite. We
originally intended to start to-morrow, but we have
put our journey off, and are to see the Emperor
and Empress again on Sunday I believe. To-morrow
we go again to Princess Lieven, and then to hear
a practice of the singers of the Emperor's Chapel
which is the finest music in the world; there are
one hundred and twenty, beginning from very little
boys, and gradually rising to the finest bass voices,

* Born Grand Duchess Mary of Russia.

without any instrument, all in perfect tune and taste, and the effect is almost unearthly. I heard it in perfection on Tuesday at a great ceremony of High Mass for the Fête of St. Alexander Neffsky, in the Neffsky Chapel. I went with the Disbrowes *en grande parure ;* the church was full of Cossacks and soldiers ranged in order; all the officers and generals &c., in the centre, all the diplomats on one side of the altar, and on the other the Emperor with the young Grand Dukes Alexander and Michael, but not the Empress. The service was magnificent. Saint Alexander Neffsky is the great saint of the country, so they all kissed his shrine afterwards. To-morrow we dine with the Nesselrodes, and shall start on Wednesday for Berlin, a sweet little journey of eighteen days. I hope to find the Duchess of Cumberland there. If it were not that the season is getting on, and must not be trifled with, we should like to stay a little longer; but though the last few days have been fine and pleasant, to our great satisfaction, it will not be safe to delay.

*Sunday,* 16*th.*—I put in a postscript to say that we went this morning to take leave of the Emperor and Empress at the Palais d'Hiver, in the prettiest and most beautifully furnished rooms I ever saw. The

Empress received me in her private sitting-room, and was very amiable and agreeable, and showed me her other rooms. The Emperor came in to see and take leave of me, and then the Empress sent for Belgrave (who had seen the Emperor), and after more conversation, took leave of us both in the kindest manner, begging us not to forget her. The dinner at the Nesselrodes was very agreeable and very *recherché*—a plum-pudding made of ice amongst other things ; we went to the French play with Countess Nesselrode after dinner, and saw some very good acting.

*Monday,* 17*th.*—We set out soon after breakfast, and went to the bankers and to the Disbrowes, but found them not up. Belgrave called on Count Zichy ; then we went to the Ecole des Mines, which is a very large establishment for boys, sons of officers and soldiers; some pay for their own education : those who do not are bound to serve the Emperor in the mines for ten years, after leaving the school. We saw first several rooms full of models of the mines themselves and all mining operations, the way of washing the gold, &c. ; we saw also a very fine collection of specimens of every sort of stone and mineral, among others, a piece of pure gold so heavy, that one person can hardly lift it ; one of the rooms contains, among other things, some swords, &c., made in Siberia. We went all over the house, saw all the boys go to dinner in one large room, went into the kitchen, where the dinner was being prepared by steam. When ready, it is wound up by a lift to the dining-room. We went quite to the top of an observatory, from where we had a beautiful view over the whole of St. Petersburg and the Neva, and out to sea as far as Cronstadt. When we came down again we went underground through an artificial mine very well contrived, the walls being done over so as to imitate the strata in which the copper, gold, &c., are found; thence we emerged into the garden, which is a pretty one, and in which is a handsome pavilion with several apartments fitted up in the perfection of neatness and cleanliness as the hospital for the school, with baths, hot and cold ; from this place we went into several laboratories, where the boys study chemistry, and where the Government send specimens to be analyzed, in order to ascertain whether they are worth the trouble of working them. The department of apothecaries was equally neat and well arranged ; on opening one of the drawers hoping to find some gum or perfume, I fell upon a collection of dried centipedes, which they use for the croup. We were shown all over

the place by two officers belonging to the establishment; we then went away and stopped at the
Académie des Sciences, which was open for the Ex-
position des Tableaux. There was an immense
crowd; one room was filled with Mr. Dawe's
pictures of the Imperial family, and of all the
generals who were employed in the late campaigns;
the other rooms, of which there were a great many,
were full of the performances of Russian artists
wretched, hard, and bad specimens for the most part.
We then again called at the Disbrowes, and found them
gone to the Modenas, where we were also going to
make a visit, in the Summer Palace. Accordingly
there we went, and found everybody at home; it
was the day of the *fête* of the Countess de Modena;
Madame Paschcoff, Madame Nesselrode, &c., were
there; we went with them into the garden, where
we found more people; there was a beautiful little
tame antelope tethered to a post in the garden. The
garden is very pretty, and the Emperor and Empress
are very fond of it, and whenever they have time,
come to pass a few days at the Palace, it being here
that they lived as Grand Duke and Duchess. We
stayed there some time, then came home, and went
at five to dine with Mr. and Mrs. Disbrowe. Monsieur and Madame Segnavine and Mr. Kennedy and

Mr. Kaly were there after dinner; we went to Madame Segnavine's house next door to see it, as it is just fitted up, and all very pretty. Returned to coffee at Mrs. Disbrowe's; Monsieur Rochefoucault and Monsieur Guerrieno and Monsieur Fontenay came in the evening; we looked at some books of caricatures of Madame Segnavine's, drank tea, and came home.

*Tuesday,* 18*th.*—Belgrave got up at half-past six, and sailed at nine in the steamboat for Cronstadt. I got up at ten, packed all my things, drew, &c., till between one and two, when Mrs. Disbrowe called to take me out; we went to get some warm travelling boots, and succeeded in the Russian shops; called at Madame Guerrieno's, but she was not at home; called at Mrs. Middleton's, at home; called to leave a note at the Palais d'Hiver for Mademoiselle Kotchedorf, we then went to the confectioner's, bought dried cherries, barley sugar, chocolate, and lemon syrup for the journey; a sandal wood toothpick case, and a purple leather souvenir pocket-book; we bought some white gloves at Madame Turin's and came home. Belgrave returned about seven, and we dined in the expectation of setting out next day; but some difficulties about the passport arose to prevent us.

*Wednesday,* 19*th.*—As soon as we had breakfasted,

we set out on foot and went to find Le Directeur
des Postes, Monsieur Bulgalow, but he was not at
home. Then we went on to Mr. and Mrs.
Disbrowe's, and found them just preparing to come
to us; we stayed there some time, and then went
with them in the open carriage to a picture dealer's
in the *Perspective.* We made our way up dirty
staircases in a horrid *masure* of a strange-looking
house, and found the man at home, he had one
picture, a Herodias by Titian, which he imagined
to be a counterpart of that in Mr. Baring's*
gallery; but it was quite different; the picture was
perfectly beautiful, especially the head with both
the arms raised supporting the head of John the
Baptist in a dish on her head; a delightful picture,
both as to colouring and expression; he had other
pictures, but all ugly. After this Mr. Disbrowe
went away. Belgrave went after his passport, and
Mrs. Disbrowe and I to the Russian shoe-shop;
from thence we called on Madame Nesselrode in
*la campagne,* near Kamien Ostroff, we found her
at home and Madame Hetroff with her; we made
a long visit, and then went to Madame Elmdt,
whom we also found at home, (I must remember
to send her some English canvas for working)

* The late Sir Thomas Baring, Bart., M.P.

and then to Anthoni's, then home. I found Belgrave returned, having arranged everything about the passport for departing next day. Mrs. Disbrowe came in and Mr. Disbrowe directly after ; they bad us good-bye with regret on both sides ; they had been most kind to us during the whole time of our stay in Russia. I then walked to the English "magazine" to pay my bill, and came home. Belgrave went at half-past five to take a Russian bath. When he came home we dined, and finished our packings.

*Thursday, 20th.*—We got up at half-past four ; breakfasted, and were off from St. Petersburg by seven ; we had a fine clear day, and a very good road all the way to Narva, where we arrived about nine ; we had already dined in the carriage, so we had tea, and went to bed. The inn very tolerable.

*Friday, 21st.*—Got up at half-past four, and after we had breakfasted walked down to the bridge, to look at the old fortifications, as it was dark when we arrived the night before ; they were very pretty and picturesque, and the town is charmingly situated on a height above the river. The whole appearance of the country on this side of St. Petersburg is quite different from, and much better than that on the Moscow side, both as to the towns, and the country itself; the villages are not such dull, long, wooden things, and the country much diversified, and with a good deal of wood. The first three stages were good to-day, and we had deep sand afterwards to Neunal, where we stopped about half-past eight and had tea as usual. We met to-day Baron and Baroness Strogonoff and their suite travelling in a very heavy chariot, and an enormous coach, each with eight horses. The post-masters on this road keep eighty horses. Before we came to Neunal, we arrived suddenly, after dragging through sandy woods, on the borders of the Lake Peipons which from its large size on a dark evening had the appearance of a melancholy sea; we went along its shores for a long time. The inn very tolerable, as all seem to be on this road.

*Saturday, 22nd.*—We were awake soon after four, and were off at half-past six, our carriage drawn by six white horses; we had constant sand for the first two stages, and then a good road as far as Ondern, where we arrived about eight. The morning had been rainy, and a thick fog succeeded; but this cleared off in the middle of the day, and the evening was beautiful.

*Sunday, 23rd.*—We were up soon after two, and off at half-past four ; Belgrave was awakened in the middle of the night by a prodigious noise made by a French *courier*. The road was good in parts, and in others very sandy ; we reached Leugenhof about ten. Belgrave's bed consisting of a mattress ; our two leather pillows, and a pair of sheets having slipped out of the little carriage three stages from Leugenhof, between Valx and Goulben ; Gartner went back to search for them, but quite in vain, as we never heard of them more, which was very provoking. Gartner arrived at Leugenhof, about two in the morning. At Leugenhof there was a tame green parrot.

*Monday, 24th.*—Count Orloff passed in the morning on his way to Warsaw, with the news of the Empress having a second son.* The road the whole of the way to-day was deep in sand leading us through a great deal of wood ; we passed long lines of little carts each with one horse, toiling through it, and arrived about half-past nine at Riga. On finding the Hotel de Londres full, we went to the Hotel de St. Pétersbourg, the landlord of which gave us a tolerably clean apartment.

*Tuesday, 25th.*—We did not get up early, being

---

* The present Grand Duke Constantine.

glad to have a good sleep after our journey.
While we were at breakfast, Mr. Cumming, the
English Consul, came to call, and very kindly gave
us his assistance in the matter of Gartner's passport,
about which there was a good deal of difficulty.
As it was probable that it would not be settled in
time for us to go next day, we accepted Mr.
Cumming's invitation to dine with him next day
in the country. Belgrave and I then went out to
walk over the town; we went first to the floating
bridge, which is a very singular one and very
broad, with the ships sitting on each side of it.
We saw many English flags; one was from
Arbroath, one from Dundee, &c. The traffic on
the bridge is immense, many carriages, hundreds of
carts, Poles, Russians, Jews, &c., cross daily; there
is a fruit-market on the Quay, with piles of water-
melons, and legions of apples. We then walked
through the streets which are narrow and dirty; the
town however is much more German in appearance
than Russian. We then walked through one of
the six gates, over the moats, along a sort of
Boulevard, then to the Citadel, then home, and had
rather a bad dinner at seven.

*Wednesday, 26th*—We got up at half-past seven;
breakfasted, read, wrote and worked till Mr.

Cumming and his son came. Mr. Cumming had been labouring for about three hours to get Gartner's passport, which at last was effected. We then took a walk with him round the ramparts : the fortifications are very large and very strong, with wide moats and numerous drawbridges. There are always six thousand men in the garrison. We went to Mr. Cumming's town house, which is a very nice one; met there Mrs. Cumming, who came to town to fetch us to dinner. I went home to get ready, and Belgrave went to the banker's ; Mrs. Cumming then called at the hotel in a barouche and pair for me, and Belgrave went in another carriage with Mr. Cumming. Their country house is about four English miles from the town; it is prettily placed over a river, with a garden and fine oak-trees. The Cummings seem fond of dogs, for they have two Spaniels, five Newfoundland dogs, and plenty of Truffle-hunters. There was nobody there but themselves and their three sons ; we had a very pleasant dinner, and after coffee, walked over the garden, which is very pretty, and like an English one; we then had tea, and came home in their carriage.

*Thursday, September 27th.*—We left Riga at seven in the morning; went two stages entirely of deep sand to Mittau, a neat and rather pretty town; from there the road becomes better and prettier, but we did not reach Frauenbourg till half-past twelve. We found there a neat and clean, nicely furnished little room; the people being tenants of Monsieur de Lieven, were very civil. As we had dined in the carriage, we wanted only hot milk, and water, and bread and butter, which they soon gave us.

*Friday, 28th.*—We set out at half-past seven; the first part of the way was sandy, but it grew better afterwards; a good road to Oberbartau, a passable inn, and an amiable dog who would sleep while we were at tea, wrapped up in a counterpane on one of the beds. We got to Oberbartau about eight o'clock.

*Saturday, 29th.* — Set out at seven, reached Polangen, the Russian frontier, about the middle of the day; had no trouble with the custom-house people: from thence to Immersalt, the Prussian frontier; for four miles it is a continued series of fine white, powdered sand. Polangen is a remarkable place, inhabited by dirty, wretched-looking Jews. We got to Memel soon after seven, and found a most excellent inn, "Die Sonne." As soon as we had arrived, Belgrave went to the bankers to get Prussian money, and then off to the post-masters.

*Sunday, 30th.*—Left Memel at half-past seven. It is a nice, pretty little town, and the change in the appearance of comfort and cleanliness on leaving Russia and entering Prussia, strikes one immediately. We crossed a very well-managed ferry on leaving the town, and proceeded with eight horses across the passage of the Strand, which is merely a strip composed entirely of sand between two seas, to which, on the right hand, ones goes so near, as to have the wheels of the carriage occasionally in the water; the road is most desolate, nothing but a plain of sand, here and there blown and drifted up into large hills; no living thing, or trace of vegetation, is to be seen, except now and then a starved calf trying to eat dried up rushes; in the middle of this waste we met a Russian with whom we changed horses. General Patgul, with five carriages, returning to St. Petersburg from Wurtzburg, with a suite of twenty people.

The weather during the whole of this fortnight has been most charming, though sometimes with a little frost in the nights; yet the days were almost too hot, and the moonlight evenings were quite beautiful. We had sent on an *estafette* to order

horses for us at Swartzort, the first stage, but quite
in vain, as the innkeepeers were all out ; we therefore
had to wait about two hours while our own horses
were baiting, and employed ourselves in walking
on the seashore. We then went on, and found
horses at Nidden, and proceeded in a beautiful
moonlight to Rositten, where we arrived at half-
past eleven, and were very tolerably lodged.

*Monday, October 1st.*—We left Rositten at eight,
and crossed by some fields to the other side of the
strip of sand already mentioned, and then went
dragging along a dreary shore with the sea on our
left; we saw in several places hooded crows tied by
the leg to entice their companions, who, when
assembled, are caught by having a net suddenly
flung over them, by means of a rope, one end of
which is held by a man, who is lying concealed in
an artificial bosquet, erected for the purpose close
to the sea. These birds are then used as food by
the inhabitants of this wretched place.

At the first stage, Sarkau, we were glad to exchange the seashore, which had become very
marshy and disagreeable, for a large wood, and
finally left the shore, and had a better road to
Königsberg, where we arrived at six. We stopped
to dine at the " Deutsche Haus," a very good inn, and

walked before dinner to Mr. Douglas's to buy
amber. We found here a magnificent dog, a large
dun-coloured hound, by name Hector; they said
he was English. Mr. Douglas showed us all his
amber, of which he had an immense quantity in
baskets; we bought some rough bits and some
worked pieces also, and then walked back through
the old castle of the Margraves, a curious large,
very old building. As soon as we had dinner we
set out for Quilitten, passing through Brandenbourg,
and arrived at Quilitten about twelve, and found a
small inn, very clean and quite new.

*Tuesday, October 2nd.*—We set out at seven,
passed through Bransberg, a pretty town, and
Elbing, which is also very pretty; got to Marienburg at six. We put up at the "Hochmeister," a
tolerable inn, and exactly opposite the old château,
built by the Teutonic knights in the fourteenth century, and dismantled by the Poles in the next; it
has lately been in part restored by the Crown Prince
of Prussia,* *i.e.*, the side which was the private
abode of the Grand Master, consisting of a number
of pretty but tiny apartments, with very thick
walls; they are now paved with coloured tiles, and

* Afterwards King William IV. of Prussia, elder brother of the
present Emperor of Germany.

the arms of the knights are inserted in coloured glass in the windows. There is here a small chapel, and a very large and handsome hall, which served as a dining-room for all the knights, about four hundred in number.

We then walked through the court, over a small bridge, and through a very old gateway into the town, and returned by the road on the outside of the moat which surrounds the castle. The opposite sides of the court, in which were the rooms of all the knights, are now arranged as magazines.

*Wednesday, October 3rd.*—We left Marienburg at seven, crossed two ferries, one at the end of the first stage, Drischan, where they are building a bridge over the Vistula. The villages are miserable, like some of the old French towns. The first part of our road to-day was tolerable ; but the last stage of four and a half German miles lay through deep sand, so that we did not arrive at König till half-past twelve. We stopped at the " Poste," where we found a very civil landlord in his nightcap, and a very clean inn with good beds, to which we betook ourselves as soon as we could.

*Thursday, 4th.*—The road the whole of the day was one of deep sand, in which it was im-

possible to go out of a walk ; the *chaussée* was not
yet allowed to be used for travelling, as they have
had no rain. This day's journey was the most
tedious we had had, there being a hot east wind
behind, which carried the dust along with us,
choking us the whole way. We arrived at " Deutsche
Krone" at half-past eleven, a good little inn. Next
year the *chaussée* will be completed from Berlin to
Königsberg, and there will then be an excellent
road.

*Friday, 5th.*—After one stage of sand we got on
the *chaussée*, and went through Hochzeit, which
appeared to have an excellent inn, and large garden.
Bought some fruit, arrived at Landsberg at nine,
and found a civil old military landlord, who had
a gentleman visiting him, whom we heard singing
extremely well in the next room. We had some
bitter grausvogel, *alias* fieldfares, for supper, and
after that went to sleep in very good beds.

*Saturday, 6th.*—Left Landsberg at seven ; at the
first stage met a Mr. Bent, or Bunt, who was
travelling into Russia. We gave him some intelligence respecting the inns, pitied him sincerely,
and went on each our respective ways. Passed
through Custrin, a very strongly fortified place in
the middle of a dead flat, and reached Berlin about

ten. We found at Jagers that Mr. Temple* had not got Belgrave's letter, begging him to secure rooms for us, but as there was a small apartment vacant on the third floor, we established ourselves there, and found it, though small, very clean and comfortable.

*Sunday, October 7th.*—We received a good many letters from England, before we were up. Mr. Temple called while we were at breakfast, after which we read and wrote our letters, walked out by the Brandebourg Gate in the gardens before dinner, and had a visit from Count Alopèus and his daughter.

*Monday, 8th.*—After breakfast Belgrave went out with Mr. Temple, and I went in Lord Clanwilliam's† carriage, of which he had written to give us the use, to Countess Pauline Neale, whom I found at home and quite ready to go out with me to shops, &c. We met the Duke of Cumberland,‡ who was

---

* The Honourable Sir William Temple, K.C.B., afterwards Minister Plenipotentiary at Naples. He was a brother of the late Lord Palmerston, and died in 1856. In 1827 he was Secretary of Legation at Berlin.

† The present Earl of Clanwilliam; he was then Minister at Beriin; but in his absence Mr. Temple supplied his place temporarily.

‡ Ernest, Duke of Cumberland, afterwards King of Hanover; he died in 1851.

charmed to find we were come. We went to many
shops to get divers articles, such as gloves, patterns
for embroidery, and coloured canvas; then I set
Countess Pauline down at her mother's, and came
home; we dined with Mr. Temple, nobody there
but himself and another member of the Embassy,
Mr. Somerville, and were to have gone to the Opera
afterwards, but as Mademoiselle Sontag was ill and
could not sing, we went to the play instead, and
saw three German farces. The King and Princess
Lignitz* were in the King's private box, and
Prince Augustus† in the large royal one. After the
play we went to drink tea at Countess Pauline
Neale's, where we met her father and mother, and
about twenty other people; the Duke of Cumberland came to meet us, and brought me a very kind
note from the Duchess, in answer to one that I
had sent her, inviting us to dine with them
next day. After staying some time we came
home.

* Second and morganatic wife of the King, to whom she was
married in 1824.

† A second cousin of the King.

We are very glad to find that we had arrived at
the end of our long journey, in as fine a state of
preservation too as that in what a most curious
case of mummies lately arrived here, but I suppose
we are not so much worth seeing ; at least I daresay
Monsieur Humboldt will say so. Our journey has
been most prosperous, and quite free from serious
difficulty, or mis-adventure. We stayed two days
at Riga, where we were very kindly treated by the
English Consul, Mr. Cumming, and by his wife,
a very agreeable Russian woman. They gave us
a dinner at their country house, where they have
five Newfoundland dogs, and two English spaniels.
From Riga we came through Memel, a nice pretty
little town with an excellent inn ; and then across
the Strand, a most extraordinary, wild, desolate
tract, made of every variety of sand, loose-sands,
sand-hills, and quick-sands ; it lies between two seas,
to one of which you drive so close as often to have
the wheels in the water, and you fag on at a foot's
pace for a day and a half with eight horses.
Thence there is an excellent new road making to

this place; it will be finished entirely next year, but where it is still unfinished the sand is tremendous and incredibly tedious. We did not find the inns so very bad even in Russia; but certainly the moment you leave Russia and get into Prussia, the change for the better is immediately visible. Our weather has been charming, almost too hot in the day, with delicious moonlight nights; we travelled from very early till very late, but stopped for a few hours every night to sleep, and have been on the road fifteen days altogether, exclusive of the two which was spent at Riga. I found there a letter from Lord Clanwilliam, giving us the use of his carriage and horses, and we have had a visit from Mr. Temple, with whom we dine and go to the Opera to-morrow. We see clearly that we cannot get away under a week from this place. There are many royal people to see, among whom you may be sure I shall not omit the Duchess of Cumberland. I have brought her an embroidered reticule from Russia, and am going to write to her to know when she will see us. Then I have a letter from the Empress-mother to Princess Charles, she was Princess Marie of Saxe-Weimar, and is only just married; then there are the King,* and

---

* The then King was Frederick William III., father of the late

the Prince and Princess Royal, &c. I have a letter to Madame Alopèus, the Russian Minister's wife, who is very much liked; and I am to see Countess Neale, the friend of the Duchess of Leeds. Except people, however, there is not much to be seen at Berlin. I have seen some beautiful horses in Russia, and have always meant to tell you that both there and in Sweden I have frequently seen beautiful hedgehog pigs, exactly like those in the Orkneys. You wished to know about the winter life in Norway. The Wedels shut themselves up with a great deal of salt meat, dried bread, &c., in a remarkably comfortable house some twenty miles in the interior, with a boiling, rushing river, and a broiling iron foundry close to it; then they go about in *traineaux*, when they *do* go out at all; and sit and work very comfortably at home in the long winter nights. Then it is that they make bear-hams, while they hear the wolves howl outside, and see the Aurora Borealis! We were very glad to hear of the Empress having a son, for which she had been wishing so much, and all belonging to her hoped for it also.

*Monday.*—I must end my letter now, as the post

King of Prussia and of the present Emperor of Germany. He reigned from 1797 down to 1840.

goes early. I have been out all the morning with Countess Pauline Neale, who has taken me to all the shops; we drink tea with her this evening after the Opera. She goes into the country the day after to-morrow to be with the Radzivils, who are in the deepest grief at losing their favourite son, only twenty-eight years old. We met the Duke of Cumberland in the streets; he stopped the carriage thinking I was Lord Clanwilliam, but knew me directly, and was overjoyed, and said the Duchess would be perfectly delighted at my arrival. I had just sent her my letter, and Belgrave had been to call on him. They are staying in the country about four English miles off.

*Monday night.*—We are just come from Countess Neale's (after the Opera), where the Duke of Cumberland came to meet us; nothing can be more cordial and good-natured than he is. He is looking very well, and his eyes are perfectly recovered, which puts him in high spirits, and makes him very happy. He brought me a very kind note from the Duchess, and we dine with them to-morrow. We leave here at the end of the week, and mean to pass a few days at Dresden and Weimar.

*Tuesday, October 9th.*—Countess Pauline came at eleven to take me out, and we went to several shops, while Belgrave went out with Mr. Somerville. We dressed and went soon after three to dine with the Duke and Duchess of Cumberland at Schönhausen, about four English miles from the town. We found the Duke and Duchess looking very well, and rejoiced to see us ; there were the Countess Schleppenbach, her Lady, Count and Countess Neale, and Countess Pauline, one of the Prince de Solms, the Duke's aides-de-camp, and the tutor of Prince George.* Before we had quite done dinner, they announced the Princess Royal,† and the Duchess of Mecklenburg-Schwerin,‡ as being arrived ; the Duke and Duchess went out to see them, and brought them into the dining-room, where we were introduced to them. Afterwards we went into the drawing-room, and they very soon went away. Prince George, who is a handsome and vivacious boy, came in to dessert. The Neales went early to join the Princess Royal. We remained some time sitting with the Duke and Duchess, and then took our leave, and went to drink tea with Countess Alopèus. I had not seen her

---

* The late blind King of Hanover.

† Elizabeth of Bavaria, wife of Frederick William IV., the late King of Prussia.

‡ A daughter of King Frederick William.

before, and thought her, though unwell, the most
beautiful person I had ever seen, and with charming
manners. There were very few people there, the
Count and Countess Strogonoff, Countess Santi and
her sister, and a few besides; we walked home, it
being next door but one, about eleven o'clock.

*Wednesday, October* 10*th.*—During breakfast, as
usual, the shop people brought their bills. At
eleven, Belgrave and I left a little parcel of a Torjok
reticule that I had bought for the Duchess at the
Duke of Cumberland's, and then went to Mr. Temple,
who gave us some more letters just arrived from
England; after that we went to a sculptor's close by,
to see a statue of the Empress of Russia; then he
went to the coachmaker's, and I to the stables with
Mr. Temple to see Lord Clanwilliam's horses. There
are some very handsome ones, and a delightful white
English terrier puppy. After that we all three went
into the carriage to call on Count and Countess
Woronzow,* at the Hotel de Prusse, who arrived

* Afterwards Prince and Princess Woronzow; she was the wife of
Prince Michel Woronzow, to whom belonged Aloupka, a beautiful
residence near Odessa. He had been brought up in England, and had
imbibed English tastes and principles, taking pleasure in improving
his immense property near Odessa, and devoting himself to the good of
his people and his country. His wife the Princess, still living, after a
long widowhood, in 1879, was the daughter of Princess Branitska, one

last night, but they were gone out to see us. We then
went to the château, to leave my cards with Countess
Reede, the Lady of the Princess Royal, and Madame
Kalmeique, Grande Maîtresse to the Princess Charles ;
then to a statuary's to see a large granite vase in
making for the King, then to Professor Rauch's,[*]
where were different busts of the Royal family,
Blucher, &c. ; and lastly to sundry shops. We then
came home to dress for dinner at the apartments of
the Crown Prince and Princess, where we went at
four o'clock. They live on one side of the Palace
in some handsome rooms ; besides themselves, there
were Prince William,[†] and Prince Charles[‡], Count
and Countess Strogonoff, Countess Reede, Mademoiselle Brockhausen, Prince Labanoff, Count
Goöben (General Daunbach's son-in-law), Baron
Humboldt, the traveller and naturalist, Mr. Bonar,
a Monsieur Darril, and some aides-de-camp. The
dinner was very pleasant, we stayed a little while in

of the seven nieces of Prince Potemkin, some of whose wealth she in-
herited from her mother.

[*] Professor of the Fine Arts in the Berlin University, and himself
an eminent sculptor.

[†] The present Emperor of Germany.

[‡] Next brother of the present Emperor. He married the Princess
Marie of Saxe-Weimar, mother of Prince Frederick Charles, and sister
of the Empress of Germany. She died in 1878, he still survives.

the drawing-room afterwards; the Prince Royal said that we must come back another day, as he would show us the very room of " The White Lady,"* and then everybody went off to the Opera. We came home first · for Belgrave to take off his uniform; I dressed over again, and we went to the Opera, where we found Mr. Temple. The opera was one of Winter's, " Le Sacrifice Interrompu," in German. Mademoiselle Sontag sang, and her beauty and voice were quite equal to what we had expected; Count Neale and Count Woronzow came into our box. The Duke of Cumberland brought a note for me, to tell me officially what Prince Charles had told me before, that Princess Charles would see me next day at twelve, and that we were to dine there on Friday. After the opera there was no ballet, but we came home immediately to receive the Duke of Cumberland, who came to drink tea with us, and sat talking till a late hour.

*Thursday, October·11th.*—We wrote after breakfast till a little before noon, when Madame Schleppenbach called to go with me to Princess Charles. Accordingly we went, and she received me in a per-

---

* An apparition said to manifest itself before any misfortune to the Royal family of Prussia; the room is a large hall in the " Alte Schloss," at Berlin.

fectly plain morning gown. She is very pleasing and pretty with charming manners; I gave her the letter from the Empress-mother, and after some time we came away.

Belgrave went to dine at two with the King at Charlottenberg, and he carried Count Woronzow there in Lord Clanwilliam's carriage. He met all the Royal family there, Princes and Princesses, the Duke and Duchess of Cumberland, &c., and was introduced to the Princess de Lignitz.* Mr. Temple called for me at four to go to dine at Count Alopèus', there I met, to my great joy, Countess Woronzow, as we had been two or three times before prevented from meeting; Dr. Granville, Mr. Somerville, Count de Ruffo, and a few more people Belgrave and Count Woronzow arrived soon after dessert was begun; they had called on the Duke and Duchess of Cumberland on their way home. We came home before nine, and Mr. Temple sat down with us to tea.

. Soon after Mr. Temple was gone, we received a note from Baron Humboldt, inviting us to a dinner at twelve o'clock next day at his brother's at Tegel, to meet the King and Royal family, and announcing that he would call himself at ten in the evening upon us; and accordingly he came.

*Friday, October* 12*th.*—On getting up, Belgrave received a message from Prince Augustus* to ask why he had not dined with him the day before. On inquiry, we were shocked to find that he had sent a message to ask him to dine yesterday, which through a mistake had not been received. Belgrave went as soon as he had done breakfast to the aide-de-camp of Prince Augustus to explain, and at a little before eleven we set out in a carriage and four, which we had hired for the day, for Tegel, about ten miles off, the first five *chaussée*, the rest sand. The King passed us *en chemin*, in a barouche and four. When we arrived, we found Monsieur and Madame Humboldt, Baron A. Humboldt, Monsieur Bulow,† and Madame Bulow, the King, and Princess de Lignitz, and her lady, the Duke and Duchess of Cumberland, their lady and gentleman, Prince William, Prince Albert, the Duke of Mecklenburg,‡ Prince Radzivil; and Prince and Princess Charles arrived soon after. We walked over the garden, and then came in to dinner; we sat at a large round table, at which were the King and all the Royal family ; the suite sat at another table in another

---

* Cousin to the King.

† Afterwards Prussian Minister in England.

‡ The brother of the Duchess of Cumberland.

room. The repast finished, we went again into the drawing-room, looked at the statues and pictures, and finally made our escape about three o'clock. Prince Charles with whom we were to dine being already departed, we got home at four, and dressed as fast as we could. Belgrave hurried on his uniform, and we went to Prince Charles's, where we found them already gone to dinner. There were there, Prince William, Prince Radzivil, Count and Countess Woronzow, Prince Labanoff, and a good many more. I sat by Princess Charles, who was most gracious and kind ; after dinner the circle was short, as everybody was going to the Opera, to hear Mademoiselle Sontag in the " Barbiere." We went to the Duke of Cumberland's box, where we found him and the Duchess, her lady, Madame Schleppenbach, the Duke of Mecklenburg, and one of the Princes of Solms. The box was exactly opposite the King's, who was there with Princess Lignitz. Mademoiselle Sontag sung delightfully, but the rest was very ill-acted. Prince Charles, and Prince William, and Prince Albert came to our box between the acts. After the opera we came home for Belgrave to take off his uniform, and then went to a ball at Count Neale's, where were the young Princes, and Princess de Lignitz, who danced the mazurka with Prince Charles, and we came home between eleven and twelve.

*Saturday, October 13th.*—As soon as we had done breakfast, Belgrave and I set out to walk to the Hotel de Prusse to see Count and Countess Woronzow before they went, and we met Count Alopèus, who was going there too ; we found them at home, and Belgrave took leave of them. I stayed with Countess Woronzow till the Duchess of Cumberland's carriage came to fetch me to her house in town, where I found her and the Duke, Prince George, and the Duchess's three sons, the Princes of Solms; we stayed there a long time, the Duke had some chocolate, the Duchess and I some grapes. She showed me all her rooms, which are very comfortably and ·prettily furnished. The Duke and the young Princes then set out on foot, and the Duchess and I followed them in the carriage with Madame Schleppenbach, and another lady of the Duchess's, to the Exhibition of the Manufacturers of Berlin, which takes place every two years. It consists of every kind of article of manufacture, steel, porcelain, iron, papier-maché, pictures, cutlery, silver, leather, &c., silks, velvets, &c., there were some beautiful *gros d'étés*, of which the Duchess ordered a pink gown for me, and blue for Mamma.* Belgrave and Mr. Temple joined us there very soon after we arrived. We stayed a long time, and when we had finished our purchases it was time to go to dress. We had hardly time to look at the pictures of the Giustiani collection, which are also here. The building is a handsome one, divided into several large rooms, and well adapted for the purpose, but the King is building a new and better one. After we came away, Belgrave and I took a walk down the Linden as far as Blücher's monument, then back, and dressed. At half-past three Mr. Temple called for us, and we went to Schönhausen to dine with the Duke and Duchess of Cumberland,—there were Prince and Princess Charles, Countess Kalmin, her Grande-Maîtresse, Baron A. Humboldt, Baron Bulow, Madame Schleppenbach, Countess Voss, Mr. Darril, Baron Linsing, and Mr. Jelf,† Prince George's tutor, and the usual suite of the Duke and Duchess. We had a very pleasant dinner, and stayed a long time after Prince and Princess Charles went, saw a sort of lighthouse called a "fanal" exhibited in the garden, lighted, which we had seen at the exhibition in the morning, and after tea came home.

* My mother, the Duchess-Countess of Sutherland.

† Mr. Jelf afterwards married Madame Schleppenbach. He died a Canon of Christ Church, Oxford.

*Sunday, October 14th.*—After breakfast, we read prayers. At ten o'clock Belgrave walked to the monument of the late war on the Kriegsberg, and I went thither in the carriage. The monument is Gothic, of bronze and very handsome; after that he walked back to the hotel. I came back in the carriage, and we then walked to see the wild beasts in their "garten:" there is a very good collection, including two fine lions and a lioness, with a very lively young cub, plenty of monkies, a beautiful lama, a fine family of young crocodiles of all ages, a boa-constrictor, and a most beautiful collection of parrots, parroquets, and macaws. After this it was fully time to dress for dinner, and we went soon after four to dine at Mr. Temple's; the Duke of Cumberland, Count Alopèus, Count Neale, Count Perponcher, Colonel Poten, Prince of Solms. and a few more were there. We had a very pleasant dinner, and they all set off for the Opera; we came home between six and seven, and passed our evening very comfortably in writing our letters for England. I also wrote to Lord Clanwillian and the Landgravine of Hesse-Homburg.*

*Monday, October 15th.*—We set out at half-past ten in a very smart barouche, and with a pair

* The Princess Elizabeth, daughter of George III.

of pretty grey horses belonging to the inn, to go
to Charlottenburg, about four English miles from
town, to see the monument by Rauch to the late
Queen ; we waited some time for the man to show it,
and found Prince Labanoff in the same situation.
He went with us to see it; we walked through a
large, flat garden divided into long alleys, and arrived
at the cemetery, which is a small and pretty building at the end of a long straight wall bordered with
fir trees ; immediately before it is a circle of gravel
surrounded with weeping willows; the monument
is on an eminence which is approached by steps on
each side; in the centre is a flight of steps which
descend into the vault. The monument is beautiful,
but if there is any fault it is that the figure is rather
too large. We walked back to the palace ; Prince
Labanoff departed, and we returned straight to the
hotel, where we found Lord Clanwilliam's carriage
waiting, so we set off for Moubijou, where is a
most curious collection of mummies. Mr. Temple
met us there ; the mummies were shewn by
Monsieur Passalagna who found them himself in
Egypt. There are several in wonderful preservation, with their ornaments upon them, and with
baskets full of fruit, birds, cats, reptiles and
household utensils ; several complete mummies

were unpacked others lay still in their mummy en-
velopes. We saw a curious tomb of a priest, with
two carved boats by its side, and the horns and
bones of the ox which had been sacrificed at his
funeral; with many other things equally curious;
the whole collection is by much the most interesting of the kind that we ever saw.

From here we went to see Mr. Solly's collection
of pictures, lately bought by the King. They
range from the first *enfance de l'art*, and include
some curious, and a few fine ones. We then went
to the Magasin de Porcelaine and the iron shop,
then to Quittels', where I stayed while Belgrave
went to the bankers, and we sent the carriage away.
We then walked home, dressed, dined, and Mr.
Temple called for to us to go to the Cenerentola,
at the Königsteater: Mademoiselle Eva Bamberger
acted the principal part, and well, considering that
she is very young; the music was beautiful.
Mademoiselle Sontag was in the next box to us.
After this we went to drink tea at Madame Alopèus's,
where there was nobody but themselves and ourselves.

*Tuesday, October 16th.*—We passed some time
after breakfast in packing up, and went at eleven
with Mr. Temple to see the arsenal; there are arms
ready for sixty thousand men; some curious old

T

arms of different kinds, and a fine statue of Blücher.
We then went to the booksellers and bought some
books, got through some more packing; at half-
past two went to dress, Belgrave dined with Prince
Augustus, where were Prince Labanoff, and a few
others, at a pleasant dinner. I went on to Schönhausen to dine with the Duke and Duchess of
Cumberland, where Belgrave also was to have joined
us, but he was prevented by Prince Augustus's
dinner. There were only themselves, the three
Princes of Solms, Baron Linsing, Mr. Temple and
Mr. Jelf. I stayed a little while after the dinner
was over, and then took leave of the Duchess, who
had loaded us with kindness, came home, found
Belgrave, finishing our packing, after which we had
grapes and went to bed.

*Wednesday, October* 17*th.*—We got up at six and
left Berlin at nine ; reached Potsdam soon after
eleven, and as we had failed in getting the rooms
that we wished at Einsedel, we went to the Hotel
de Prusse, where the rooms were full of lady-birds,
and dirty enough, but we were obliged to be
content; here we dressed for the fête at Potsdam,
and drove to the Palais Neuf, where we arrived at
half-past one; the party consisted of about seventy.
The Prince and Princess Royal, Prince and Princess

of Saxony (who had arrived the night before),
Prince and Princess Charles, Prince William, Prince
Albert, Prince of Hesse, Duke of Mecklenburg, two
Princes of Solms, the Duke of Cumberland, Prince
Labanoff, the Duke of Brunswick (the second
holder of that title), Prince Augustus of Prussia,
and their respective aides-de-camp, Baron Humboldt, Princess de Lignitz, Marquise de Bruges,
and Madame de Roche-Lambert, and a good
many more. The King came into the room a little
while after we arrived, there was *cercle* for some
time, while he walked about and talked ; and at
two o'clock we all went to dinner in an immense
and handsome room, lined with shells and all sorts
of marine ornaments, called " La Grotte." I sat at
dinner between Prince William and the Prince of
Hesse, Belgrave and Prince Labanoff opposite the
King ; the dinner was very pleasant. After spending
a due time on our meal, we rose up, and there
was again *cercle* in the drawing-room ; after which
the King and Royal family all went to their
respective apartments, and the Duke of Cumberland
took us over the Palace, which is very handsome,
though not much furnished ; we went over the
rooms of Frederick the Great, who built this
Palace at the end of the Seven Years' War, to

show that he had still money left in his exchequer; the rooms are very handsome, in long enfilades like those at Castle Howard or Worksop, and are said to be four hundred in number. After we had seen all this, Belgrave and I drove to Sans Souci, where we saw the gallery, with some good pictures; among them a Rembrandt, of a Prince of Asturias threatening his father; several good ones by Rubens, &c. The gallery is separate from the Palace, where we went next, and saw Frederick the Great's rooms—which except having belonged to him are in no way remarkable—and those of Voltaire. The view from the terrace is very pretty, and the environs of Potsdam in general are extremely so; with a great deal of wood and water, and very different from the country round Berlin; the quantities of hot-houses belonging to these palaces are incredible; they are built on the sides of hills and mounted in rows of terraces, one above the other. After seeing Sans Souci we returned to the Palais Neuf, and fell in with some of the young Princes, with whom Belgrave went to walk, whilst I went to sit with Countess Reede, the Princess Royal's *grande maîtresse*, and the rest of the ladies. I remained till a little before six; when we went up-stairs to the rooms on the first floor, where all the company were again assembled. The King soon came, and at six we all went to the theatre, which was quite full, all the surrounding inhabitants being allowed to come. The King and his company sat on circular benches, in the front of the pit, exactly opposite the stage, where one saw and heard very well; the play was " Jocondi " in German ; Mademoiselle Sontag sung; between the acts, the King and Royal family stood up by the orchestra, and we were all treated with tea and ices—the play lasted till about nine. We all returned to " La Grotte," where supper was prepared on a number of small tables. The King and Princesses supped at the centre table; the Prince Royal took me to another, where were Prince William and Prince Augustus, Madame de Bruges, Madame de Roche-Lambert, Prince Charles, and the Duke of Brunswick. After supper the Royal family all took leave of us, saying a great many kind and civil things. Prince and Princess Charles settled that we should come to see them next morning at their house at Glienike, about a quarter of an hour's drive from Potsdam. Here the party ended and everybody went away. We arrived at our inn at half-past ten.

*Thursday, October* 18*th.*—We got up early, had

some coffee, and went to Glienike by half-past
nine, where we found Prince and Princess
Charles, and a very pretty house, nicely fitted up,
and full of pictures, drawings, and objects of beauty
and interest ; the house and place, with the garden
full of flowers, rather reminded us of Bromley
Hill;* after they had shown us the house, Prince
Charles walked with us over the garden, where
are pavilions full of antiques, and beautiful views
over the water.  We then returned to the house to
take leave of the Princess, who gave to our care a
Spaniel puppy to carry to her sister at Weimar ;
Prince Charles then walked with us to the kennel,
and showed us his dogs, among which were some
Newfoundlands and Mount St. Bernards.  We then
took leave of him with a grateful remembrance of
the kindness which we had experienced from himself and the Princess, and indeed from all the Royal
family ; and got into the carriage to go to " L'Isle
des Paons," about a mile from the gate of Glienike ;
we were ferried over the river to this prettiest of
islands, which is a charming mixture of forest and
flower garden, and like a scene in a fairy tale.  The
flowers in the greatest profusion, and the finest

---

* In Kent, now the seat of Colonel Long, son-in-law of Edward,
thirteenth Earl of Derby.

possible, magnificent dahlias, twelve and thirteen feet high; blue hydrangeas, and enormously large bushes of salvia splendens in the open air, and lovely walks, through oak woods, and a fine collection of birds and beasts, in different parts of the wood. A round building with a pond, and space of grass is enclosed for all sorts of water-birds and tortoises; in another place there is a pit with two magnificent bears, both in excellent condition. They were very gentle in appearance, and at the command of their keeper climbed up a tree in the centre of their habitation, and sat on the top of it to receive as a reward branches of leaves and fruit fastened to the top of a long stick; they eat no meat. Farther on was an aviary with all kinds of birds, not so good, as they had no grass, but only sand. There is a very good collection of monkeys, parrots, eagles, &c., and walking on one of the lawns we met a large flock of sheep and goats, of all sorts and all countries, all so tame as to follow us to have their noses rubbed. There is a small palace behind, with more enclosures for other animals. The fallow deer came to eat acorns and chestnuts out of one's hands, (I picked up some enormous acorns to plant at home); kangaroos, a she-wolf, who when the keeper went into her

den, gave all the signs of pleasure that a dog
expresses, licking his face and jumping about him;
this she-wolf had with her two large young half-
bred cubs. A fox, who also played like a puppy,
letting the keeper take him up in his arms. There
were also wild boars, and different sorts of deer;
after we had seen all this delicious place, we were
ferried back again, then got into the carriage, and
stopped at Glienike to pick up the puppy that we
were to carry from Princess Charles to Princess
Augusta at Weimar; he was very well secured in a
basket. We then returned to the inn at Potsdam, had
our things put up, and set out at three. The environs
of Potsdam are extremely pretty; we reached Treun-
britzen at seven o'clock, and found a passable inn.

*Friday, October 19th.*—We left Treunbritzer at
half-past seven, had an even day's journey without
any event, and got to Leipsic at half-past nine;
here we found an excellent inn, " l'Hotel de Saxe,"
as good and clean as any English one.

*Saturday, October 20th.*—After breakfast walked
round the town, which is a remarkably clean and
pretty one, full of curious old German houses,
pleasantly mixed with gardens and trees. We
walked round the market, then round by the
Promenade to a private garden, in order to see the

small River Elster, where the body of Count Poniatouski was found two days after the Battle of Leipsic, Bonaparte having blown up the bridge after he had made his own escape from the town. Poniatouski endeavoured to rejoin the French by going through the stream on horseback, but being wounded, it is supposed, his strength was not sufficient for the struggle up a steep bank, and so he was drowned; the horse escaped, and is now in the possession of the King of Bavaria, who bought him from the Russians. After this we walked back through the town to the bankers, where I left Belgrave and walked home; he came soon after, having bought some white gloves by the way. We set out soon after eleven, got out of the carriage to see the stone near Lutzen which marks the spot where Gustavus Adolphus fell; and then travelled on without any event, the postillions driving so miserably slow, that we did not get to Weimar till past one, went to the "Hotel of the Erb Prinz," which looked dirty and disagreeable; we looked at the "Hotel de l'Eléphant," which not being better, we remained at the "Hotel de l'Erb Prinz," and got to bed as soon as we could, which was not till three o'clock.

*Sunday, October 21st.*—Got up between nine and

ten, received messages from the Court, and wrote to the two *grande-maîtresses* about being presented; we received a notification that we should be presented to the Hereditary Grand Duchess of Weimar* at three, and dine afterwards with the reigning Grand Duke and Duchess.† Accordingly at three we went, and were taken first to the Imperial Grand Duchess, who received us very graciously, and to whom I presented my letter from her mother, the Empress-mother of Russia. Her daughter, Princess Augusta,‡ was with her, and the Grand Duke came in soon after; the Grand Duchess is very deaf, but has the most delightful manners. Princess Augusta is also charming, handsome, full of gaiety and good breeding, with a great deal of conversation. After remaining here a little while, the Grand Duchess said she would present us to the Grand Duke and Duchess; we accordingly went all together, and found a large circle, and the old Grand Duke and Duchess, who received us with great kindness. After talking for

---

\* Grand Duchess Mary of Russia, daughter of the Dowager Empress and the Emperor Paul; born in 1786.

† The Grand Duchess was Princess Louise of Hesse-Darmstadt, who personally opposed the great Napoleon.

‡ The present Empress of Germany.

some time we all went to dinner, the number about forty-two. A Count and Countess Remhardt, who were going to Frankfort, where he had just been appointed French Minister, all the suite of the Court, and a good many other people. We dined in a very narrow long gallery; after dinner we returned to the drawing-room for a little while, and then were all dismissed till six o'clock. Belgrave and I returned to the inn in the same carriage, which was sent for us. At six o'clock the carriage came for us again, and we returned to the palace, where we were ushered into a different set of rooms. There was a large circle formed, in addition to the former party, of some of the inhabitants of Weimar. Belgrave played at whist with the reigning Grand Duchess; the young Grand Duchess played at another table also at whist; and the Hereditary Grand Duke played at casino in a circular room at the end. There is a custom here that when the Royal people sit down to cards, all the company go successively up to the table to make a bow or curtsey to them. As I was obliged to own my ignorance of all games, I sat with Princess Augusta and some other ladies in the circular room, and had a very agreeable evening, though it was desperately cold; the reigning Grand Duke went away early. At length the games at cards were finished, and after some more conversation, the Grand Duchess took leave of everybody. We followed the young Grand Duke and Duchess into their apartments through a long suite of rooms ; and after some time went to supper, and at half-past eleven we returned to our hotel.

*Monday, October* 22*nd.*—The Hereditary Grand Duchess having very kindly arranged that we should pay Göthe a visit, the poet wrote that he would receive us at eleven. Accordingly Belgrave and I walked there after breakfast, and found him in a comfortable home ; he was very amiable and agreeable ; talked in French rather with difficulty, but pleasantly, and on literary subjects ; he seemed quite alive to everything, and sent messages to my brother Francis,* who had paid him a visit last year. He has a fine head, with great expression, and does not give one the idea of being seventy-eight years old.

We walked a little about the town, and when we returned to the inn, found the Grand Duchess and one of her ladies already waiting to take me to the Palace. When we arrived there, I went up first to Princess Augusta, who showed me her

* Lord Francis Leveson Gower, afterwards Earl of Ellesmere.

rooms, which had also been those of her sister, Princess Charles; then we saw the puppy that we had brought from Princess Charles, and which, as Princess Augusta had desired me to christen him, was named Carlo. After I took leave of her, I went to the rooms of the young Grand Duchess, where I found the Grand Duke, receiving a visit from a French lady. Here I was also introduced to Monsieur Kanikoff, the Russian Minister, whom Belgrave had known at Dresden ten years ago.

After this the Grand Duchess prepared to go out ; when she was ready I went with her and her lady in a coach and six to the Belvedere, a small country Palace about two miles from the town, which they often visit in the summer. Here we met Belgrave and one of the Duke's gentlemen, who had been sent to fetch him in a barouche and four. The Grand Duchess took us all through the quantities of hot-houses, which are full of the finest plants, and of the most curious kinds I ever saw. The orange trees, four hundred in number, are prodigiously fine, very tall, immensely large, and in the most flourishing and healthy condition ; they are of all sorts, and covered with fruit ; one of them is said to be five hundred years old; it is enormous in the trunk, and the rest of it equally fine, though after the Battle of Jena the French cut off nearly all its branches close to the stem. On a cactus in another house we were shown the cochineal insect, which looked like a white mould, but on being removed and scraped, turned into a scarlet juice. The Grand Duke joined us in the garden, and we .walked through some pretty woods close by, where we saw three roe deer. After this we went back as we came ; and got back to the inn just in time to dress for the three o'clock dinner at the Palace, to which we were again invited. The day was cold, miserable and raw ; and this considerably helped to increase a bad cold which had begun at Potsdam. We sat down to dinner at three, the party of about twenty consisting principally of the Court, and General Kanikoff. The Grand Duchess (Hereditary,) being deaf, I had great difficulty with my hoarseness to make myself intelligible, and she had a great deal to ask about the Empress, her mother, whom she had not seen since the Emperor's death, and also about Princess Charles, her daughter, whom she had also not seen since her marriage. We dined in another room to-day ; the Grand Duke was very cheerful, talked much about London, remembered dining at Cleveland House and seeing the Claudes there; after dinner and conversation we were again dismissed at five, the Grand Duchess inviting us to come to the play in their box at six ; we therefore returned to the inn, and put in an appearance at the play at the due time ; after we had waited a few minutes in the outer room, all the Royal family arrived, with the addition of Princess Augusta, who had not dined with us, as being very young she does not dine at table except on Sundays. The box is very large, exactly in front of the stage. The theatre is pretty and small : the play was " Katan of Heilbron " in German, and most entertaining. After it was over we took leave of our friends, and received many invitations to return. We then went home.

*Tuesday, October 23rd.*—We were very glad to set out again, and left Weimar at nine, with most pleasing remembrances of the gracious kindness we had received from the Royal family. It was a much finer day than the preceding. I was perfectly mute from my cold, and my head so oppressed that I could hardly see out of my eyes. Our first post was Erfurth, a fortified town, and not an ugly one by any means ; here we bought some very good pears. Gotha was our next halting-place, still in an ugly country, as indeed is most of what we have hitherto seen; but the town is certainly pretty, being full of nice gardens and walks. While we were changing horses, Belgrave walked into the town and up to the Palace, which stands very well on the top of a bank overlooking the town. I could not go with him on account of my cold. We bought two Almanacs de Gotha. After this stage, the country begins to be pretty with wooded hills and valleys. We got to Eisenach at six, and found a good inn, the "Half Moon."

*Wednesday, October 24th.*—My cold better. We got up early, and after breakfast walked up the Wartburg to see the castle where Luther lived, belonging to the Dukes of Saxony. The morning was very mild, damp, and pleasant; it had rained a good deal in the night. The walk was very pretty up a very steep path for above a mile, through beautiful little woods. Eisenach lies in a valley in the middle of wooded hills, and is the first pretty country we have seen since we left Sweden. The castle is perched on a very steep cliff, looking down over all the surrounding country; there are within it curious old rooms full of armour, belonging to the Margraves of Thuringen, and to Henry II. of France. The Knights' Hall is full of very old, and curious portraits, of no great merit; we were shown the room once inhabited by Luther, and the injury done to the wall by his having, in a fit of generous indignation, thrown his inkstand at the Devil! We walked down again, and departed about half-past ten. Travelled through a fairly pretty country, the last stage in perfect darkness; consequently we got our wheel entangled in that of a cart; we were however soon extricated and arrived at Fulda at nine.

*Thursday, October 25th.*—Left Fulda at half-past seven; travelled through a pretty country with many vineyards, and reached Frankfort at eight. We found very comfortable rooms at the Hotel of the Romische Kaiser.

*Friday, October 26th.*—Got up after a very comfortable night's rest; received two letters from Princess Elizabeth* at Homburg; dressed a little before twelve, and set out soon after, (Belgrave not in uniform by her desire), to go to Homburg in order to dine with her and the Landgrave. We got there before two, and found Princess Elizabeth looking very well, and were most kindly received by her, my family being very old friends; the Landgrave came in soon afterwards; the castle is small, built round a square with long cold passages.

---

* Daughter of George III.

U

Princess Elizabeth's own rooms, drawing-room, &c., are very tastefully furnished, and filled with all her pretty things; she showed me her bed-room, dressing-room, &c.; on returning, we found two ladies belonging to her in the drawing-room, and an aide-de-camp of the Landgrave's. We then went to dinner up-stairs, through long passages, into a large, long room. All the dinner was put on the table at once, and carried round one dish after the other, *selon la Russie.* Princess Elizabeth talked a great deal of England, and of our travels, and was as agreeable as ever; in the dining-room we found more guests belonging to the Court; and after dinner we went for some time to another drawing-room, where the ladies sat and the gentlemen stood. After coffee, and talking for some time, we again went down to Princess Elizabeth's room, but only with herself and the Landgrave. What became of the company afterwards I know not. Princess Elizabeth again took me to her dressing-room, and gave me some pretty onyxes which are found in this country. They are sent from a place called Oberstein to Italy, where they are carved, and thence again trans-shipped to England as antiques. In a little while we took our leave, and were charged by Princess Elizabeth with a thousand messages to her friends in

England, particularly to Lady Grosvenor, Mamma, and Lady Derby. The country between Frankfort and Homburg is flat and full of fruit trees; there are also large quantities of mangel wurzel; behind Homburg the country all consists of wooded hills, and looks very pretty. We got back about six.

*Saturday, October 27th.*—After breakfast we went out in a cold raw day to some shops in order to look for stones; we were recommended to a Monsieur Buoz in an obscure alley; but, as he was not at home, we were forced to return later. We went to the banker's, then home, then between one and two, to Monsieur Buoz again; we found him living up two pair of stairs in an out of the way old house, and himself a very odd-looking, little old man, like the picture of a miser; he showed us quantities of shells, old pictures, and collections of all sorts of old rubbish, but nothing very tempting, except some fine cornelians, of which we bought some, and a small onyx which was the sort of stone we wanted; but unfortunately he had only one. We went home, Belgrave wrote letters, we dined at half-past four, and a little before six, Mr. Coke, of the bank, called for us to take us to his box at the Opera, where we saw "La Preciosa," the music by Weber, and pretty ; the actresses large and clumsy. The play was over by nine, when we came home and packed up our goods.

*Sunday, October* 28*th.*—Left Frankfort early ; the first part of the way ugly, thought it began to be pretty at Wiesbaden ; it rained almost all day. Just as it grew dark we passed through the old town of Nassau, which seemed very pretty and picturesque, with the ruins of the old castle perched on a high, wooded rock over the town. In the middle of the town we suddenly turned through an archway, down a very steep hill to the banks of a river, over which we were ferried, and passed through the modern town of Nassau ; the country about it is hilly, wooded, and beautiful ; and reached Coblentz about ten ; a good inn the " Poste." We passed the fortress of Ehrenbreitstein before crossing the bridge at Coblentz.

*Monday, October* 29*th.*—Left Coblentz at eight, a cold morning, nothing particular, except that the first part of the way lies along the banks of the Rhine, and is very pretty ; arrived at Cologne about six, ordered the stove to be lighted, and had some dinner.

*Tuesday, October* 30*th.*—After breakfast we went to the Cathedral, which is of exquisite architecture,

and in the course of being repaired. We saw the
tomb and shrine of the "Three Kings of Cologne"
behind the altar, then walked a long way to Saint
Peter's Church, in order to see an altar-piece by
Rubens, representing the Crucifixion of Saint Peter.
The picture usually left visible is a copy, but on
spinning it round the original appeared; it is a
disagreeable picture, and scarcely worth the trouble
of a long, dirty walk through narrow streets. We
found our way back to the hotel, the "Kaiserliche
Hoff," and then set out, intending to sleep at
Liege, but half way in the stage to Aix-la-Chapelle
a nail in one of our springs gave way, and we
were forced to stop for some time to get it repaired,
so we arrived at Aix-la-Chapelle after six on a
rainy night; and as it was too late to go on to
Liege, we remained in the "Grand Hotel," which
we found an excellent inn and very comfortable.

*Wednesday, October 31st.*—Left Aix-la-Chapelle
early, passed the Netherlands custom-house without difficulty, and through a hilly country, went
down a very steep hill into Liege, a large, nasty,
dirty town; a good *pavé* all the way from thence
to Brussels. As we did not reach Louvain till half-
past ten, we stopped there, it having been a wet

stormy evening. We found a clean inn, and our beds ready made.

*Thursday, November 1st.*—Left Louvain before nine, a stormy morning; got to Brussels at half-past twelve, found a comfortable apartment at the "Hotel de Bellevue," and had a real fire, not a stove. Went out to some shops, got our English letters, and went out again. It was the Fête of the Toussaints, the shops not ostensibly open, but business was going on all the same. We looked into a church hard by, walked round the *parc*; it was very wet. We left our names at Sir C. Bagot's,* but he and all the Court were at the Hague for the year.

*Friday, November 2nd.*—A very stormy morning, Belgrave went to the banker's, and also to get some money changed. We set out at twelve; after some severe hail-storms, the day cleared and became quite fine. We reached Ghent at six, but as it was a very fine moonlight evening, we thought it better to go on to Bruges; arrived there (at "La Fleur de Blé") by eleven.

*Saturday, November 3rd.*—At ten o'clock set off, with three horses and a postillion; at Furnes we took four horses, and came by a very wild road

* Sir Charles Bagot, then British Minister at Brussels.

along the seashore, and some part of the way in the water, among the sea-gulls; on the beach met the *douaniers*, one of whom mounted on the carriage to accompany us to Dunkirk; heard the firing of guns from a ship in distress out at sea; there had been a great storm the three preceding days, and a small vessel had perished off the coast only the day before. It was quite dark before we got to Dunkirk; we stopped at the "Hotel de Ville" for Belgrave to declare who he was, whence coming, where going, &c., and then proceeded to the "Hotel de Flandre," which we found as well furnished and as comfortable as an English one, with carpets, fire-places, and a large sitting-room. The *douaniers* came there and looked at some of our boxes, but gave us very little trouble; we had some supper of soup, whitings, and mutton chops, and found our beds very comfortable. It being the eve of the King's birthday, a salute was being fired.

*Sunday, November 4th.*—After breakfast we went to some shops to get some long gold earrings, such as the peasants here wear on fête days; we succeeded in getting some pretty ones. Set out soon after ten, passed through Gravelines, which looks the very abode of melancholy, and reached Dessins, at Calais, at two, made ourselves very comfortable with a fire, then took a very pleasant stroll through the town, and upon a very long pier, stretching out across the sands into the sea; saw a greyhound and two companions rushing about on the sands; walked back and wrote letters.

*Monday, November 5th.*—Got up and had the carriage packed and sent down to be put on board the steam-packet between eight and nine. Embarked ourselves exactly at half-past ten, and departed in a French steam-vessel, the 'Duc de Bordeaux,' with not many passengers besides ourselves, and only one carriage; the wind and tide being against us the vessel heaved a good deal, and I was horridly sick; however, in five hours we were safely landed on the Dover Pier, and went to the "Ship" Inn. Our boxes were delayed for a long time in order to be examined at the custom-house; this was owing to the Boulogne steamboat having come in just before us. After waiting two hours we settled to dine, and had just finished when the Commissioner came to say thàt the men were ready to begin with us, accordingly Belgrave went down; the people were very civil, and matters were very easily and speedily arranged. We then set off for Canterbury, and arrived at the " Fountain Inn" a little before ten o'clock.

*Tuesday, November 6th.*—Walked out early to see the Cathedral, which is under repair, and is being restored in very good taste. We ordered our post-horses, and set off afterwards and reached London by six o'clock, after a most pleasant and interesting journey, having been absent from England about five months and three weeks.

THE END.

London: Printed by A. Schulze, 13, Poland Street.